FitzDuncan's Hope

JOHN J. SPEARMAN

DEDICATION

To Gus, my faithful companion for eight-and-a-half years. There were no strangers in your world, only friends you had yet to meet. No one could ask for a more loyal friend than you. You asked for little and gave so much in return. I miss you, old buddy. Ave atque vale!

OTHER BOOKS BY THIS AUTHOR

The Halberd Series

Gallantry in Action
In Harm's Way
True Allegiance
Surrender Demand

The Pike Series

Pike's Potential
Pike's Passage
Pike's Progress

The FitzDuncan Series

FitzDuncan
FitzDuncan's Alchemy
FitzDuncan's Enlightenment
FitzDuncan's Fortune
FitzDuncan's Gambit
FitzDuncan's Hope

The Perseverance Andrews Series

The Defense of the Commonwealth

ACKNOWLEDGMENTS

Dear Reader,
You are the purpose of this and all my books. Thank you for reading. If you like what you have read, please leave a positive review on Amazon.com or goodreads.com. If you did not like it, I'm sorry.

If you would like to stay abreast of my latest activity, please visit my website: johnjspearmanauthor.com

1

The month of Ylir was upon us, and with it came the cold of winter. There was not much snow yet—that usually came later, after the Winter Solstice. The ground was only thinly covered, but the cold was more than enough to convince anyone that winter clutched the country in its icy talons.

Lucy and I had just arrived at our house in the city of Aquileia after a journey made twice as long by the intense cold we encountered. Five hours of riding a day were all we could manage in the bitter chill, leaving both our horses and us exhausted. By the time we reached the city, we were at our limit.

The previous few weeks before we left Easton, there was nothing pressing, and there were no demands on my time. That was a welcome break for me. It seemed I'd danced from crisis to opportunity and back to another crisis for the last year and a half.

Before leaving the Eastern March, I had taken some short rides, trying to find traces of old roads that lead from different farming communities to the Pheas River. Over a hundred and fifty years earlier, the March used to ship grain to the rest of the kingdom of Aquileia. That became less profitable over time. The harbor at the end of the river, Port Charles, filled with silt because it cost too much to dredge it. The river became less of a vital artery, and the roads linking the different farming communities to it became overgrown.

The population of the kingdom had grown since then. This year, harvests in the rest of Aquileia were poor, but in the March our crop yields were as bountiful as ever. If we had been able to ship our produce economically, we would have alleviated shortages in the rest of the realm, and our farmers would have enjoyed an extremely profitable year. As a result, I'd had the notion of seeing how difficult it might be to reopen the river and Port Charles. The king also took an interest, and we would be investigating the feasibility of dredging the harbor and clearing the river. With winter upon us, that project would need to wait for a couple of months.

My scouting forays into the countryside had been fruitless. Where the old roads went through forests, enough time had passed that the trees which grew in the roadbed made it indistinguishable from the rest of the woods. Only in open country could I trace the faint indication of where the road had been. We would need to start from the beginning and hire surveyors to lay out the best routes.

Lucy and I were in the city to attend the joint wedding of two couples who were our friends. The wedding was scheduled in four days—the first full day after the Winter Solstice, an auspicious day in our religion. The celebration after the wedding was to be a bal masque. That meant that all the guests would be dressed in costume. It promised to be a memorable event.

Once the wedding was over, I would return to Easton. Lucy might stay in the city for a time—we had not needed to decide that yet. The following month, my father and I would then visit every community in the Eastern March. As earl of the March, that was his duty. Since the king decreed I was now heir to the March, it behooved me to join him for these meetings.

If you are new to my stories, you might be asking, *He's your father. Why did the king involve himself in making you the heir?* The problem was that my father and mother never married. She was a maid in Easton manor, and he was a young man sowing his wild oats. That makes me a bastard—by birth, not by deportment. I have always striven to be a gentleman, despite my illegitimate birth.

Father later married an awful shrew of a woman, and when she gave birth to a son, I was sent away. It wasn't an easy life for me from that point but it helped shape me into the man I am today. I carved my own path and was doing well. My father's wife turned out to be a nightmare and the two sons they produced ended up taking after her at her worst. Between the three of them, they bankrupted the March.

During the same period, I enjoyed financial success in my quirky "business." Eight years earlier, after retiring from the Rangers (who protect the western border), I came to the city to make my way in the world. My old school friend Freddy, Lord Rawlinsford, came to me with a problem. I was able to help him and, through word of mouth, assisted a few others in retrieving items of value when the law could not help. As compensation, I charged half the value of the item I recovered.

About a year and a half ago, I came to the king's attention through a series of circumstances—some pleasant, some not. Freddy introduced me to his cousin Lucy at the same time. Both of these developments changed my life dramatically—for the better (though my life up to that point was certainly not unpleasant at all).

The king later presented my father and half-brothers with an ultimatum—they had six months to prove they were capable of managing the defense of the March. Instead of rising to the challenge, the boys complained to their mother, who hired an assassin to kill me. He nearly succeeded.

At this point, His Majesty stepped in. Just after Lucy and I married, not quite six months earlier, His Majesty named me Lord Oritur, after a town on the border of the March. He decreed that I was hereby adopted by my father and the legitimate heir, then charged me with defense of the March against the depredations of the horse nomads.

You can read all about that in my earlier chronicles. I certainly do not want to waste your time, dear reader, by scratching ground that has already been well-plowed. There is a new tale to share, so let me move on.

Despite being chilled to the marrow, after I brought our bags into the house, I needed to take our horses, Andy and Bella, to the stable behind the Foaming Boar. The Boar was an inn owned by Carl Stensland, a former sergeant in the Rangers with whom I served years before. The horses seemed happy to be returning to the tender care of Jerry, the stable boy at the inn. I'm sure they were also pleased to get out of the cold and under some blankets. Jerry and I did not engage in much conversation—it was too cold to linger. I did not even ruffle his hair. There was no point in stopping inside the inn. If I did, I knew I wouldn't leave until I was warm again. Lucy was waiting for me, so I trudged home instead.

Walking back to our house, I held my cloak tightly. The bitter chill we rode in had seeped down to my bones. I wanted nothing more than to get back to our house, hoping Lucy would have a fire kindled and I could bask in its warmth.

I was not disappointed. When I entered through the kitchen, Roberta, our housekeeper, had already stoked the fire in the stove and the warmth embraced me as soon as I shut the door. On my way to the parlor in the front of the house, Roberta met me and took my cloak, jacket, and sword.

The hearth in the parlor was ablaze, and Lucy had dragged the sofa to face it. She beckoned me to her. I slid next to her, and as I did, she squirmed onto my lap, holding me close. Most of the air in the room was still chilly, but here, in front of the fire, we were cozy as we held one another closely and comfortably. Lucy wrapped an arm around my neck and tucked her head under my chin.

The two of us dozed off at some point. A noise woke me, and I found we were now stretched out on the sofa. Lucy was draped on top of me, and Roberta must have covered us with a blanket while we napped. The fire had died down, but the room felt warmer.

"Milord?" Roberta called softly from the door.

'Yes?" I mumbled, coming more fully awake.

"There's a gentleman to see you," she said.

"Thank you, Roberta, but I'm no gentleman," Fenwick declared as he strode in. "Don't get up," he said to me, though I had no intention of moving—I was too comfortable to contemplate it.

Lucy shuffled a bit and moved her head to see. "Hello, Fenwick," she said.

"Your Loveliness," he replied, bobbing his head to her. "You're late," he directed to me. "We expected you three days ago."

"The cold slowed us down," I explained. "We could only stand it for so long. Who is this *we* you mentioned? And what happened to your accent?"

Aloysius Fenwick is the assassin who tried to kill me. After I captured him, the king offered him the choice of being executed or serving as the royal assassin. In that new role, we worked together and developed a friendship of sorts. One of his peculiarities was his ability to speak a variety of languages, but in the past, his Aquileian used to be marked by the clipped, laconic speech common to the Eastern March where we both grew up. There was no trace of that accent now.

"The *we* is the royal *we*, as I am certain you would have reckoned once you dislodged the sleep from your brain," he said. "As far as the accent, I am keeping more lofty company these days. It is advantageous for me to ape my betters."

The first piece of information made me groan as I realized it meant the king had an errand he wished me to perform with Fenwick. There was no possibility of begging off—it was the king, after all, and I was well aware I owed my current position to him. My groan was somewhat covered by Lucy's interested response.

"You are still seeing Miss Traval, then?" she asked in a chipper tone.

"I am," he acknowledged, "and as a highly valued, irreplaceable, confidential assistant to His Royal Majesty, my mode of speech must reflect that lofty position."

"You took my advice, then," I said, "using that phrase to describe your employment."

He looked at me skeptically. "I don't remember you saying anything along those lines. It was your treasure of a wife who suggested it."

"Nonsense, Aloysius," I countered, purposefully using his given name, which he detested. "I believe I offered you those exact words while we were still on the boat after retrieving her when I suggested you become better acquainted."

"I assure you, I don't recall the conversation," he said airily.

I was planning on protesting, but Lucy dug her elbow into my ribs to silence me. "We are so glad to hear you are still courting her," Lucy said. "Things are going well?"

"I believe so."

"Her father?" I asked.

"Herbert is predisposed to like me since I have shared with him I am a man of independent means," Fenwick replied, "*and* I organized her rescue."

He looked at me for a reaction to that last statement. Traval had actually contacted me, asking if I would deliver the ransom to the Rhetian pirates who abducted her. I asked Fenwick for his assistance, and, I freely admit, he played a bigger part in leading the expedition than I.

"Herbert is the easy part," Fenwick continued after determining I was not planning on objecting to his earlier comment. "He would approve even if I were the royal assassin."

I chuckled.

"Her mother…?" Lucy said.

"Her mother is exhilarated that such an important personage is courting her daughter," Fenwick stated.

I laughed out loud. Madam Traval was a social climber of the worst sort. Her intense desire to become associated with the nobility led her to arrange a marriage for her daughter to one of the worst examples of the Aquileian aristocracy. That particular tale was the first I chose to commit to pen and paper.

"And Julienne?" Lucy asked. "How does she feel about your profession?"

"She is an adventurous soul," Fenwick answered.

"Something else I told you while we were still on the boat," I remarked.

"I'm sorry, but I don't recall," he replied blithely.

Lucy nudged me again with her elbow, but I was not planning on responding. I knew he was just trying to tease me. I would have done the same, positions reversed.

"And the two of you?" Lucy asked.

Fenwick paused before answering. "I am besotted with her," he said quietly and humbly.

"And she?" I pressed.

Lucy sat up, jabbing me sharply enough to make me gasp as she did. "Hush, you," she warned. "Fenwick is every bit as handsome and charming as you are, and you know it. Add in the spice of his dangerous mode of employment, not to mention the sheer pleasure of pulling the wool over her mother's eyes, and she is undoubtedly head over heels."

"I can only hope," Fenwick uttered in a forlorn tone.

I laughed out loud again, realizing he was overplaying his role as a lovesick paramour. Lucy joined me with a giggle herself. Fenwick smiled as he realized we understood his act. Lucy rose and headed for the kitchen.

Once I stopped laughing, I asked, "Where are you taking me this time? And we had better not leave before the solstice."

"Queen Liliana is well aware of our social obligations, Caz," Fenwick replied. "She convinced the king to allow us a few days, but we must depart the morning after the wedding."

"Where are we headed?"

"Dunland, on the other side of the Downs," Fenwick answered. "According to reports, something is amiss there. There is no solid information—just some grumblings from travelers and merchants who complained of their treatment while in the area and the hostility of the locals. The first complaints came over a year ago but they have increased in frequency and intensity recently, according to His Highness, Albert."

"So?"

"Count Dunland is a Braintree," Fenwick explained. "The Braintree clan had as strong a claim to the throne as the king's family, as far as consanguinity. What they have always seemed to forget is that the support of the other leading noble families was more important and still carries more weight. The only people who ever threw in with them were the families who were passed by and powerless. The king did not think Count Dunland was part of the recent plotting that brought much of the rest of the family low but hearing these complaints moved him to want to investigate. After all, no one in the Braintree faction was ever known for being clever or subtle. Knowing that you were coming to the city for the weddings, he decided you should join me. He knows you do not need to return to the March until the end of Morsug and thought to take advantage of your idleness."

"That's so kind of him," I replied sarcastically. "What is happening with the rest of the Braintrees?"

"The rest of the group that was actively plotting against the king is still in the cells below the castle. The trial is scheduled to begin in Morsug while we are away."

"Could Dunland be plotting some sort of armed insurrection in the hope of freeing them?" I asked.

"Unlikely," Fenwick stated. "Dunland does not have the resources—either financially or in terms of men. To reach the capital, he would need to take an armed force in the dead of winter through five different holdings whose loyalty to the king is unquestioned. The nobles in control of those holdings have all been alerted. Count Dunland is probably just unhappy, and his people are feeling the effect of his displeasure."

"Why do you need me?"

"I don't, quite frankly," Fenwick said with a shrug. "I expressed that opinion, and His Majesty ignored my utterance. He simply restated his wish for you to join me."

"Huh," I grunted. "Did you pick up anything from Albert or the queen that there might be more to the situation?"

"No," Fenwick replied, shaking his head. "I sensed they were also a bit puzzled at his insistence that you accompany me. They don't know anything more than I do."

"Fenwick," Lucy said as she returned, "will you stay for dinner?"

"Thank you for your kind invitation, Your Loveliness, but I have already made other plans," Fenwick answered.

His face showed the faint trace of a blush. From that, I suspected those plans included Julienne Traval. Lucy read the same signs I did.

"I would offer to include Miss Traval," Lucy said, "but I suspect she would prefer more advance notice. Would tomorrow evening suit?"

"I will need to ask," Fenwick stated, "but I know of nothing that would interfere."

"Splendid," Lucy said. "I'll see what Freddy and Greta are doing, and we can have a small gathering."

2

The following day the cold snap broke—thank all the heavenly beings! It was still chilly but not the knife-edge, take-your-breath-away freeze of the past week. I took advantage of the improvement and headed for the Foaming Boar to confirm arrangements for the horses. I had no doubt Jerry would have communicated with Carl, but it was a simple courtesy and no great burden.

When I finished chatting with Carl, I looked for Jerry, but he was not there. I guessed he was at school, which gave me an idea. One of my holdings in the city was a bookstore I owned. Originally, I rented the upstairs from the owner. When I came into some money, I offered to buy the building and the discussion expanded into buying the business too. Lyle Forteney still ran the shop, and I made arrangements over a year earlier so that Jerry could borrow any used book to read.

Lyle was pleasantly surprised to see me. It had been quite some time, and so much had changed in my life. We spent the morning drinking tea while I told him stories. Finally, I remembered the reason I came.

"Lyle," I inquired, "the boy Jerry—how often does he come in?"

"Every few days. More often than that, when school is out," Lyle replied.

"So you expect him soon?"

"Actually, today or tomorrow would be a good guess. This is the last day of school before the holiday, and they get a week off. I'll probably see him three or four times in the next week," Forteney answered. "He's a voracious reader."

"Are there any books he has expressed interest in that he can't borrow because they are new?"

"I can think of five right off," Lyle said, rising from his stool.

"You don't need to get them this minute," I said. "Just tell me what I would owe you for them."

"In order to do that, I need to pull them, Caz," he said with a wag of his finger.

"When he comes in, give them to him," I requested. "Tell him Grandfather Frost wanted him to have them."

"I don't think Jerry has believed in Grandfather Frost for a long time," Lyle admonished.

"I know. As an orphan, I don't think Grandfather Frost paid him many visits over the years," I agreed. "Still, the idea tickles my fancy—the spirit of the season."

Jerry's choice of books was intriguing. There was an atlas, a history of the kingdom of Aquileia, a book about an itinerant knight I remembered reading as a boy, a book on pirates, and a book on horsemanship. The total came to two ducats, seven florins, and four coppers, with the atlas accounting for almost half of that. I paid Lyle with a smile, feeling good about what I just did.

When I returned to the house, a marvelous assortment of smells greeted my nose upon entering the kitchen. Sadly, Lucy shooed me away immediately but not before I saw Roger, Freddy and Greta's man, working in the kitchen alongside Roberta. The aroma of pies and roast fowl, among other things, reached my olfactory sense.

"Out! Out!" Lucy said, her hands on my chest pushing me through the door.

"But it smells so good," I complained.

"I'll not have you bothering Roberta and Roger the way you torment Laurie at Easton Manor," Lucy stated.

"Why is Roger here?" I asked.

"Since I invited Greta and Freddy, they lent him to us for the day," Lucy explained. "Ratty and Inger Fairchild are also coming. Their parents are going to announce their betrothal the day after the solstice."

"At the wedding?"

"No. They are hosting a late breakfast for all the out-of-town wedding guests that morning. We are invited. Tomorrow night, remember, we are invited to the Earl of Dorch's gala and the night of the solstice to the castle as we were last year. The following evening we attend the weddings."

"I remember," I said. "You made me buy new clothes for them."

"You did remember to bring them?"

I growled at her and chased her upstairs. When we reached our bedroom, I was unsurprised to see Chauncey asleep on his perch. Wherever Lucy went, Chauncey was usually not far away. Chauncey was an owl but not a pet, according to Lucy. She had explained their relationship to me earlier in only the most vague terms.

His presence did not trouble me in the slightest. I caught Lucy in my arms. She kicked and squealed while giggling madly. I bundled her onto our bed. She quit squirming when I kissed her, and I forgot entirely about what was cooking in the kitchen.

The dinner was a success. Ratty had an inkling regarding Fenwick and his role before this, but Inger did not. Hearing that he was a confidential advisor to His Royal Majesty satisfied her curiosity. It also prevented her from asking too many questions since she understood a confidential advisor certainly would not be allowed to speak about what he did.

Inger did ask, "How did you end up in that position?"

"Caz actually brought me to His Majesty's attention," he said, giving me a grateful nod.

That was actually the truth, in a way. Of course, Fenwick omitted explaining that he was trying to kill me and had earlier kidnapped Freddy to draw me in. I managed, with great difficulty, to subdue Fenwick, and he was taken to the king in chains, but I suppose I was responsible for their meeting. I needed to avoid eye contact with everyone until I regained my composure, or I would have burst out laughing.

Julienne Traval fit right in with the group. Her father was a competitor of Greta and Ratty's father in merchant trading, so they shared a common frame of reference. When she told Greta she was working in the family business, Greta was intensely curious. It also turned out that Julienne and Inger had some mutual friends.

A great deal of the conversation revolved around the impending weddings of Quint Pompeo to Siobhan Harper and Linc Ellsworth to Nellie Fassbender. It seemed the ladies all knew the costumes they would be wearing. We men were kept in the dark except for our own.

The first awkward moment came when Inger asked how Quint and Siobhan met. After a brief uncomfortable silence, Lucy said, "Caz introduced them."

"Why is everyone looking at me?" Inger asked.

"There's a whole story behind it, Inger," I explained. "Last year at the Earl of Dorch's party, Lucy told me that Siobhan's parents were negotiating to marry her to Lord Barrowton and Siobhan was not pleased with the prospect. I arranged for her to meet Quint Pompeo that night and might have dropped a word in Earl Montgomery's ear about the suitability of such a match the same evening."

Inger's eyes grew wide, and her mouth opened. "Oh! You're the one! I heard the whole story a long time ago, but I didn't know it was you who engineered Quint's entrance and saved Siobhan from marrying that turd, Barrowton. Oops," she apologized for her choice of words.

"Quite alright, Inger," I said. "He was a turd."

Poor Inger was also responsible for the second uneasy moment when she later asked how Julienne and Fenwick met. Noticing the lack of an immediate response, Inger turned red. "I've done it again, haven't I?"

Julienne reached across the table and patted Inger's hand to put her at ease. "Not at all, and this is a much better story," Julienne said.

Julienne then told how she traveled to Nagah, was captured by pirates on her return, and how Fenwick rescued her. "Of course, Fenwick would not have been there except for Caz," she stated.

Julienne explained how my former business brought me to her father's attention, and he thought to reach out to me in this crisis. I asked Fenwick for help, and he took command of the whole operation. I thought she handled it deftly, leaving out the tricky bits that were to remain unspoken. I gave her a wink to let her know I appreciated it, and she smiled in response. When Julienne finished, Inger looked at me, then at Freddy and Greta, and then raised an eyebrow, questioning me.

"I had nothing whatsoever to do with Freddy and Greta," I protested. "Nor with Linc and Nellie. And Freddy is responsible for me meeting Lucy—for which

I will be eternally grateful. As far as you and Ratty, blame Freddy and Greta for that."

"You and Lucy are somewhat responsible for Ratty and me," she said. "It was your wedding where we became better acquainted."

The evening was enough of a success that we discussed getting together again in the future. We left things vague since I would be traveling with Fenwick on the king's errand and did not know when I would return. After our guests departed, Lucy and I retired to bed. As we lay there, we discussed the evening.

"Fenwick certainly seems to be an adaptable sort," Lucy remarked. "He seemed right at home with our company."

"That was his reputation," I said. "According to Sir Oliver, Fenwick had the ability to fit in, no matter what his surroundings."

"He came from the Eastern March, didn't he?" she asked.

"Yes. From a town away from the eastern border—Northrup, he told me."

"Did you ever think to find out more?" Lucy inquired.

"I did, at one point," I answered. "But as we have become better acquainted, my desire to dig into his past lessened. I would not feel comfortable doing it now. He is the man he made himself, similar to me in some ways."

"Good," Lucy said as she snuggled closer to me. "I feel the same way."

The next evening was the Earl of Dorch's annual gala. For many, it was the highlight of the holiday season. The guests wore their absolute finest attire as it was an opportunity to see friends and to be seen. Freddy and Greta were sharing a carriage with Ratty and Inger, so Lucy and I arrived in one I hired for the evening.

Lucy looked exquisite, of course. She wore a dress of blue and silver, matching two of the traditional holiday colors. My outfit was more subdued, though my waistcoat was of the same fabric as her dress.

It was a wonderful evening. I took the opportunity to spend time with Linc Ellsworth and Quint Pompeo since they would not have time to chat with me at their wedding. Quint's father, Earl Montgomery, made a point of seeking me out and thanking me for introducing his son to Siobhan Harper the year before.

The music began, and I danced not only with Lucy but many of our friends (and their mothers). That was nothing new—these people were my long-time friends. What was interesting was how people I knew only slightly reacted to my presence.

In years past, my illegitimacy was too much of an impediment for them to ignore. When they could not avoid being introduced, I could feel the cool reluctance in their handshakes. It was something I was accustomed to, though I will admit it irritated me that so many were willing to judge me on the circumstances of my birth and not on my character.

Before the evening, I wondered whether the king's decree of my adoption and legitimacy six months earlier would change their attitudes. I observed that it did not. Their continued snobbery bothered me not at all. These people would never be my friends, and I would not allow their small-mindedness to affect my enjoyment of the evening or of my life.

Lucy and I had a marvelous time. When the hour came to clamber into our carriage, we were both a bit footsore from dancing all evening. On the ride home and while we were undressing, we discussed the evening and laughed at the antics of our friends. We slid into our cold bed, happy and tired, but not so tired that we didn't think of a way of warming ourselves up quickly.

3

After a lazy day, the following evening found us heading to the castle. For the second year in a row, Lucy and I were invited to join the royal family at a gathering of some of the most important and influential people in the realm. Last year, Lucy's parents and her aunt and uncle were present, and helped calm my nerves at being in the midst of such an august group. This year they stayed home.

When we arrived at the castle, the driver stopped at the gate. I helped Lucy down and showed our invitation to the guard. Pages were standing by to escort us across the short bridge to the castle proper. The bridge was swept clear of snow.

Arriving inside, attendants took our cloaks. I saw what Lucy was wearing—a dress of black with white accents. Her hair was gathered in a corona around her head. Seeing Lucy always took my breath away but seeing her dressed for a more formal occasion was even more arresting.

A page led us to a drawing room. A herald, standing at the door, asked our names. He then announced us to the room.

"Lord and Lady Oritur," he bawled.

Upon entering, Lucy was whisked away by Queen Liliana almost immediately. That left me in a bit of a spot. I knew few of the other guests and those to whom I had been introduced I did not know well. Still, it would be to my advantage to get to know them better. Fortunately, it was a relatively small gathering of only about two dozen. Earl Montgomery saw me as I was mustering my resolve to wade into the fray. He crossed to me quickly and offered a friendly greeting.

"I saw you girding your loins to take on this assembly," he commented, "and I thought it would be unfair for you to do it alone. Your father should be here to smooth your way."

"We discussed it at length, and he felt more comfortable staying in Easton," I said. "The last few years have been difficult for him, and his embarrassment is such that he is not yet ready to face his peers. At this very moment, though, he is hosting a gathering of the leading citizens of the March—something he has not done in decades. Our plan is that he will come to the capital next year, and Lucy and I will stay behind and entertain the March."

"After your stunning successes this year, don't you think the people of the March would like to see you?" the earl asked.

"There is only one small problem with that," I replied. "I still know very few people. That will change once the month of Morsug is over. Beginning in Porri, my father and I will call upon every community in the March."

"Huh," he grunted. "In Montgomery, we do that in Heyannir."

"In Heyannir, we are usually plagued by the horse nomads and cannot afford to lose focus on them. Porri is the month when the annual levy for the militia is conducted, and one purpose of the visit is to swear the new men in," I explained.

"Ah," he replied, nodding in understanding. "I heard you enjoyed unusual success this year with the defense of the March. The gathering last night was not the proper venue to discuss such things, but this certainly is. Please tell me more about the campaigning season."

From my expression and posture, along with my delay in responding, the earl realized I was reluctant to extol my accomplishments. He laid his hand on my arm and whispered, "Don't worry Caz. When some of these other men overhear what you're talking about, they'll be drawn in like bees to honey. We've all heard rumors, and there is a great deal of curiosity. A subject that includes horses and bloodshed? They can't resist, and it provides me a way of introducing you without awkwardness. Talk a bit louder than normal, as though I were deaf."

Feeling self-conscious, I began explaining to the earl about the challenges we faced at the beginning of the campaigning season—primarily our lack of numbers and poor morale. As our neighbors in the room overheard me discussing military actions, they dropped their conversations and began to listen in. In a few minutes, there were three other men listening. The earl asked me to pause and introduced me to them briefly, then bade me continue.

Our little gathering formed a knot in the midst of the party, drawing more notice. A couple of others drifted over to learn what was happening. When Prince Albert caught sight of me holding forth, he brought his group over, giving me an audience of ten men. If it weren't for Count Brisset, who was currently bending the king's ear about something, all the men would have been present.

"Damme, Caz!" Albert exclaimed. "I've been dying to hear all about this. Would you mind getting the rest of us caught up on your narrative?"

I had already shared all the details with Albert when we traveled to Scaramouche, but I understood he was trying to help. Earl Montgomery seized this opportunity. He sent the original three to get drinks (and one for me) and made sure everyone knew my name, and gave his in return. I had not progressed very far, so when the men returned with a glass of wine for me, it was enough time to get the newer part of the audience to the same part of the story.

As the earl mentioned, horses and bloodshed had their attention. I looked over their heads and was not surprised to see Lucy surrounded by a group of women. I returned to my description of the events of the summer. As I finished, I intended to describe the celebration we conducted in honor of the Minor God Andvar. I was interrupted by the ringing of the bell for dinner, however. Before heading to the table, I thanked Earl Montgomery for introducing me to the others.

"Now they have a face to go with the name," he said, "and an engaging tale of derring-do. Your path will cross theirs repeatedly over the years, so it was important to make a good impression. I believe you are off to a solid start."

He clapped me on the back and then strode away. I joined Lucy at the table where my place card was waiting. Lucy introduced me to the woman on my left, the Duchess of Caurus. She was pleasant looking, though slightly plump.

Once we sat, the duchess asked if I would get Lucy's attention, and when I did, the two began conversing right over me. I offered to switch seats, and she moved in an instant. The duke looked at me and laughed when I sat.

"She's eager to learn more from your wife about her dress," the duke said. "Did she purchase it locally?"

"No," I replied. "She found a seamstress in Easton who is marvelously talented."

"Easton is about as far away as it could be," the duke stated. "So it wouldn't do my wife much good. I have heard other things about you than just your adventures with the nomads, Lord Oritur, and am curious to know more."

"What sort of things have you heard?" I asked cautiously.

"Well, you spoke about your success against the horse nomads, but I think that is only one facet of your life. I sensed there were other things you wished to talk about but did not have the opportunity."

"Very astute, milord," I replied. "You are not wrong."

"If your audience had wanted to hear something other than blood and guts, what would you have wished to discuss?" the duke asked.

"I would have liked to talk about things that Lucy and I hope to do to help the entire March beyond defending it," I said. "Things like the harvest fair my wife organized. There is another project we will be investigating that could benefit the kingdom as a whole. We need to learn a great deal more before we proceed, but I'm optimistic."

"Really?" the duke inquired. "Now I am curious. What sort of undertaking?"

"Before I answer, allow me to ask a few questions," I countered.

"Feel free," the duke replied.

"I know where Caurus is," I said. "I made a pilgrimage to the Temple of Bellona not quite a year ago. Beyond that, I know very little. What is the economy like in your holding? Is your territory largely self-sufficient? Do you export? What are the things that trouble you on a long-term basis?" I asked.

"We export timber, mostly fir, some ore, including gold, and animal pelts," the duke replied, "and Caurus is blessed to be one of the more prosperous duchies in Aquileia. Our soil is fair, but our growing season is shorter than most. As our population has grown, we have needed to import more food every year, and every year, prices have risen. This year, weather wreaked havoc on our crops. I am finding that there are widespread shortages throughout the rest of the kingdom as well, and prices are outrageous. Enough about my woes. Tell me about the Eastern March. All I know is you are plagued by horse nomads every year."

"And countering those incursions has commanded the entire attention of my father and his father before," I said. "I am hoping to broaden my focus though, of course, that will depend on the military situation. The March would be prosperous, but the expense of countering the nomads makes it difficult to get ahead. Our soil is incredibly fertile, though, and this year we had better-than-average crop yields. Unfortunately, we have no way of shipping our grain and produce economically to the rest of the kingdom. I hope to change that but won't know whether it makes sense financially to pursue the idea for months, at least."

"When you do learn more, please contact me," the duke asked. "I might be willing to invest, especially if it will help me feed my people."

At this point, the duchess rose, and I returned to my seat. Dinner was being served. It was the traditional roast of beef accompanied by roast potatoes, batter pudding, onions, carrots, and gravy. The dinner was followed by a flaming pudding.

We rose from the meal and waited for the royal astronomer to announce the exact moment of the solstice. When he rang the small gong, couples turned to one another and kissed. The king offered a toast to a prosperous new year, and Albert offered a toast to his father's good health. With that, the evening was ended. I made sure to say goodbye to the Duke of Caurus. Lucy and I joined the line of guests saying their farewells to the king and queen.

The next evening was the wedding and bal masque. Lucy and I spent a lazy day together. My only pressing task was to pack my saddlebags for my trip the next day with Fenwick. I would miss the breakfast where the betrothal of Ratty Hawkins to Inger Fairchild would be announced.

Lucy and I shared a carriage that evening with Freddy and Greta. We were all covered by cloaks, so none of us could see what the others were wearing. Lucy and I were dressed as characters from a storybook romance, the Huntress and the Woodsman.

The costume Lucy designed for me had me feeling self-conscious. It consisted of a shirt, a thick woolen tunic that reached the middle of my thighs, long stockings that covered the entirety of my legs, a very comfortable pair of low boots, and a felt hat to which my mask was attached. As exposed as I felt, Lucy's outfit as the huntress covered less, if you can imagine. She wore a blouse that was unlaced to her décolletage, a leather vest that fit snugly and enhanced her cleavage, a scandalously short skirt, and high boots of a buttery soft leather that extended nearly to the skirt's hem. She, too, had a felt hat with her mask sewn on. When we dressed earlier, I was so smitten with her appearance I chased her briefly around the bedroom.

I had never attended a bal masque before, but Lucy had. She explained to me that the pretense of disguising one's identity with a mask encouraged guests, particularly the women, to dress more outrageously and far less modestly. According to Lucy, her outfit would not be one of the more daring ones I would see tonight. I did not believe her.

We arrived at the house belonging to Nellie Fassbender's parents. Before leaving the carriage, we donned our masks. Like ours, Greta and Freddy's masks were part of their hats. Unlike ours, Freddy's also included some sort of a wig.

Freddy was wearing a conical hat of blue, with moons and stars in gold and silver. Long white hair fell from the edge of the hat, and his mask included a bushy mustache and scraggly gray beard. Greta's hat was also conical, in black with a wide brim. Servants met us inside the front door and took our cloaks, revealing the attire beneath.

As I suspected from the hat, Freddy was also wearing a gown of sorts, decorated identically to his hat. He clearly dressed to look like "The Amazing Doctor Flamel," who claimed to see the future. Lucy and I had encountered Flamel twice before and, in my case, his predictions were eerily accurate. Other friends of ours also visited the man and received nothing meaningful, so Lucy and I could not determine if he possessed any real clairvoyant ability.

Greta's hat hinted that she was dressed as a witch, but any resemblance to a storybook character was shattered when she removed her cloak. I did not notice how my jaw dropped until Lucy reached over and pushed my mouth closed with her finger. Greta's dress was black and cut low in the front, nearly exposing her bosom, and there was even less fabric in the back. From her shoulders to her waist, nearly all of Greta's back was exposed. Her short skirt only reached the middle of her thighs and was resting on petticoats that flounced the skirt outward. She wore black and white striped stockings that covered as much as I could see of her leg and dainty black shoes.

When we traveled to Scaramouche a few months earlier, Greta went in disguise as Freddy's saucy maid. Her appearance created a useful distraction at a key moment. Upon the return journey, she lamented that she did not have the opportunity to wear her naughtiest outfit. I guessed I was seeing it now, only repurposed to make her a witch of the most wickedly seductive sort.

With our cloaks taken, other servants directed us upstairs. When we reached the third floor, we heard the buzz of many people in quiet conversations. Following the sound, we found a large ballroom. There was a small stage on one end of the room and an open space before it. The rest of the room was filled with round tables decorated magnificently, each surrounded by eight chairs.

We were by no means the first to arrive. The room was already three-quarters full. Looking around, Lucy and I spotted a couple waving to us. As we neared them, I could tell it was Fenwick and Julienne Traval. They seemed to be attired as highwaymen, with black breeches, waistcoats, and jackets, wide-brimmed black hats with flamboyant black feather plumes, and knee-high black leather boots. I noticed Julienne's waistcoat was tailored to enhance her bust, much as Lucy's was.

RJ Sweetland was also at the table with a young lady named Camilla Winsor. She was dressed as a pretty shepherdess, and RJ as a black sheep. The two other place cards were for Thomas Gibson and a woman named Sophie Cohill. We were in the midst of introducing each other when they arrived. Gibson was dressed like the Grand Vizier of Scaramouche and the young lady as a dancing girl from his court. Having just visited Scaramouche, I was impressed with the accuracy of their costumes.

In surveying the room, Lucy's prediction of daring modes of dress was certainly in evidence among the ladies present. At first glance, I thought Greta's attire was the most audacious. Sophie Cohill's outfit hinted at much but ultimately revealed little. Still, I was eagerly looking forward to the dancing that would begin after dinner when I might get to examine some of these bold young ladies more closely.

The wedding itself was brief, the dinner was delicious, and the dancing was everything I hoped it would be. Fenwick and Julienne fit into the group seamlessly, and I observed that Fenwick danced well. I wondered where he learned.

The evening passed quickly, with good food, excellent friends, costumes that ranged from hilarious to outrageous, and an abundance of laughter. The only thing to dampen my good mood was when Fenwick reminded me as we were departing that he and I would be setting off for Dunland in the morning. On our ride home with Freddy and Greta, we all complimented Greta on her boldness in wearing such a naughty dress and predicted that others would try to outdo her for years to come without success.

4

When we arrived home after the weddings, Lucy and I had dragged our weary selves up to bed, stripping off our clothes and falling asleep immediately. The following morning came far too early. The dim light of false dawn must have registered in my brain even though my eyes were closed. I found myself awake, seemingly against my will.

Remembering that Fenwick and I needed to leave at a decent hour, I forced myself to swing my feet down to the floor. I moved gingerly, not wanting to disturb Lucy's slumber. My efforts were in vain, though, as she called out to me as I went to wash my face.

"Oh, good. You're awake," Lucy said as she rose to join me in my morning ablutions.

As I dressed for the day, Lucy draped her arms over my shoulders from behind and rested her head on my neck. She sighed and I paused, just enjoying feeling her leaning against my back. Lucy turned her head and stuck her chin into the muscle where my neck and shoulders joined. As she did, she opened one of her hands. It contained the egg-shaped piece of topaz on a silver chain that Queen Liliana gave us before we departed on our mission to destroy a grimoire of the dark arts. The topaz acted as a ward against them, and I knew from experience how effective it was.

"Dear heart," she said, "I don't have any idea what you will find in Dunland, but it would help me sleep better at night if you wore this, just in case."

I took it from her hand and looped it over my head, then pulled my hair up and over it.

"I don't think we will find anything so awful that I will need it," I said, "but if it gives you peace of mind, I'm happy to wear it."

"Good," she said, turning me by my shoulders and planting a solid kiss on my lips.

Lucy headed downstairs as I gathered the toiletries I would take on the journey. I added those items to my saddlebags, so only needed to eat breakfast and go to collect Andy from the Foaming Boar. Roberta was already at work in the kitchen and announced breakfast would soon be ready. I poured some qava and went into the dining room.

The weather was cold, and a very light snow was falling as I trudged to the inn to collect Andy. Jerry was already up and about, and my horse was saddled and waiting. I attempted to ruffle his hair, but he dodged under my arm.

"Thank you for the books, Mr. Caz," he said.

"What books?" I replied, playing dumb.

"The books Mr. Lyle gave me. He tried to tell me they were from Grandfather Frost, but I know it was you," he said smugly.

"I don't know anything about any books," I replied, using a gruff tone of voice. "But I do know that only people who say they believe in Grandfather Frost get presents from him. What makes you think I gave you some books?" I added with a wink.

"I dunno, Mr. Caz," he said, catching on. "The more I think on it, maybe it was Grandfather Frost after all."

"It must have been, Jerry," I agreed. "After all, if I were to give you a present, it would probably be something dull and unimaginative, like money."

I took his hand and pressed five golden ducats into it. Jerry opened his hand and looked. He tried to give the coins back.

"It's too much, Mr. Caz," he protested. "I don't even look after Andy for you except when you come visit."

"It's the season of giving, Jerry," I stated. "It makes me happy to give this to you since I suspect there might be some new tack you want to buy for Thunder and maybe some new clothes that you won't need to bother Mr. Carl about."

Jerry kept his hand outstretched for a moment, then slowly withdrew it as a smile grew on his face. "Well, if it's for Thunder," he said slyly, "I suppose it would be mean not to accept it on his behalf."

"Exactly, Jerry," I agreed. "After all, the finest horse in Aquileia should have tack that suits him."

When I returned to the house, I found Fenwick sitting at the table in the dining room, enjoying a hearty breakfast that Roberta must have cooked for him. From the smirk on his face, he must have thought this might irritate me. It didn't bother me at all.

Lucy came in, and I met her at the door and gave her a kiss. "Fenwick said he missed breakfast."

"Thank you for arranging to feed him," I said. "It means we won't need to stop for hours."

"Fenwick, what do you expect you'll find?" Lucy asked.

"Nothing important," he mumbled as he finished chewing his last bite. "As a member of the Braintree clan, Count Dunland was probably aware of the conspiracy against the king. As a rule, that extended family is unpleasant, and the residents of their territories tend to reflect that. The count's unhappiness is probably increased due to the arrests of the leaders of the plot."

"So, you think that is the reason for these reports?" Lucy asked.

"Almost certainly," Fenwick stated.

Fenwick rose, intending to return his now empty plate to the kitchen. "I'll take that," Lucy offered.

Fenwick shook his head. "I cannot allow you to sully your pretty hands with my dirty dishes, Your Loveliness," he said to her. To me, he added, "Grab your bags, Your High-and-Mightiness, it's time to leave."

I went to the hall, put on my cloak and gloves, then shouldered my saddlebags. Lucy trailed after me. At the door, I embraced her with my free arm and kissed her goodbye. By the time I finished securing them to my saddle, Fenwick had mounted Davy, his striking piebald gelding. I swung up onto Andy's back, and we set off for the north gate of the city.

"Don't take this the wrong way, Fenwick, but how did someone like you, from no particular background, from Northrup, a town of no importance, become so versed in the kingdom's politics?" I asked. "I'm envious of your knowledge and familiarity. I've always been intrigued by these sorts of things but even now that I have a title, access to information has been an obstacle."

"King Mark is the source of most of my knowledge, Caz," Fenwick replied. "He feels it is important for the Royal Assassin to know how all the different threads are connected. The more I know, the better I can serve him. He values precision. I think he also intends me to share my knowledge with you. He knows that your geographic location and the recentness of your appointment have given you a handicap."

"It has," I admitted. "I am just now meeting people with whom I should already be well acquainted."

"Which is why he invited you to celebrate the solstice at the castle," Fenwick said.

"I suspected as much," I agreed. "Tell me more about this precision he desires."

"Well, the whole Braintree mess is a perfect example," Fenwick said. "If the king had the services of someone like me two years ago, I doubt things would have become as messy as they are."

"How are they messy?" I asked. "He has the chief conspirators locked up."

"He has the heads of five different families in cells below the castle," Fenwick confirmed. "That is messy. All five will need to be tried, and all five will end up being executed. That leaves five important territories needing noble vassals—a significant upheaval in the order of things and creating a problem of distributing these holdings fairly between the king's supporters."

"How could you have made a difference?" I asked.

"The king first learned of this over two years ago," Fenwick said. "He had enough information to know with absolute certainty what the duke was planning. Some of the evidence King Mark possessed was sensitive and could not be used in the courts without exposing the sources of that information. It took another two years to compile additional proof that could be shared in a trial. During that time, the duke dragged the others from the extended family and some allied clans deep enough into the plot that they could not escape, resulting in the five men being held below the castle. If I were in the king's employ two years ago, he would have directed me to arrange an accident for the duke. The conspiracy would have been thwarted. The king would have summoned the other participants to let them know the duke's death was not due to random misfortune. They would still be in place, suitably chastened, and the king's power and influence would have been augmented."

I thought about what Fenwick shared. "I think I understand. Resolving the matter in the legal arena does nothing to enhance the king's authority, does it?" I suggested. "It's separate and distinct from the crown."

It was an eight-day journey to Dunland. Along the way, Fenwick shared with me what he learned from the king about aristocratic politics. Both of us realized that was the reason for the king's insistence that I join Fenwick on this errand. Before the king's intervention, naming me as heir to the Eastern March, I only concerned myself with the machinations of the aristocracy on a surface level. In my new role, it would be to my advantage to know much more.

My father had little, if anything, to teach me. He had been mired in his own problems for too long. Between the trouble caused by his late wife and the annual incursions by the horse nomads, that was enough to command anyone's full attention.

I intended to bring the nomads under control. How I would accomplish this, I had no idea, but that was my intention. Once I gained command of that situation, I wanted to work with Lucy to make sure all the residents of the March enjoyed the healthiest and most prosperous lives possible. In order to make that come to pass, I would need to work with my counterparts within the nobility.

The journey was not difficult. The weather was cold but not unreasonably so. For three days we rode through moderate snowfall. The fifth and sixth days, we traversed the Downs. This was an immense piece of gently rolling terrain with no trees and only thin grass. Below the thin layer of sod was chalk. No crops could grow here, and it was weak pasturage at best.

The evening of the fifth day, we stayed in a grubby inn located in Center Downs. Center Downs was a collection of shabby buildings at the crossroads where the north-south road through the Downs intersected the east-west road. The only purpose of the residents was to extract as much money as possible from travelers forced to spend the night.

It was not until the last day that Fenwick asked, "How do you want to go about this investigation?"

I'd actually thought about it, so I had a ready answer. "First, we go to see Count Dunland. When he throws us out, we book rooms in town. We start asking questions that make people uncomfortable. Someone will come to chase us away. We grab them and work our way backward until it leads back to the count. We threaten him. When we're convinced he's learned his lesson, we leave."

"What if that doesn't work?" Fenwick asked.

"Which part?"

"Him learning his lesson."

"Surely the king gave you instruction," I said.

"Well, he did," Fenwick admitted. "I just want to make sure it won't bother you if I have to—"

"Arrange an accident?" I interrupted. "As long as you don't drag me into it, I'm fine."

We arrived just after midday. Count Dunland's manor complex was clearly visible on a rise to the east. We headed to it straight away.

There was no one at the entrance, and the gate was locked. Fenwick had it open in seconds, and we rode to the house. After dismounting, I used the knocker on the front door.

A querulous wail came from within. "Leave me alone!"

I knocked again.

"Leave me alone, I say! You've taken or ruined everything I have. What more could you want? Leave me alone!"

I jerked my head at Fenwick, indicating he should use his picks to open the door. He dismounted, and I heard the click of the lock quickly. I opened the door but stayed out of the doorway. I don't know why I did that, but I was instantly glad I did. A crossbow quarrel whistled past, chest high.

I quickly connected to my link with Bellona and tried to cast my senses outward. As far as I could determine, there was only one person there. I drew my sword and stepped into the doorway.

Sitting on the floor was an older man. His gray hair was stringy and unwashed. He had a scraggly gray beard, and his eyes were sunken into his cheeks from either lack of food, lack of sleep, or both. After I took a step in his direction, I realized he had not bathed in quite some while. His hands were scrabbling, trying to reload the crossbow in his lap.

"Stop!" I hollered as I laid my sword on top of the crossbow.

The man quit his fumbling at my shout and looked at me fearfully. His mouth opened and closed, but he said nothing. I pulled my sword away.

"Why did you fire at us?" I demanded.

"I— I—thought you were one of them," he said so softly and quietly that I nearly did not hear him.

"And who are *they*?" I asked.

"People," he said. Before I could respond, he must have realized how inadequate his answer was. "People who serve him. Some I recognize from town, others… strangers."

"Who are you?" I asked.

"I am… I was, Count Dunland," he whispered. "Who are you?"

"My name is Ca—Lord Oritur," I replied, catching myself. "My companion is a Privy Advisor of the king's. His Majesty sent us to find out what was happening in your holding."

"Oh, thank all the heavenly beings," Dunland murmured.

I caught Fenwick's eye. "These people who have threatened you," Fenwick asked. "You said they serve someone. Who?"

"I don't know his name," Dunland replied, shaking his head vigorously. "These people call him their master, as in, 'The master wants this. The master wants that.' I don't think they know his name either."

"Where is this person, and when did he arrive?" Fenwick asked.

"I don't know where he stays," Dunland replied. "He showed up in town sometime in Morsug. What day is it now?"

"The ninth of Morsug," I answered. "Did he just arrive?"

Dunland's eyes opened wide in surprise. "It's been a year?" he gasped. Before he said anything else, his eyes rolled up, and he fainted.

5

I looked at Fenwick as if to say, *Now what?* Fenwick shrugged his shoulders in response.

"The man looks like he hasn't eaten or slept for days," I said.

"He clearly hasn't bathed in months," Fenwick added.

"I'll try to find something he can eat. Why don't you go through the place and see what you can learn."

I made my way to the rear of the house, where I expected the kitchen to be. On the way, I passed a dining room on one side and a small study or library on the other. In the dining room, every piece of furniture was smashed to pieces, including the large table. There were brown splotches and smears on the walls. From the lingering funk in the air, I guessed the brown substance was feces. In the study, the furniture was also destroyed, and all the books had been ripped from the shelves. Torn-out pages littered the floor. The violence of the destruction troubled me.

The kitchen was in a similar state to the other rooms. What few pieces of furniture there were had been smashed. Pots and pans and cooking utensils were strewn about. In poking through the wreckage, I noticed there were no knives or cleavers. The stove was still in place—probably too heavy for the marauders to bother with.

The pantry was a shambles. Every tin or sack had been emptied, and its contents tossed on the floor. I nudged some of the mess with my foot, and a rat scurried past. I continued to the root cellar. There was no longer a door. It, too, was ruined, lying in three pieces below. Like the pantry, everything was dumped on the floor, and it looked as though they attempted to stomp everything into a paste of gunk.

Climbing back into the kitchen, I realized there was nothing edible in the house. While that explained the count's gaunt appearance, I wondered how he managed to keep himself from starvation. I would need him to return to consciousness to tell us.

When I returned to the front of the house, Dunland was still unconscious. Fenwick was coming down the stairs, shaking his head. When he reached the floor, he blew out a sigh.

"Every room is a shambles," he said, "like a pack of wild animals was set loose inside."

"That's what I saw, too," I confirmed. "There isn't a bit of food that is unspoiled. I'm reluctant to go into town without more information from our sleeping friend here. I have some jerky, dried fruit, and cheese in my bags— enough to feed us today and tomorrow."

"I have the same," Fenwick said. "What do you think is happening here?"

"A great deal more than I was expecting," I said. "Beyond that, we need to wait for the count to give us more information. In the meantime, we should take care of the horses. I hope the stable hasn't been torn up the way the house has been."

Fenwick and I went out the front door, untied our mounts, and led them behind the manor where we found the stable. The doors were all shut, which I took as a good sign. Opening one of the stall doors, I learned my optimism was not in vain.

The stall was empty, with an unsoiled covering of straw on the floor. Leaving Andy there, I went through the rear of the stall into the rest of the building. I found a lantern hanging from a hook and used my flint to light it. Fenwick left Davy and found another lantern.

The tidiness of the stable stood in clear contrast to what we saw in the manor. The floor was swept. Looking up, I could see hay and straw stacked neatly on separate sides of the loft. Bags of feed grain were also arranged along the back wall in an orderly way.

"At least the horses will be fine," Fenwick said.

I returned to Andy and unsaddled him and began his grooming. When I finished, I found where some blankets were stored and draped some over his back. Using a scoop, I filled the bottom of a small trough in his stall with grain and then added hay to the rack above. With that done, I went looking for buckets to fill with water.

There were none in the stable proper, so I went through a door into a small storage room. I found buckets, then went outside to look for the pump. As I did, I worried that it might be frozen.

There was no pump, but there was a well with a windlass. I cranked the rope up and tied it to the handle on the bucket, then dropped the bucket in the well. It hit something solid with a thunk. Fenwick was approaching with two more buckets and heard the sound.

"Ice," he said. "I'll find a rock."

He returned after a minute with a stone the size of a loaf of bread. Leaning over, he let it drop into the well. A satisfying crash and splash resounded up the walls.

"Funny that it's still as much fun to do that as it was when I was a boy," he commented.

I smiled. There was a sense of boyish naughty fun from dropping a large rock into a well and making a big splash. I sent my first bucket down again and pulled it up full.

When we finished and watered the horses, we returned to the manor. Dunland was still where we left him. Fenwick grasped the count's shoulder and gave it a gentle shake. With a flutter of his eyes, Dunland woke.

His first reaction was fear. His eyes opened wide, and he began to scrabble away from us. After a moment, his wits returned, and he stopped moving, though he was far from relaxed.

"How have you been living?" Fenwick asked.

Dunland gave us a fearful look, twitching his eyes back and forth between us. "I... I live in the groom's quarters," he said hesitantly. "He left with all the others."

"The rest of your staff?" I inquired.

The count nodded.

"When did this happen?"

"They all left in Porri after the master's people came the first time," Dunland explained quietly. "I don't blame them. I couldn't protect them. The master's gang beat all the men to a pulp and raped all the women. They tied me up and made me watch. They told the staff that anyone who stayed would suffer worse the next time. Everyone left as soon as they could. They told me if I left, though, they would do to the whole town what they did to my staff. For months someone came every day to make sure I was still here."

"Is that first visit when they ravaged the place?" Fenwick inquired.

"No," Dunland said sadly, shaking his head. "That happened not too long ago. I'm going to guess it was three- or four-months past. I'm sorry, I haven't been keeping track of time very well. The one they call their master came with them."

"So, you've met this person?" I asked. "Tell us about him."

"I only caught a brief glimpse of him. Even so, I can't remember what he looked like. Almost immediately, I was on the floor."

"Someone knocked you down?" Fenwick questioned.

"No," Dunland said with a tone of despair, "I could not control my body. My body went to the floor. I crawled to him and," Dunland sobbed, "I licked his boots. I think he asked me some questions, but I don't remember what he asked or what I answered. He kept me frozen on my hands and knees, and later, I could hear his people wrecking everything. I decided afterward it was very strange. The only sounds were of things breaking. When he departed, and I could stand, I looked at the destruction and thought it was odd that I never heard any shouting or yelling while it was happening."

"Has anyone been here since?" Fenwick asked.

"For a time, they continued to send someone every day to check that I was still here. Those visits became less frequent. I'm going to guess it has been at least a week since the last one. Someone comes and knocks on the door, and they leave once I answer. They don't come in. I've been waiting with that crossbow for weeks and weeks in case they did," he said. "I still need to wait here every day. It's like an overwhelming compulsion to sit here all day."

"How have you fed yourself?" I asked.

"The gamekeeper is still around," Dunland said. "He drops off some dried meat and other things every so often. I've also been making porridge from the feed grain in the stable. I don't know how to cook, so it's pretty awful. It's just enough to keep me alive."

"Do you have any other clothes?" I questioned. "Would you like to clean yourself up?"

"They destroyed all my clothing along with everything else," Dunland said. "As far as washing up, I can't."

"Why not?" I said in bafflement.

"I can draw water, even heat it and fill a tub," Dunland explained, "but when I try to enter the bath, my body will not obey me. I end up on my hands and knees until I decide to leave. When I give up, I can stand again but only to exit the room. If I try to return, I'm on all fours again as soon as I cross the threshold."

"Do your minders ever visit after dark?" Fenwick asked.

"No. It's always the middle of the day until about the time you arrived," Dunland said. "I would not expect someone now."

"Then let's get out of here to where we can have a fire and warm up," Fenwick suggested. "We have some food, too. It's not much, but it's edible, and we will share it with you."

We left the house and crossed to the stable. The groom's quarters were on the left side of the building. It was a large, plain room. There was a bed, a couple of wooden chairs, and a small stove for heating and cooking. I saw Dunland had brought over a couple of small pots from the wreckage of the kitchen. In the smaller space, the count's lack of hygiene assaulted our nostrils.

"This won't do," I said. "Fenwick, come with me a moment."

"What are you thinking?" Fenwick asked.

"We need to clean him up and wash his clothes, or I can't stay in that room," I said. "I'm going to draw some water and heat it up. You find some rags and soap and grab a stack of those blankets. Something that person did prevents him from washing himself. I think if we do it for him, we can work around that. Once he's clean, we can boil his clothes."

I found the buckets and filled two of them. When I returned, Dunland had rekindled the fire in the stove, and I could feel the warmth. Fenwick returned just after I did. I poured the water from the buckets into two pots atop the stove.

"Right," I said. "Strip, Count Dunland."

"What?"

"Strip," I repeated. "Mr. Fenwick and I cannot stay here with you smelling the way you do. I reckon if you merely stand still, we can clean you up. Then we will deal with your clothes."

Dunland took off his clothing sheepishly. He was clearly embarrassed to be naked in front of us. Though the water we were heating was still cold, I did not wish to wait. I took a rag from the pile Fenwick brought, soaked it in one of the pots, and worked some soap into it. Fenwick did the same.

"I'll take this side," I said to Fenwick. "Raise your arms," I told Dunland.

He stood with his arms up while Fenwick and I scrubbed him. We needed to rinse our rags often as Dunland was filthy. We only used one of the two pots, keeping the water in the other clean. We saved his face and hair for last.

When we finished his face, we used the rags to wet his hair. I took the soap and worked it into his scalp and beard. By now, the water on the stove was warm. I removed the pot with the clean water.

"Right. Outside now," I instructed Dunland.

"I'll freeze," he protested.

"We need to rinse the soap off," I explained, "and we can't do that in here. We're using warm water, and it won't take long. C'mon—outside."

Dunland exited reluctantly. I prodded him further away from the door. I didn't want the water to freeze right on the doorstep and have one of us slip the next morning.

"Squat down on your knees," I instructed. "We're going to rinse your hair first and your beard. As the water flows down, use your hands to try to get as much of the soap out of your hair and off yourself as you can."

Fenwick and I both took hold of the heavy pot. We did not want to merely dump it on Count Dunland's head—that would still leave him covered with soap. It would take both of us to control the flow out of the pot due to its weight.

We started to trickle the water on Dunland's head, and he worked his hands vigorously. It took nearly half the pot to rinse his hair. We then began to pour it over one shoulder, then the other. By now, Dunland had caught on and was doing a good job of distributing the clean water to eliminate the remaining soap. We finished with his hips and groin, then bustled him back inside and gave him a blanket.

I took the pot of dirty water out and emptied it, then refilled the buckets at the well. I used a little bit of the water to rinse the dirty pot, then set both pots back on the stove. His blouse, breeches, and underthings went in one pot. His jacket in the other.

With Count Dunland scrubbed and his clothes soaking, the airflow from the fire in the stove removed the stench from the air quickly. Fenwick and I retrieved our small stocks of food from our saddlebags and brought it inside. We distributed an even amount of jerky, dried fruit, and cheese to each person. It was enough to keep hunger away, but none of us would feel satisfied when we finished. Still, it was all we had, and I was guessing that dining in town was probably not an option.

When we finished our meager meal, Fenwick and I returned the remaining food to our bags. On the way back into the groom's quarters, we each took another stack of horse blankets. He and I would sleep on the floor. Half the blankets were to provide a cushion against the planks and the others to keep us warm in the night when the fire died.

Count Dunland was poking at his clothing in the two pots with an iron prong. "How much longer?" he asked.

"Is the water boiling yet?" I asked.

"Just started."

"Give it a couple of minutes, and then you can take them off the stove," I said. "Wring them out—outside—as best you can, then hang them somewhere near the stove to dry. They may still be damp in the morning, but once we get the fire lit again, you'll be able to get dressed."

"I really can't thank you enough," he said. "I apologize for trying to shoot you. You're the first decent people I've seen in months, and I know it made me dotty. You've fed me and cleaned me and, more importantly, given me the first glimmer of hope I've had since this all started. I seem to remember you saying His Majesty sent you?"

"He did," Fenwick confirmed. "Beginning about a year ago, some travelers through Dunland started to report that they were getting an unpleasant reception from the locals. More recently, those reports included assault and theft and were happening to everyone instead of merely occasional individuals. His Majesty was concerned. He sent us."

"And us is? Please pardon me, but I was not myself when you gave me your names," Dunland asked.

"Lord Oritur," I replied. "And this is Mr. Fenwick, Privy Adviser to His Majesty."

"Oritur?" Dunland asked. "Where in the seven hells is that?"

"The Eastern March," I said. "I am the Earl's heir."

Dunland looked at me with a puzzled expression. "He had two sons," he commented, "both of them spineless degenerates. What happened to them?"

"I don't know exactly," I responded, only smudging the truth a little. "I am also his son, from before he was married. The king commanded that he formally adopt me and named me his heir and charged me with defense of the March."

"Oh? You're a bastard, then," he said, then realizing how that sounded, quickly followed with, "By birth, I mean. All the heavenly beings know that you're obviously a fellow of the highest quality based on the kindness you've shown me. And clearly, a young man of promise for King Mark to involve himself directly like that. But why on earth would he send you here to check on Dunland? It's about as far away from the March as can be."

I turned to Fenwick to allow him to answer Dunland's last question.

"Before you became a prisoner in your own home, milord," Fenwick began, "how much contact did you have with your Braintree cousins?"

The count looked blankly for a moment, then began to laugh. "You're here because I'm a Braintree? And you thought the negative reports were tied to that? Those clodpates must have reached a new level of stupidity. To answer your question, sir, it has been years since I last communicated with them. What have they done?"

"Four of them, along with Count Morningvale, are about to undergo trials for treason, milord," Fenwick replied.

"Majors and Minors," the count exclaimed softly. "What a bunch of suet-brains. They can't even manage their own holdings properly, let alone a kingdom. I assume their guilt is certain to be proven in a court of law?"

"Without question, milord," Fenwick replied.

"Then they will receive what they deserve," the count said.

6

"What do you think is happening here?" Fenwick asked after we determined Count Dunland was asleep.

"Well, it's fairly certain that the person known as 'master' has well-developed magical ability," I said. "And from the way we have heard he wields it, I'm going to guess his dominant is the Lord of the Seven Hells."

"That's what I was thinking, too," Fenwick agreed. "I wish I knew more about how this all works. What do you think we should do?"

"Get on our horses tomorrow morning and get as far away from this place as we can," I said. "If this 'master' is tied to the Dark Arts, we require help. We may need to get the queen involved."

"You don't want to at least try to bring this guy to heel?" Fenwick wheedled.

"No. And neither should you try anything," I stated firmly. "Did Queen Liliana ever tell you what we did in Eatonford?"

"No. Why?"

"She, Lucy, and I went to Eatonford because Liliana suspected someone unearthed a grimoire of the Dark Arts."

"What's a grimoire?" Fenwick asked.

"A comprehensive spell book. From what Lucy explained, spell books that are that detailed are incredibly powerful and can actually possess someone with an affinity for the type of magic in the book."

"So, if you or I came across a spell book like that for Bellona, the book could control us?" Fenwick asked.

"I suppose," I said. "We only ever spoke about it in relation to the Dark Arts, but I guess it would apply to any affinity. Anyway, from reports that made it to the castle, a powerful practitioner suddenly appeared in Eatonford. From the abruptness of how this happened, Liliana suspected someone with affinity came into contact with a grimoire of the Dark Arts, and the book took control. That is exactly what we found. In Count Grafton's library, there was a grimoire. A young lady working on the staff had an affinity for the Lord of the Seven Hells, which she didn't even know about. The book took control of her and woke her ability. We had a difficult time severing her from the book's influence. We then needed to destroy the book. In the process, we were almost killed. It was terrifying—I'm not ashamed to admit it."

"Is that what is happening here?" Fenwick asked.

"I don't know," I replied, "but I don't think so. This 'master' probably had some ability when he arrived in the town a year ago. He knew enough to be able to bend people to his will. From what we've heard, his ability increased a few months ago. I have a feeling that he found something useful in Count Dunland's library—not a grimoire, but information that taught him more about his ability and how to use it."

"Do you think he knows we are here?" Fenwick inquired.

"We needed to ride through town to reach the estate," I said. "He probably controls the whole town now, so, yes, he knows. That's why I want to make a hasty retreat. Staying here any longer only increases the danger to Count Dunland and to us."

"Should we take him with us?"

"He doesn't have a horse, so he would slow us down," I said. "In addition, there is the threat the 'master' made. I hate to say it, but I think it's safer for everyone except him if we leave him behind."

"Even though this person might kill him?" Fenwick said.

"If he leaves, the 'master' will wreak vengeance on the whole town," I said. "Better one than many."

"Are you sure there is nothing we can do?" Fenwick asked. "It's just one person."

"We would never get close enough to him," I said. "He clearly controls these people. If we made an attack, he would use them to make sure he escaped.

I know you are confident in your ability, as I am in mine, but this would not be a normal fight."

"So, we leave in the morning?" Fenwick confirmed.

"After we tell Count Dunland," I said.

I will confess I did not sleep well. Even though the count said no one came after dark, I was half-expecting trouble. When morning arrived, my eyes were scratchy from lack of sleep. Looking at Fenwick, he passed a similarly restless night.

Fenwick rekindled the fire, and I took two buckets for fresh water. Dunland heard us moving about and woke, wrapping his naked body in blankets. We shared some of our food with the count, and when we finished, I cleared my throat.

"Count Dunland, Mr. Fenwick and I are certain we were spotted when we rode through the town yesterday. We think the safest option for you and your people is for us to leave quickly. Our plan is to go back to the capital, obtain the assistance we need to subdue this 'master' and return as swiftly as possible."

"Is there nothing you can do?" Dunland whined.

"Milord, I asked the same question. Lord Oritur and I are both accomplished swordsmen," Fenwick said. "Lord Oritur has personal experience in facing someone with power in the Dark Arts, and he assures me that dexterity with a blade is near-useless in a situation of this type. We know people who possess the magical ability to counter this 'master,' and we will bring them with us on our return."

The count was not pleased with our answer but understood its necessity. Fenwick and I saddled our horses, wished the count well, and set off. We had not made much progress when we encountered a lone man waiting in the middle of the road. He was astride a handsome brown mare. I guessed the horse belonged to Count Dunland not long ago.

His appearance was in no way physically intimidating. He seemed nondescript and unprepossessing. When Fenwick and I drew within a half of a furlong from him, Andy started to become nervous. I noticed Fenwick's horse acting in a similar fashion. At roughly fifty yards distance, Andy stopped and would not go further. He was shaking and began taking sidesteps back and forth. I looked over at Davy and he was also rolling his eyes in addition to trembling.

Rather than wait for Andy to calm down, I slid down from the saddle. From the corner of my eye, I saw Fenwick do the same. Both of us had our right hands on the hilts of our swords. I accessed my connection to the power of Bellona and withdrew a small tendril as I started to advance slowly toward the man. When I had taken five steps, he raised his hand.

"That's close enough for two dangerous-looking men like you," he said. "What brings you to Dunland?"

I did not plan to answer, but Fenwick spoke immediately. "The king asked us to investigate reports of trouble in the region," he said.

"Oh, my," the man replied, exaggerating his distress. "Did you find any trouble?"

"No. Just a crazy old man," Fenwick answered.

While I would expect Fenwick to answer with such words, knowing his craftiness, in this case, I did not detect his usual sly tone. I looked over at him. He was staring straight ahead at the man.

"And you, sir? What did you see?" the man asked.

"I've seen evidence that a practitioner of the Dark Arts arrived in the area about a year ago," I replied. "While he was already skilled to a degree, his power increased a few months ago. He holds a number of people in his thrall and demands they call him 'master.' I reckon that's you."

Out of the corner of my eye, I saw Fenwick standing immobile, still staring at the man.

'That is indeed me," the man stated. "Will you call me master?"

"No," I said.

At the same moment, Fenwick answered, "Master."

As soon as I heard that, I drew my blade, turning toward Fenwick. I was just in time to parry his first slash. Before my eyes, Fenwick's appearance changed. He seemed larger, his features sharper, his eyes glowing red, and his expression was exultant.

I drew upon my ability and imagined a net enveloping Fenwick and drawing tight to restrain his power. The queen had taught me this, and it enabled me to capture Fenwick the second time he and I met. Fenwick snarled in frustration. I sensed my net was ripped apart as Fenwick's appearance began to shift back to that other-worldly aspect. I glanced quickly and saw that Fenwick had touched the tan-zyan gem in his ring to the diamond in the pommel of his sword, accessing a reserve of numinous energy.

That was all I had the chance to see as he attacked again. He began with a coulé, sliding his blade along mine. Then he forced my blade down with a croisé. His strength was greater than I had ever experienced from him. I realized he was attempting to disarm me. Skittering backward, I broke contact before losing my sword. When I had enough distance, I snapped the tie of my cloak from my neck and quickly wrapped the cloth around my left forearm. Fenwick imitated my action.

I touched the tan-zyan stone on the ring on my right hand to the diamond in my sword and felt magical power flow into me. Using that power, I cast imaginary nets around Fenwick, one after another, and pressed forward with my first attack. Fenwick parried my lunge and replied with a riposte. I countered with an esquive which he needed to use his left arm to block.

While doing this, I kept casting my supernatural nets as I sensed Fenwick was shredding them as quickly as I created them. It was a distraction for both of us while we were also fighting for our lives against one another. Fenwick attempted a counter-time move that fooled me, and I needed to block his following thrust with my cloak. Before he withdrew his blade, I tried a prise with my left arm and a counter as I drew him slightly off-balance.

The tip of my sword sliced along the top of his right shoulder. It was only a superficial wound—cosmetic more than structural. Fenwick roared with rage, the red glow returning to his eyes. I retreated, drawing more power from my diamond, and tried to imagine heavier and tighter nets.

I don't know how long we fought. Time was not a consideration—survival was what mattered. The longer we continued, the more our battle moved away from pure fencing. Both of us were trying every trick, feint, kick or punch we could think of. At the same time, there was a psychic battle as Fenwick fought to use his power and I struggled to prevent him. All my supernatural power was being used to control Fenwick's access to his own. It was skill and against skill, and Fenwick and I were a match for one another.

We broke momentarily, and I touched my ring to the diamond in my sword and felt nothing. My store of numinous energy was exhausted. I did not know whether Fenwick had anything left but could not take any chances. My mind whirled desperately, trying to think of a way to disable him without killing him. It came to me in a flash.

He lunged, and I dodged more slowly than usual. His blade pierced me, just under my left clavicle and continued upward, missing my scapula. Ignoring the burning pain, I then took a half-step toward him and punched him square in the face with the swept hilt of my sword as hard as I could. Blood spurted from his broken nose as his body collapsed to the ground like a marionette whose strings were cut.

For the first time since the fight began, I was able to turn my attention to the man on the horse. I tugged Fenwick's blade from my shoulder and began advancing upon the man with a sword in each hand. He pulled the reins of his horse and rode away before I took three steps.

After I watched him ride away, I turned in the other direction to see where Andy and Davy ended up. They were roughly a furlong away. I whistled for them, and they walked toward me hesitantly. Whatever the 'master' did to spook them was no longer present, and they eventually reached me.

I sheathed my blade and stuck Fenwick's through my belt. Searching his boot, I found the knife I knew he concealed within and took it. Then I dug in my saddlebags and found some leather thongs. With them, I bound Fenwick's wrists and ankles as tightly as I could. I was unwilling to risk having him regain consciousness and still want to kill me. When I felt I trussed him as securely as I could, I heaved him up and draped him over his saddle. It was difficult with the use of only my right arm. I unwound his cloak from his left arm and covered him with it.

I picked up my cloak and retied the ends of the fastening back together, then slipped my neck through. My left shoulder had bled all over my jacket and shirt, and the loss of blood, the wet cloth, and the cold temperature were sapping my strength. The bleeding was down to a trickle, though.

I hoisted myself into the saddle and nudged Andy over to where I could grasp Davy's reins. When I had them in hand, we started off. I did not head for the town of Dunland. I was sure the mysterious magician would have an unpleasant reception prepared for us. Instead, we went in the other direction.

There was a town, Dunbride, ten leagues away that I hoped to reach. Traveling by this route would add another day to our return journey, but that was of less concern than my pressing desire to get away from Dunland. I kept the horses at a trot as long as I could before slowing to a walk to allow them some rest.

Sometime after we traveled two leagues, I heard Fenwick groan. "Stop for a minute, please," he rasped plaintively.

I reined Andy in, bringing him to a halt. Davy followed suit. Fenwick groaned again.

"From the way my face hurts and from how you have me trussed up like a roast pig, I'm guessing that wasn't a bad dream—it really happened," he said.

"I don't know," I said neutrally. "What do you think took place?"

"Caz, did I attack you and try to kill you?" he asked.

"Why, yes, Aloysius, you did," I replied calmly. "You seemed quite intent, actually. Nearly succeeded—*again.*"

There was silence for a bit while Fenwick processed this information. I had *some* sympathy for him, but not much. In Eatonford, Esme gained possession of my mind twice. Thankfully, it was only for brief periods, and I never managed to attack my companions, but the complete loss of control was frightening. My concern was that the 'master' still might have a hold on Fenwick.

An idea came to me of how to break any enchantment that might remain. I dismounted. As I crossed to where Fenwick's upper body was draped over his horse, I fished the topaz ward from around my neck. I put the gemstone to Fenwick's neck. When I did, he shuddered as though a cold tremor coursed through his veins, then gave a sigh.

"Something just happened, Caz," he commented. "What did you just do?"

"I touched your neck with my ward against the Dark Arts," I explained. "Why did you just shiver like that?"

"Whatever you did, expelled something," he said. "It's hard to find the right words, but something I didn't even know was present inside of me was chased away."

I stepped closer and grabbed his hair. I lifted his head so I could look into his eyes. All I could see in them was fear. He had lost control of himself, which frightened him. He also realized that I was only a hair's breadth away from killing him. I don't know how much that frightened him, but I felt he understood the predicament we both were in.

After I put the ward back around my neck, I said, "Fenwick, I'm going to untie your ankles so you can ride. If at any point, I feel you are not yourself, I will run you through. I don't have any choice. The ward may have broken his hold on you for now, but I don't know whether that will last."

"I understand, Caz. And, for what it's worth, I'm sorry," he said.

7

We reached the town of Dunbride after dark. We found an inn, and I went inside to arrange rooms for us and stalls for our horses. The innkeeper seemed grateful for visitors, though when he saw the blood on my jacket, his expression grew apprehensive.

"Is there a physician in town?" I asked. "My friend and I encountered trouble in Dunland and are both worse for it."

Relief washed over the innkeeper's face. "Aye, we have a physician of sorts. Not surprised you ran into difficulty in Dunland. You're the first travelers we've had from that direction in months. What's going on there?"

"I don't know exactly," I replied, "but it was certainly dangerous. A place to avoid."

The innkeeper made a warding gesture.

"If you summoned the physician, I would be grateful," I said.

"She's not exactly what you might call a physician," the innkeeper said. "Meara is a healer, that's for certain, but not what you might be used to."

"A hedgewitch, then?" I asked.

The innkeeper nodded.

"Even better," I stated. "My companion and I will take care of our horses. Have someone come get us when she arrives."

"You don't need to do that, sir," he said. "There's a groom."

I waved his comment off. "We would prefer to do it ourselves, my good man."

"Suit yourself," he said with a shrug. "Will you be wanting dinner after?"

"Please."

Fenwick and I led our mounts to the stable behind the inn. The groom came out to meet us. He looked at Fenwick's bound wrists and bloody, ruined face and took a step back, making the same warding movement with his hands.

"Don't be alarmed," I said. "It's just a precaution. Meara is coming, and I hope she will be able to set things to rights. We will take care of our horses, though he might need some help cleaning the hooves."

"Aye, sir," the groom said hesitantly, still clearly uneasy.

Fenwick needed a bit more help in unsaddling and grooming Davy than just the hooves. The groom was extremely wary, acting as though Fenwick was a poisonous snake who might strike at any instant. For his part, Fenwick just looked glum.

Just as we were finishing, the innkeeper hollered out the back door, "Meara's here!"

We returned inside and met a pleasant-faced woman, short and a bit thick in the middle. Her hair was mostly gray, and she carried a large cloth bag over one shoulder. I introduced myself and suggested it would be better for her to come upstairs rather than have her treat us in the common room. The innkeeper showed me to my room, and Fenwick and I both entered.

"This is uncommon," Meara said after the door closed. "I don't think I've seen a Bellona-dominant in years and years, and here the two of you are."

I was extremely pleased to learn she could see our auras. It was an ability Lucy possessed that neither Fenwick nor I had.

"My friend recently fell under the thrall of a mage wielding the Dark Arts," I explained. "I think I broke the connection but is that something you could see?"

"If he were still in thrall, his aura would show it. I can see no sign of it now," she agreed. "How did you sever the control?"

"With this," I said, pulling the topaz from under my shirt.

"That would do it," Meara agreed. "That fellow in Dunland?"

"Yes, ma'am."

She shook her head sadly. "It's a bad business over there. I hope someone will do something."

"That's why we came," I said as I was untying Fenwick's wrists. "His Majesty sent us to investigate."

"And?" she asked, indicating I should strip off my jacket and shirt.

"And we need to bring others who can help us after we deliver our report," I said. "The woman who gave me this ward—her dominant is Ceridwen Sospita."

"You don't say? I've heard that there have been one or two over the centuries, but it's extremely rare. She'll be able to handle the likes of him, I imagine. Tsch," Meara said, examining my shoulder. "It's a clean in-and-out. Praise all the heavenly beings, but you're not going to be happy with me."

"Alcohol first?" I asked. "And then you'll pack the wound with a brown paste?"

"Aye," she replied. "You've been to someone like me before?"

"Someone like you," I confirmed.

Fenwick snorted. He knew I was referring to my wife. Meara turned to him.

"Don't laugh, sonny. Your turn will come when I put your nose back where it belongs," she said, wagging her finger.

Meara poured alcohol into my wound, which nearly made me howl. She then began working the brown paste into the entrance and exit, pressing it in as deeply as she could with her thumbs. It hurt like the deuces at first, but the pain dropped away as whatever the goo contained started to numb where it touched.

When she finished with the paste, she retrieved a length of linen from her voluminous bag and wrapped it around my shoulder, covering both parts of the perforation. I found a clean shirt in my saddlebag and put it on. Meara then handed me a sling for my arm.

"Keep your left arm in the sling for three days," she instructed. "Try not to use it at all."

Meara turned to Fenwick and probed his nose with her fingers gently, feeling for the point of the break.

"You have a very mild touch," Fenwick remarked.

"There's no sense in hurting you anymore than—"

"YEOW!" Fenwick shouted.

"—I have to," Meara continued. "Hold this under your nose to catch the blood. Don't touch it. Leave it be."

Tears streamed from Fenwick's blackened eyes. His nose began to bleed again. Meara handed him a clean rag to soak up the blood.

"I'm guessing you'll be leaving in the morning," she said. "Here's some more of the ointment and material for bandages. Tomorrow evening, you'll need pretty boy over there to clean it using hot water cooled off the boil enough so it won't scald you and clean cloth. He will need to express the old ointment and work in the new. You'll do that the next night as well. If it begins to smell putrescent, find a physician or someone like me as soon as possible. On the third day, you can start moving your arm again but don't overtax it. Pretty boy," she said to Fenwick, "don't touch your nose. It will heal just fine if you don't bother it. You'll have another lump in it, but it's straight now."

Meara went and rinsed her hands in the bowl of water on the dresser.

"What do we owe you for your assistance, ma'am?" Fenwick asked.

"Eight florins will do," she said.

Fenwick counted out the coins and handed them to her. We both thanked her, and I saw her to the door of the room while Fenwick washed dried blood from his face and changed his shirt. When she was gone, I turned to him.

"Dinner?"

He nodded, and we proceeded downstairs. The innkeeper saw us and took us to a table in his small dining room. We were the only guests. He asked if we wanted ale or cider. We both asked for the latter.

"Tell me good sir, are we your only patrons this evening?" I asked.

"Aye," he replied. "Winter is normally slow, but with the troubles in Dunland, no one is traveling that way. The only traffic we get is on the north-south road, and there's precious little of that until summer. In the past, we would have three or four visitors on a night like this. The summer, we would be full up. Someone needs to do something."

"Someone will," I said. "The king sent us to find out what was happening in Dunland, and we are on our way to report to him."

'Thank all the heavenly beings," the man sighed. "Thank you for sharing that. If you don't mind, I'll fetch your cider now."

After dinner was brought to us, Fenwick wanted to know more about what had happened earlier. "It seemed like a bad dream, and like a dream, I'm not sure I remember everything clearly."

In a quiet voice, I recounted our duel to Fenwick. His expression, unhappy to start with this evening, grew more dejected as I continued the narrative. When I reached the point where I decided to allow him to stab me in order to knock him unconscious, he buried his head in his hand.

"I cannot find the right words to express my apology enough," Fenwick groaned.

"It wasn't your fault," I said.

He looked at me sharply as though I had just cursed the Three Major Gods.

"It wasn't your fault," I repeated. "You were not in control of your actions. You were in thrall to this person. I recognized it immediately and was ready. I am relieved that neither of us died."

"How did you avoid being in his control?" Fenwick asked.

I pulled the topaz out of my shirt. "The queen gave me this before we traveled to Eatonford to find the grimoire. Topaz is the gem linked to Ceridwen Sospita, who was a white witch. According to what Lucy told me, she transcended into the realm of the divine when nine mages, far more powerful than the one we just faced, killed her. She is the queen's dominant."

"I overheard Meara saying that is quite rare," Fenwick said.

"Lucy has told me the same. Anyway, while we were in Eatonford, Esme managed to remove this ward twice. Esme was the girl possessed by the grimoire. Without it, I was just as powerless as you were today. The second time, I almost killed Lucy and the queen."

"What stopped you?"

"Lucy did," I said. "She sent out an overwhelming wave of love for me. It equaled the strength of Esme's hold, and I was paralyzed. I had just enough sanity to realize the two forces were at war within me. The idea of war triggered me to access Bellona, and with her strength added to Lucy's, I regained the ward and used it against Esme."

"And you've carried this ward with you since?" Fenwick asked.

"No. It has been sitting in a small cloth bag in one of the drawers in the house in Aquileia. Lucy asked me to wear it on this journey," I said.

"Do you think she knew what we would encounter?" Fenwick asked.

The thought staggered me. Up to now, Lucy had never shared any of her visions of the future. When she was young, upon learning of her clairvoyance, her grandmother had filled Lucy with fear that sharing knowledge of the future could disrupt even the present. Lucy had occasionally let innocuous bits of information slip to me, but always of an inconsequential or trivial nature.

"It's possible," I admitted. "If she did know, it took a great deal of strength for her to overcome what her grandmother taught her. I don't know whether I should even ask her."

Fenwick groaned again.

"What?" I asked.

"Your wife… she's certain to turn me into a newt."

"I think you've wormed your way into her good graces enough that she would settle for a squirrel," I teased. "We'll keep you in a little cage and show you off to our guests. Maybe we'll give you to Julienne to keep her company."

"Quit joking," Fenwick snapped. "I'm sincerely dismayed that I attacked you again. Beyond how it troubles me personally, my employer will be quite put out."

"And I know it wasn't your fault," I stated firmly. "What's more, Lucy will understand that, as will Queen Liliana. With the queen on your side, you have nothing to fear."

We sat in silence for a few moments.

"I have to tell you," Fenwick said eventually, "that I have been resentful that you never taught me how you dampen my power. Thank all the heavenly beings you didn't. Otherwise, one or both of us would be dead right now."

"You are probably correct."

"What about us, Caz?" he asked. "My relationships with you and Lucy are the closest things to friendship that I have ever experienced, other than what is developing with Julienne. You say you don't blame me, but can you forgive me?"

That was a good question, and I needed to ponder it. I chewed on it in my mind and weighed how I felt. There was also a nagging conviction I had been carrying around.

"At the moment, I can tell you I harbor no ill will, Fenwick," I said. "But I will confess the events of the day have left me rattled and unsteady. This is the third time you've tried to kill me and the third time you nearly succeeded. I believe and hope that the passage of a few days will wash away my current trepidation."

Fenwick gazed at me glumly. "There's something else, isn't there?"

I gave him an unhappy smile. "It might never happen, but there might come a day when either of us falls out of favor with His Majesty."

I could see Fenwick swallow nervously. He nodded. "Right," he said. "Then the one would be sent to kill the other. It does cast a bit of a pall over the future, but, as you said, it might never happen."

"And I sincerely hope it never does," I stated.

Fenwick extended his hand across the table to clasp mine. "Agreed."

8

The first three days of our journey back to Aquileia were subdued. Fenwick was still distressed that he attacked me. I was still wary and found it impossible to relax around him, which he noticed. From the worst sort of beginning, the two of us had managed to develop a friendship in the last year. Now that friendship seemed to have evaporated.

Mid-morning on the fourth day out of Dunbride, Fenwick broke our silence, saying, "My father died at Litchville when I was fifteen. He was in the militia—his third and last year of service. They told us it was a lucky shot. The arrow hit his neck and cut the artery."

I started to murmur something sympathetic, but Fenwick held up his hand to stop me.

"You've always been open with me about your past," he said. "I've told you as little as I could get away with about my background. I'm just trying to even the scales."

"Fenwick," I replied, "I appreciate the gesture, but you can tell me this when you're ready. It seems like you're forcing it, and that makes us both uncomfortable. What happened yesterday was not your fault."

"Then why have you been keeping an eagle eye on me?" he asked. "You clearly don't trust me."

"I'm leery of the Dark Arts," I said. "It's not you. I just don't know if he can take control of you again."

As I said this, I had a sudden thought. I reached into my shirt and withdrew the ward. After I pulled the chain over my head, I handed it to him.

"Put this on," I instructed. "If you have it on, he can't influence you."

"Are you certain?"

"Completely. And when we return to the castle, we'll have the queen create a new one. For that matter, whoever comes with us will need to have a ward."

Fenwick pulled the silver chain over his neck. Seconds after he let go of it, he suddenly began clawing at it. He was gasping as though the thin chain was choking him. I almost fell for it before I remembered what happened when I touched the topaz to Esme. She fainted.

"Nice try, Aloysius," I smirked.

"Damme!" he muttered. "I thought I'd get you with that one."

From that point, the rest of our trip back to Aquileia was filled with our normal juvenile give-and-take. He did not resume telling me his life story. I figured he'd allow tidbits to trickle out over time. He did confess that he had told Julienne everything.

"It was easy," he said, "because I've never withheld anything from her. Every question she has asked me about my past, I've answered as truthfully as possible. I've explained to her that there are things related to my assignments that I cannot share, and she accepts that."

We arrived in the city of Aquileia after dark. Fenwick was heading to the castle to make his report immediately. He returned my ward to me when we parted ways. I went to the Foaming Boar to leave Andy. After helping Jerry get Andy settled for the evening, I hoisted my saddlebags on my good shoulder and walked home through light snow. On my way, I heard the bells ring six o'clock. That cheered me, as I hoped Roberta cooked enough dinner to feed me.

Opening the front door, I hullo'd that I was home and dumped my bags. I heard a squeal of delight from the kitchen and the patter of Lucy's feet. She skittered through the door to the back of the house at the end of the hall and into my arms. Lucy peppered my face with kisses, then tugged me into the parlor where a fire was already burning in the grate. When I sat in the chair closest to the hearth, she slid onto my lap, where we exchanged a soul-restoring kiss that lasted until we gasped for breath. When we broke apart, I looked at her quizzically.

"You normally don't attack me like that," I commented. "You seem to reserve those for when we hit a hinge moment related to one of your glimpses of the future. Did we just pass one?"

Lucy nodded solemnly.

"Was your suggestion for me to take along my ward related to it?" I asked.

She nodded solemnly again.

"Can you tell me more?"

She shook her head slowly but softened her refusal by kissing me deeply again. We stayed in the chair, entwined with each other and oblivious to the rest of the world. I heard the creak of the door and then Roberta clearing her throat.

"Dinner," she said, with a small crack in her voice.

Lucy bounced from my lap with her customary grace. If I had been in the same position, I'm sure I would have floundered around, trying to get up. I heaved myself up, feeling stiffness in my legs from the days of riding.

When I joined her at the table, Lucy asked, "Tell me all about your trip, dear."

I proceeded to do just that. When I reached the point on the journey home where I gave my ward to Fenwick, a thought came back to me that bothered me at the time. I was considering how to phrase my question in a way that would not offend Lucy when she laid her finger on my lips.

"I couldn't," she said.

Once again, my wife amazed me. I was going to ask why she did not give me her ward to share with Fenwick, and she answered before I spoke. My mind raced ahead from her brief admission.

"You knew Fenwick would attack me?" I asked quietly.

Lucy did not answer. She gave me a calm look instead while my brain ticked through the logical progression. *She knew he would attack me, but she also knew I would prevail. Lending her ward to Fenwick would have prevented it. She might have warned me in advance, but she did not. Therefore, there is still something to come that required things to play out this way.* I took a deep breath.

"I think I understand," I said. "The queen knows?"

Lucy nodded solemnly again.

"She would not say anything in advance of Fenwick's return because it would make Mark uncomfortable," I offered, thinking aloud. "Still, since the two of you know, I'm going to guess unseen preparations have already been made."

"I'm so glad you're occasionally halfway clever," Lucy said and blew me a kiss.

I let her little quip pass without comment. "I should warn you that I used up all the energy I had stored. Fenwick did too. He might have been able to put some back, but I've been trying to help my shoulder heal."

"All taken into account," she said.

"Good. Then I'll just let you tell me what to do," I said. "It's easier that way. Should I write my father and tell him I will be delayed for our meetings throughout the March?"

Lucy pouted at me. She had already written him to let him know. I suppose I could have been upset that Lucy thought so far ahead of me, but I found it didn't bother me at all.

As we left the table, I made a suggestion to Lucy. "Please warn Roberta that we might have a guest for breakfast. I have a feeling Fenwick will be here early with a summons for us."

While we were eating dinner, Roberta was preparing a hot bath for me. After my long journey through winter weather, it felt wonderful to slip into the hot water. Of course, it felt even better when my lovely wife decided to join me.

Sure enough, the next morning, Fenwick strolled in just as Lucy and I were sitting down to eat. Roberta already had a plate prepared for him and brought it out immediately. He raised his eyebrows at this.

"Have I become that predictable?"

"It's not you, Aloysius," I said. "It's the situation."

"Consider it a token of my thanks for not killing my husband—again," Lucy added with a twinkle in her eye.

Fenwick blushed brightly. I believe it was the first time I have ever seen him embarrassed. He looked as though he wanted to say something but could not find words. Lucy patted his hand to reassure him.

"He was concerned about his future life among the newts and salamanders," I said. "But I shared with him that he had risen enough in your estimation that you might consider turning him into a squirrel instead."

Lucy squinched her face up as though in thought. "I don't know if he can count on that. We'll have to see how I feel if the day ever comes. It hasn't yet, so let's leave those thoughts for Fenwick to ponder in the middle of the night when he can't sleep. So, Fenwick, we have guessed that you are here bearing a summons."

Fenwick cleared his throat, relieved not to be a target for our amusement. "Indeed. Their Majesties and His Highness have requested our presence this morning, 'at our earliest convenience,' which means we must not dawdle."

Lucy and I needed to dress, which did not take long. We met Fenwick at the bottom of the steps, where we all put on our cloaks. From there, Lucy and I went down the street and around the corner to the small market square and found a hackney. Fenwick had Davy, so he rode separately.

He arrived ahead of us, so when we alit from the carriage, a page was already waiting to escort us across the bridge to the castle. The seneschal himself met us and took us inside to the room the king used as his office. Fenwick and I surrendered our swords to the guards at the door, and we were ushered inside after the seneschal announced us. King Mark rose as we entered. Fenwick and I bowed respectfully while Lucy curtsied.

"Liliana and Albert will join us," the king stated. "Quite a disturbing situation you found. We need to discuss the best strategy for dealing with this *person*."

Before the wait grew uncomfortable, the queen and Prince Albert entered. After we greeted them, we waited for them to sit. Once the king took his chair, Lucy, Fenwick, and I sat. Mark cleared his throat but did not speak.

The queen opened the discussion. "When Fenwick arrived yesterday, we all listened to his report. It is clear that this person in Dunland discovered his affinity with the Dark Arts before he arrived there. Whatever he learned about his ability was through trial and error, since there is no one of whom we are aware who could train him."

"Is there a possibility that there is a mage out there more skilled in the Dark Arts? One that we don't know about?" I asked.

Liliana laughed. "It's possible but extremely unlikely. Ability in the Dark Arts comes with a hunger for power and dominance. You saw that in Esme. For that reason, mages who use the Dark Arts have an extremely difficult time remaining obscure. Their compulsion for forcing those around them into subservience draws attention—as it did in this case. From what Fenwick shared, this man is quite powerful but relatively unskilled."

"He seemed to become more capable a few months ago," I commented. "I think he found some materials in Dunland's library—"

"He may have found some spell books," the queen interjected, "but nothing like the grimoire we dealt with. Many older families have them. They usually contain spells that anyone with magical ability can use, regardless of their dominant connection—simple things like lighting a candle with your finger. That person probably analyzed some of the spells in the book and adapted them. Again, through trial and error. It may have made him slightly more skilled but not more powerful. He was already quite strong."

Discussing magic clearly made the king and Albert uncomfortable. I could see it in their faces. Albert merely looked uncomfortable, while his father showed signs of irritation.

"The question is," the king broke in, "how do we get rid of him and set things in Dunland to rights?"

"I've given the matter some consideration, Your Majesty," Fenwick responded. "I have an idea of how we can be successful, but I warn you that you might not like it."

"Tell us what you're thinking," Mark said, "and we will decide whether we like it after."

"Yes, Your Majesty," Fenwick replied. "The challenge we face in this situation is that this person has the ability to convert anyone in the town into his thrall. This gives him a potential force of thousands of people who could oppose us. Using military force to try to reach him, even if we could find a way to prevent our soldiers from falling under his control, would result in the deaths of hundreds of people and make it impossible to reestablish any degree of normalcy in the region."

"Go on," the king said.

"I would suggest instead that we proceed with as few people as possible. In this case, I would propose a party consisting of only Queen Liliana, Lord and Lady Oritur, and me."

"The queen will not travel without adequate protection," the king stated flatly.

"I understand, Your Majesty," Fenwick said. "And it would certainly be possible for her usual escort to travel as far as Dunbride. For the last part of the exercise, Her Majesty might need to leave them behind."

"Unacceptable," the king declared.

"Hear him out, dear," Liliana suggested. "I think Mr. Fenwick has begun with the worst part of his proposal."

King Mark glowered for a moment before muttering, "Continue."

"The problem is that Dunbride is a full day's ride from Dunland," Fenwick said. "The nearest area suitable for a large group of men to encamp would be Count Dunland's manor, which we are certain is under observation by our target. My idea would be for Lord Oritur and me to go in quick and quiet, render this person unconscious, and bring him to the queen. That is possible if she is in the near vicinity. Attempting to transport him to Dunbride would surely fail as soon as he regained consciousness."

"Why does the queen need to be involved at all?" Albert asked. "If you can render this man unconscious, surely you could kill him?"

"If that is your wish," Fenwick said, "we would certainly fulfill it."

"The reason why I need to be there is to learn what he has done so we can un-do it," Liliana said. "Killing him absolutely prevents any further trouble but might leave the people he has placed under his power witless. His death might free them entirely, but if it does not, their minds will remain enslaved—only without a master. That is my greatest worry. We need to question him, and I am the only person with the knowledge of how to gain the information we need and reverse what he has done."

The king's grumpy expression deepened. In the past, I observed how discomposed he was regarding the supernatural. The thought of exposing his wife to danger heaped more distress on top of that. The room was silent while the king grappled with his misgivings.

"If you were to leave the queen's escort behind, where do you propose to take her?" the king asked. "Surely she would not accompany you and Lord Oritur when you went to collect this man?"

"No, Your Majesty," Fenwick replied. "Though you will probably think it unseemly, I believe it would be best for Her Majesty and Lady Oritur to remain behind in a portable shelter. It would certainly not be a pavilion, befitting her stature and position, but the simple type that travelers use to spend the night in the rough. We would be hidden in the woods. If we succeed in capturing this man, Her Majesty and Lady Oritur could then meet us at Count Dunland's manor if it is still standing. The Castle Shield could also relocate there once we have the man under our control."

The scowl on King Mark's face resembled a storm cloud about to unleash a bolt of lightning. Prince Albert saw it. He spoke before his father exploded.

"Please walk us through the steps, Mr. Fenwick, so we can see the logic of what you propose."

"The day before, the four of us would depart Dunbride and travel toward Dunland," Fenwick said. "Before we reached the count's manor, we would leave the road and make camp. I believe that this person has the manor under some sort of watch, but I do not think his concern extends much further from town. Before daybreak, Lord Oritur would join me, and we would find our target and abduct him. We would bring him to Her Majesty, where she would interrogate him and, ideally, neutralize his abilities. With that accomplished, we would summon the queen's usual escort, establish ourselves in town and begin restoring matters."

"Mother, is this at all agreeable to you?" Albert asked.

"Majors and Minors, yes!" she answered proudly. "I appreciate your concern on my behalf," she said, touching the king's hand, "but I am not some delicate flower that could not survive a single night like this. It might even be fun, especially with Lady Oritur, who will share the adventure and any hardship with me."

The king remained scowling and silent. Just before the quiet reached the point of awkwardness, he sighed heavily. He put his hands on the arm of the chair, preparing to rise.

"If Her Majesty suffers anything worse than a hangnail while in your care," he muttered in a low, dark tone, "I will see you flayed alive—both of you."

He stood, and we all followed suit. The king left the room without a backward glance. The queen and Albert remained.

"That could have gone better," Albert commented after the door shut.

"On the contrary," Liliana responded. "It was never going to be easy, and he granted us permission to pursue this in the most effective way. We gained the outcome we sought."

Together, the five of us worked out more of the details and logistics. The troop of the Castle Shield, bodyguards for the royal family, would accompany us to Dunbride and set up camp. The next day, the queen, Fenwick, Lucy, and I would ride toward Dunland. We would stop short, pull off the road, and erect a portable canvas shelter that would accommodate the four of us. That night, Fenwick and I would slip into town, find where this 'master' was and abduct him. At daybreak, the troop of horsemen would leave Dunbride and resume guarding the queen. If Dunland Manor were still standing, we would move everything there. If the 'master' destroyed it after Fenwick and I departed, we would set up a bivouac on the grounds.

9

We left the following day. Though Lucy and Queen Liliana were supposed to travel in the royal carriage, they also brought their horses, Bella and Tyche. As soon as we were out of sight of the city gates, the two women left the carriage to join Fenwick and me on horseback.

Reddened cheeks from exposure to the weather enhanced both women's beauty. The queen, in particular, was enjoying her freedom. She enjoyed riding and seldom found the time in her schedule to indulge.

It took us nine days to reach Dunbride. At every inn, they made a fuss over hosting the queen for the evening. I could tell Liliana would have preferred to be just another traveler, but she accepted the fawning and deference with good grace and displayed her kindness and courtesy to everyone.

In the morning, we set out in the direction of Dunland. When I judged we were still a league away from the count's manor, I looked for a place we could leave the road. Thickets and low scrub flourished under the trees at the edge of the road, but I found a game trail that provided a break. Fenwick and I went first, followed by the ladies. Two members of the Castle Shield accompanied us, their horses nearly overburdened, carrying our portable shelter and bedding. The soldiers would erect the shelter and then depart. Just over a furlong down the thin trail, we came across a glade in the woods. This was the perfect spot, and I dismounted.

It took the two men very little time to erect our temporary quarters. Made of canvas, supported by wooden poles, it was square and squat, with a pyramidal roof and an oilskin floor. There were four low cots that rested no more the six inches off the ground that folded into a surprisingly small bundle.

While the soldiers were setting up our accommodations, Fenwick and I were busy gathering deadfall wood for a fire. We dragged three small logs and arranged them to give us a place to sit off the ground. Fenwick had a hatchet and used it deftly to cut some of the larger branches we found into more manageable sizes. While he was doing that, I took two canvas buckets and went in search of water. It did not take long to find. A small stream was still running on the far edge of the glade.

We brought six buckets with us, and I filled them all, giving one to each of the horses. Fenwick had started a fire, and the two of us unsaddled the horses and gave them a cursory grooming. Though small, our shelter had enough room for us to store the saddles.

Once we put the saddles away, I stood and examined our little camp. As the sun was nearly set, it was growing difficult to see. I was fairly certain I saw the silhouette of Chauncey atop the portable shelter, though.

Fenwick then invited the ladies to come to sit by the fire, which had grown into a cheerful blaze. It was a nice winter scene with about six inches of snow on the ground. Judging by their expressions, Lucy and the queen were in high spirits. It occurred to me that neither was likely to have ever spent the night in this rough manner. During my time in the Rangers, I passed more than a few nights in worse conditions than these, and I suspected Fenwick had done as well in his checkered past.

"Fenwick," the queen said suddenly, "please put this around your neck. I've been meaning to give it to you since before we left the city. We can't have you trying to kill Caz again."

She handed him a small cloth bag. He withdrew a thin silver necklace connected to a topaz. After he slipped it over his neck and tucked it inside his shirt, he patted his chest, then bowed deeply.

"Thank you, Your Majesty," he said.

"Psst," she hissed. "We'll have none of that while we are out here in the woods. Please call me Lily. It will humor me."

Fenwick gave a wry grimace. "I'm sorry, mum, but I canna," he said, reverting to the heavy Eastern accent of his youth. "Tis too disrespectful an' twould pain me dear. The lowest I can go wi'out gratin' on me soul is 'mum' I figger. If n that's 'ceptable, mum."

The queen's mouth twisted in a smile that reached her eyes. "As long as it's 'mum' and not 'ma'am,' I'll accept 'mum' from you but there is a price to be paid. What that price will be, I'll decide later."

We spent a couple of hours in idle conversation, quite a bit of it regarding the weddings that Lucy, Fenwick, and I attended. The queen wished to know about all the different costumes. As the sun began to set, Fenwick retrieved a small kettle the soldiers brought with the other equipment.

I helped him set up the tripod of iron rods that would suspend the kettle above the fire. Fenwick added some water to it, then dumped in a small bag of salted pork, cut into cubes. He stirred it occasionally and, when he judged it ready, added dried peas, beans, chunks of carrot and potato, some onion, and some other seasonings. He let it cook for a while, stirring every so often.

"Salt pork stew," he announced when he felt it was ready.

I handed out wooden bowls and spoons and broke a loaf of bread into four parts. Fenwick took each bowl and spooned some of the stew into it, then handed it back. When he finished serving himself, he took his seat again.

"Eat hearty, mum," he said to the queen.

"This is regular fare for soldiers on the march," I explained. "Consider it part of the adventure."

As we ate, it began to snow lightly. Both women commented that dinner was good, but neither planned to ask for the recipe. By the time we finished, the snow was steady, falling at a good clip. Fenwick looked at me in the firelight with a faint smile. A strong, steady snowfall like this would make it extremely difficult for any watchmen to see us. It would also muffle any noise we might make on our errand later tonight.

The ladies stayed with us for another couple of hours. We spent the time chatting about everything except the challenge facing us. Eventually, they decided to retire for the evening. Fenwick and I stayed by the fire. With the moon and stars hidden by clouds, the best way of judging the passage of time was by how quickly the wood burned.

Eventually, Fenwick stood, saying, "Let's get moving."

We retrieved our saddles quietly so we would not wake the ladies and readied our horses. Given the darkness, I trusted Andy's eyesight far better than my own and let him pick his way along the game trail until we found the road. As soon as Fenwick and I cleared the woods, I reached within myself and tugged forth the smallest tendril of Bellona's power I could imagine.

I wasn't expecting a fight—I wanted to expand the reach of my senses. Fenwick and I had discussed this earlier. We felt our biggest challenge tonight would be finding our target. Even though Fenwick and I were not well-versed in the supernatural, using magic to find magic seemed perfectly logical.

We passed the entrance to the count's manor and knew the town was not far. The town of Dunland was home to several thousand people. The first building we encountered loomed suddenly in the darkness. There were no lights in town, which was what we expected. Fenwick and I continued slowly and silently, both of us straining, hoping we would sense where our quarry was presumably sleeping.

We both reckoned he would have established himself near the center to make it easier to manage the people he controlled. He probably took over an inn or a large private residence. Fenwick and I plodded along silently through the falling snow.

"Hsst!" Fenwick signaled. "Ahead, on the right."

As soon as he said it, I felt it too. We nudged our horses to walk slightly faster. When we were halfway from where we sensed his presence, some light appeared in the windows of the building we were aiming for.

"Damme!" Fenwick cursed softly as he urged Davy forward.

I nudged Andy to keep pace. As we rode, I pulled forth more of my asomatous energy, readying myself for conflict. We could hear shouting and doors slamming.

Lights appeared in the windows of the other buildings nearby and across the street. Fenwick steered Davy to the side of the street and reined him in. I followed. We slid off our saddles and quickly looped the horses' reins over a fence, drew our swords, and began running for the house that drew our attention.

Before we reached the door, men materialized in front of us. I sensed them before I saw them. They were without shoes and barely dressed. Fenwick and I had no choice but to cut them down. I encountered seven before we reached the building we sought. Only one had a sword. Two carried knives, and there was a fire poker, a candlestick, a shovel, and one held only a length of log as a weapon. I didn't know what Fenwick faced, but it was probably similar.

The building in question was an inn with a porch the full width of its front. We reached the front door, and I could see Fenwick in the dim light from the windows. Fenwick tilted his head at the front door and shook it, then nodded at the window on his side, raising an eyebrow in query.

I nodded in agreement and moved quickly to stand beside the window on my side of the porch. I pulled forth more of Bellona's energy. Fenwick caught my eye and held up three fingers. I nodded. He lowered one finger, then another. In the same cadence, when he would have lowered the last, we both dived through the windows, landing on the floor, and then rolling to our feet.

As I experienced before when under the influence of Bellona, time seemed to move more slowly. My senses were sharper, and my reactions almost as quick as thought. Before I even completed my somersault, I heard the twang of crossbows, then the whizz of the quarrels flying over my head. We were in the common room of the inn. There were twelve men waiting for us. Half already held their swords drawn. The others were dropping their crossbows and unsheathing their blades.

As I moved to face them, I sensed other men running to the building from the outside. Those facing us may have been skilled for Dunland, but none were a match for Fenwick or me, even without our supernatural gifts. They did have the advantage of numbers, and reinforcements were on their way, so Fenwick and I needed to be quick.

As with any large task, the key to success is to take things one at a time. I danced to the side to put one of them between me and the others and dispatched him quickly. Sliding to my right, the next man blocked his companions, and he fell on my thrust to his chest. I skipped to the left for another, stayed in place for the third, dashed forward for the fourth, stutter-stepped and moved right for the fifth, and trapped the last man on my side with his back to the stairs. Fenwick had his last man there, too, and we sent them both to the Seven Hells at nearly the same instant.

Others were climbing through the window already as Fenwick and I clambered up the stairs into the upper hallway. We sensed our objective was in the room at the left end of the hall. We ran toward it, expecting to find it locked. It was. Fenwick and I both backed up, then charged the door to smash it in with our shoulders. The door did not budge even a hair's breadth or give forth the slightest rattle from our assault. Our target must have found a way to reinforce it with his magic.

Before Fenwick and I could figure out what to do, three half-dressed men appeared in the hall, aiming loaded crossbows at us. Three more arrived a moment later. Fenwick looked at me and shrugged. He dropped his sword and raised his hands. I bent at the knees slowly and laid my sword on the floor. As I stood, I opened my cloak to show the men I was otherwise unarmed. When my hand reached my neck, I clasped the thin silver chain around my neck, snapped it easily, and allowed it to slip down my sleeve to near my elbow as I raised my hands.

"I knew it was a stupid plan," I snarled at Fenwick. "We might as well have walked right up in the middle of the day, stopped in the street, and shouted, 'Hey! We're here to kill you!' That would have worked just as well."

"At least I had a plan," Fenwick snapped back. "I don't remember you offering any brilliant ideas, and you seemed to go along with this one easily enough."

"Every time I mention something, you always dismiss it," I complained, yelling. "Every single time I make a suggestion, you tell me how stupid I am and why it won't work."

"That's because all your ideas *are* stupid," Fenwick shouted. "If we'd done half the things you brought up, we'd both be dead five times over by now."

The door opened, and the man we'd seen who had made Fenwick attack me appeared. "Now, now, children," he said in an oily voice. "There's no need to fight. Once I find out how you are able to resist me and remove those obstacles, you'll both become my willing servants. How wonderful it will be for me to have two thralls, both master swordsmen with supernatural powers."

"You're not going to kill us?" I exclaimed. "Oh, thank you, sir! Thank you!'

I fell to my knees in front of him. When I dropped, I lowered my arms, and the necklace slid back into my hand. Clasping my hands in supplication, I reached for his hand as though to kiss it.

At the last instant, he recognized a possible trick. He tried to yank his hand away, but with Bellona's strength coursing through me, I was too quick for him.

I touched the topaz from my necklace to his fingertip. The moment the gem touched him, he fainted dead away, dropping with all the grace of a sack of potatoes.

This was the moment of greatest danger. I half-expected six crossbow quarrels to bury themselves in my flesh. I turned around slowly, only to see the six men, still armed, standing stupefied, seemingly stuck in place. Queen Liliana had thought this would be the case when we rendered the mage unconscious. His control over them remained, but with him being unconscious, they were frozen, unable to act without his direction.

Fenwick and I retrieved our blades and sheathed them. I put my ward into my money pouch while Fenwick was fishing leather thongs from his boot. He handed some to me, and while he was binding the mage's hands, I worked on the ankles. When we were satisfied, Fenwick darted into the room. I heard cloth ripping. He returned and gagged our captive.

I took the feet, and Fenwick grasped him under his shoulders, and we carried him downstairs and out the front door. Passing through the common room, I felt a twinge of regret over the men we killed. It was necessary, but they were not acting of their own will.

I stayed with the unconscious mage while Fenwick fetched our horses. He returned in a matter of minutes. We hoisted the limp body onto Fenwick's horse in front of the saddle. Fenwick and I both mounted and headed back out of town. The snow was still falling steadily.

"If he stirs, remember, bonk him in the noggin," I reminded.

"I will," Fenwick replied. "I have to give you credit. Things worked out just as you predicted."

"I wish I could claim the idea," I said. "The queen warned us that he would probably be able to sense our presence. I'm just sad that he put so many in our way."

"Any one of them would have killed us," Fenwick pointed out.

"I know," I agreed. "Still, when we straighten out this mess, how many families will be missing husbands, sons, and fathers?"

"You can't blame yourself, Caz," Fenwick said. "Remember who is at fault here."

"That's true."

10

As we left town, the dim light began to grow, even as the snow still fell. When we reached the entrance to the count's manor, there was no one there. I hoped the count was still alive.

We saw a light in one of the windows of the manor as we rode up. That was a good sign. Fenwick and I rode to the front door and dismounted. We tied the horses to a post. Fenwick went inside while I stayed with the unconscious mage. Fenwick returned with Lucy and the queen, still wearing their cloaks.

"We've started a fire," Lucy said, "but it is still cold inside. Count Dunland has gone to get a chair for the mage. You can bring him inside."

We carried him in and followed Lucy to the drawing room. She and the queen had largely cleared it of the wreckage we saw when we were here before. The count entered a moment later, carrying a wooden chair I last remembered seeing in the groom's quarters. There were also four folding camp stools. A fire was blazing in the hearth, though the room was still chilly. Fenwick and I tied our captive to the chair securely. We did not remove the leather thongs from his wrists and ankles.

"Did you have any difficulty?" the queen asked.

"Nothing we didn't anticipate, thanks to your warning, Your Majesty," Fenwick said.

The count appeared only slightly less disheveled than when we first met him. His expression was much happier, though. He came rushing over to us and seized Fenwick's hand first, then mine, pumping vigorously.

"Thank you!" he babbled, "Thank you! A thousand times thank you!"

I patted the count's hand to get him to release mine. He looked past me and saw our captive trussed to the chair. The count took an involuntary step backward.

"He is unconscious," I said, "and with the queen here, he won't be able to hurt anyone ever again. Did it go poorly for you when we left?"

"He came and tortured me," the count said in a quavering voice. "He never touched me, but he made me feel such pain as I never knew existed. I felt as though I had been whipped, flayed, branded, and beaten, but when he eventually tired of hurting me and left, I had no injuries."

"Caz, what happened when you disabled him?" the queen asked.

"As you predicted, Your Majesty, his thralls were stunned and immobile, incapable of thought or movement. They remain in that condition," I answered.

The queen pulled a large book from a bag I hadn't noticed, resting next to one of the camp stools. Several ribbons of different colors extended from the top of the pages. The queen opened the book to where a green ribbon lay. With the book in hand, she went to each window and the doorway of the drawing room, holding up her ring, which featured a large topaz, and murmured an incantation. When she finished with those, she went to each corner of the room and made a similar gesture, but the spell she chanted was slightly different. When she finished, she turned to us.

"I just sealed the room. When I wake him, his influence will be trapped inside these four walls and unable to affect anyone outside. His thralls will remain stupefied. Count Dunland, I do not have a ward for you, so you should leave the room. Do you have your wards?" she asked Fenwick, Lucy, and me.

They nodded. I pulled mine from my money pouch and held it in my hand, then I indicated I was ready. The queen removed the gag from the mage's mouth, then flipped to a different section of the book and read aloud. When she finished, the mage opened his eyes. In an instant, they turned the same glowing red I had seen in Fenwick's eyes when he was trying to kill me. The man twisted his head to look at each of us, snarling with rage.

"Your powers are confined to this room," the queen told him. "The four of us are protected by wards, and you cannot influence us. I suggest you test my claim, so you realize the futility of your situation more quickly."

The mage uttered something in a language I never heard. The light in the room dimmed, and the fire in the hearth nearly died. After a moment, the light returned, and the fire blazed again.

He muttered something else and struggled against the bonds tying him to the chair. Whatever he said had no success, and his eyes glowed even more fiercely. He then tried another incantation that had no effect. The chair shook slightly as he strained against the ropes, the cords in his neck and the redness of his face showing the physical effort he was exerting, but he made no progress. He stopped and seemed to compose himself.

"You're going to kill me," he said. "You should just get on with it."

"That has yet to be determined," the queen replied. "We need to learn how poisoned your soul is first. If you are irredeemable and the entirety of your soul is the possession of the Lord of the Seven Hells, we will be forced to end your mortal life and condemn you to an eternity of torment. You should know by now the Dark Lord has no tolerance for failure."

The fire in the mage's eyes flared, and he snarled like an animal. The queen calmly opened another section of her book and began reading. The words and language were unknown to me and sounded similar to the mage's earlier incantations. As the queen continued, the red in the mage's eyes began to dim. At length, he appeared to relax. His eyes returned to a normal brown.

"If it is possible, I would like to speak with the man or boy you were," the queen requested. "Is there still a trace of him remaining in this body? Or have you destroyed him utterly?"

Various expressions flitted across the man's face. When they stopped, his eyes glowed red again. He glared at the queen defiantly.

The queen calmly read through the passages she had recited before. When the man calmed, she repeated her request. It took four more attempts before she received a response.

"I—I am here," the man said in a weak voice with the high pitch of boyhood.

"Who are you?" the queen asked.

"D—Donald. Donald Entremont."

"Hello, Donald," the queen said in a kindly tone. "My name is Liliana. Will you talk to me?"

"I—I guess."

Gone was the snarling, straining, red-eyed mage. In his place, a grown man but with the posture and voice of a shy boy—a boy who knew he was in trouble for doing something naughty, slumped and squirming in the chair. It was fascinating to see.

"What did you do, Donald?" the queen asked.

"Me? I didn't do nuthin'—I swear," he responded.

"I think we both know that's not true, Donald," the queen replied in a motherly tone. "What did you do?"

"They were making fun of me," he whined. "It's all their fault."

"That was mean of them," the queen agreed. "Why were they making fun of you?"

"They make fun of me since my dad is a drunk. My mom got so tired of him she up and left. It's just him and me and he's either drunk, or sleeping or mad all the time. It ain't fair for them to tease me."

"So you made them stop?" the queen inquired.

"I sure did," came the little boy's voice, full of pride. "I hurt 'em, real bad. Made 'em run away, cryin'."

"And that felt good?"

"Real good."

"Did they keep teasing you?" the queen asked.

The man's posture straightened slightly, and he was no longer squirming. "They knew if they came after me, I'd hurt 'em," he said with more confidence.

"Did they stay away after that?"

"Yes'm." His tone took on a sad tinge, "I din't want that, though. I just wanted 'em to treat me reg'lar, like everyone else. But they din't even talk to me. They just run away."

"What about your father?"

"He was still a mean ole drunk but when he tried to hit me, I hurt him, too," the man said. "He was stupid. I had to keep on hurting him 'fore he stopped trying to hit me. Then he was scared of me. Said I was a devil-child. The others started callin' me that, too. Devil-child. I din't like it, so I hurt 'em some more."

I found this uncomfortable to observe. Fenwick did not seem troubled by it; he appeared fascinated. I looked at Lucy with pleading eyes. She shook her head slightly and nodded at the queen, indicating I should have patience and pay attention.

"When did you find out you could make people do what you wanted?" the queen asked.

"Not long after," he replied. "There weren't no food in the house and I hain't eaten in two days. I went to the baker but I din't have no money. I sorta wished him into giving me a load of bread but as soon as I walked out, he came chasin' after me, sayin' I stole it."

"Did you hurt him?"

"Nah. I just wished him to stop hollerin' and quit chasin' me."

"Did he stop?" the queen asked.

"Yes'm. He looked like he ran into a wall, he stopped so sudden," the man replied, a bit of youthful pride coloring his tone.

"How long was it before you learned you could keep someone from getting upset when you *wished* them to do something for you?" the queen asked.

"A couple of years," the man responded, his voice now deeper and more adult. "Everyone hated me, though. People crossed the street to stay away. The shops would lock their doors if they saw me coming. It didn't do 'em any good, though, because I'd just make 'em let me in."

"When did you figure out how to make them your slaves?" Liliana asked.

Suddenly, the mage's eyes glowed red again. "They're slaves, alright. *My* slaves."

The queen sighed. She crossed to the mage and touched his cheek with her ring. The instant the topaz contacted him, he slumped, unconscious.

"This will take time," the queen said.

"It did not seem like you made much progress," I commented.

"On the contrary. I learned a great deal," Liliana replied. "First, he's very powerful, though relatively unskilled. We suspected that, but this confirms it. Thank all the heavenly beings he did not conduct the ritual of awakening, or he would be immensely stronger. Second, since he looks to be in his mid-twenties, he's been using his abilities for over a decade, based on what we just saw."

"Is that good or bad?" Fenwick asked.

"It's not good," the queen answered. "You saw how the Dark Lord reestablished control of him?"

We nodded.

"I need to learn if enough of his true self remains for him to survive when I cast the darkness out," the queen explained.

"If it doesn't?" Fenwick asked.

"We will wait and see," the queen said. "It will be less unpleasant if I can get his true self to tell us what we need to know about how to free his thralls. In the meantime, Caz, Fenwick, I need the two of you to return to where you found him and see if you can find a spell book. That may provide us with the information we need. Lucy can keep me company."

Fenwick and I donned our cloaks and exited the front door. It was no longer snowing, but the sky was still overcast. The fresh snowfall made it so quiet the only noise was the horses breathing. That silence became eerie when we entered the town. We could see no sign of activity.

There were several people we saw still stuck in place without the will to move. None of them were dressed for the weather, and snow crowned their heads and shoulders. The bodies of the men we killed in front of the inn were now covered over. Entering the inn, everything was as we left it. On the upstairs level, two of the motionless thralls had lost control of their bladders while we were away.

We walked past them into the room from which the mage came. It was the largest guest room in the inn, and we found it well-kept and tidy—not surprising since he had people to pick up after him. On a small desk, we found three old books.

Flipping them open, I saw they were handwritten journals. Each one was written in a different hand. Two of the three were easily readable. The handwriting in the third was a scrawl. For all three, the edges of the pages were discolored by age, and the pages themselves were brittle.

Fenwick took a pillowcase from the bed and put the books in it. We searched the rest of the room and found nothing interesting. There were clothes and toiletries but no amulets, medallions or other interesting trinkets, and no other books or writings.

By the time we returned to the manor, it was nearing midday. The Castle Shield had arrived. We rode around back to the stable and left our horses. The soldiers offered to groom them. Fenwick and I were tired enough that we did not protest. There was a large heap of rubbish outside the kitchen door, a sign that the soldiers were already busy tidying things. When we went inside and made our way to the drawing room, Lucy met us. She took the pillowcase with the books and handed us a small sack.

"The soldiers supplied lunch, and I grabbed some for you," she said. "It's not much—meat, cheese, and bread—but better than starving. The two of you should eat and then get some rest. I understand they put our cots in the groom's quarters."

Lucy gave me a kiss and then turned to go to the drawing room. Fenwick was holding the sack, and he gestured with his head toward the rear of the house. Food and sleep sounded fairly attractive, so I followed him outside.

11

The count came to wake us before the sun set. He apologized, saying the ladies asked him to do it since the soldiers were going to serve dinner soon. Though I was groggy, I also realized that if Fenwick and I slept much longer, we would be awake all night again.

While we were sleeping, the Castle Shield established camp in the area between the manor and the stable. We could see a cooking fire with kettles larger than the one we used the night before. From what I could smell, the meal would be the same.

"You should watch the mage," the count suggested, "while the ladies eat. When they finish, you can take your turn."

Fenwick and I went to the drawing room and found Lucy and the queen sitting next to one another, peering at the same book. As we drew closer, we could see it was the one with the difficult handwriting. The other two books were on the floor, clearly discarded. The mage was unconscious.

'The count suggests you eat, mum," Fenwick said, "and you too, Your Loveliness. We will watch our friend until you return."

Both women looked up, slightly startled. They had been concentrating so hard, trying to decipher the handwriting, that they did not notice us come in. They laughed—embarrassed to have been so engrossed.

"Did you learn anything more while we were gone?" I asked.

Lucy shook her head.

"It was more difficult to reach his true self than the first time," Liliana said. "And the darkness regained control more quickly. We decided not to try again until we saw the books. Those two," she gestured at the books on the floor, "contain nothing more than parlor tricks, though you both might find something useful in them. This book, with the terrible handwriting, seems promising, from what we have been able to make sense of."

The ladies departed, and Fenwick and I sat. Bored, I picked up one of the two books. Leafing through it, I saw what the queen meant. The book did not address the supernatural at all. It showed various sleight-of-hand techniques, explained how to perform certain card tricks and how to build boxes with false bottoms or mirrors to enable different types of "disappearing" tricks. I discarded it rather quickly.

The second book had an uninteresting title: *Simple Magic for the Home*. I had nothing better to do, so I scanned the table of contents. Half the entries seemed to concern removing different types of stains from a variety of fabrics. Others promised to slow the tarnishing of household silver or keep knives sharper for longer periods or other insipid things.

I was about to close the book and drop it on top of the other when something caught my eye. Opening it back up, I saw the entry for "Lighting Candles." This was something Lucy did routinely. I don't know why I never asked her to teach me, but I hadn't. Turning to the proper page, the instructions were surprisingly simple.

"Fenwick," I said, "have a look at this."

I handed the book to him, open at the proper page. Looking around the room, I did not see any candles. With darkness falling, we would need some. Planning on going to ask where candles might be found, I tried to stand from the low camp stool on which I was sitting, but I lost my balance. Stumbling slightly to my left, without thinking, I reached out to steady myself and touched the mage's knee.

It was as though I had entered a dream. The same lack of logic that we often experience in dreams was present. I suddenly felt compelled to draw my sword and cut the mage's bonds. After I freed one of his hands and one of his feet, Fenwick interrupted me by trying to disarm me. His battute was unsuccessful. I responded with an esquive and croisé, forcing his blade downward.

Killing Fenwick was now my burning desire. His failed attempt to disarm me left him extremely vulnerable. It was a simple matter to flick my blade up, and I would pierce him under his ribs and reach his heart and lungs in a single blow. Before I could complete my thrust, everything went black.

When I woke, darkness had fallen outside. The drawing room was lit with a handful of candles and the light of the fire. I was stretched out on the floor. My last memory was of the very bizarre dream, and I was quite befuddled.

Lucy was holding my hand, and the queen was peering down at me. *I should not be lying down in the queen's presence*, I thought, and tried to stand so I could bow properly and apologize. Lucy put her other hand on my shoulder and prevented me from getting up. My thoughts were a jumble.

"I know how you light candles," I said.

Why that was the first thing out of my mouth, I don't believe I will ever know. Lucy looked at me as though I suddenly sprouted a second head from my neck. The queen began to giggle. Behind her, I heard Fenwick chortle. When I realized how ridiculous my statement was, I began to laugh as well.

When I recovered, I asked, "Did I nearly kill Fenwick?"

"You would have," Lucy answered, "except Lily stopped you."

"Sorry, Fenwick," I said. "You put me to sleep?" I asked the queen.

She nodded. "More or less."

"I was under his control, wasn't I?" I asked. "That's not good."

Lucy nodded. I looked over at our captive. He was once again unconscious and lashed to the chair.

"Something good came from it," the queen said. "We learned how he controls some of his thralls, perhaps all of them. In a moment, Fenwick is going to the town with some soldiers to free the men who were trapped outside. I hope they have not already died from exposure to the cold. In the morning, we will attempt to lift the mage's command over the rest. We will need all the soldiers in town to help reduce the confusion that is bound to follow."

After Fenwick departed, the queen woke the mage and made another attempt to connect with his true self, the man named Donald Entremont. It took longer, and she had to repeat the spell she had employed before many times before the red glow in his eyes faded. When he spoke, he sounded weary.

"Donald, you still remember the difference between good and evil, don't you?" the queen said. "Is that why the Dark One suppresses you so tightly?"

"I guess," he replied.

"You knew what you were doing to people was wrong, and it troubled you, didn't it?"

"They were mean to me," the man stated. "They deserved it."

"Later, after everyone knew not to be mean to you, did you ever consider whether they still deserved it?" she asked.

"I could not hold those thoughts in my head," he said.

"But it did disturb you," the queen stated.

"The wolf sheds no tears when he kills the rabbit," he snarled, his eyes glowing red again.

The queen touched her ring to the mage again. He fainted, as before. She returned to her seat, looking at Lucy and me with a chagrined expression.

"I fear there is not enough left of Donald to survive," she sighed. "I will try again in the morning. In the meantime, we need sleep, and we need to watch him through the night. How do you propose we divide the watches?"

"Am I free from his influence?" I asked.

"Yes," the queen confirmed.

"I'll take the first watch then," I offered.

"No," Lucy countered. "Lily will take first watch. I will take second, then Fenwick. You will have the last—because I can tell you are exhausted."

For a split-second, I thought I would argue, but I realized my wife was right. I was drained, both physically and emotionally. Lucy took my hand and helped me stand, then led me through the manor toward the stable. A small city of portable shelters was now located outside the rear entrance. We walked through them into the groom's quarters where our cots were waiting. Lucy pointed to one, and I stretched out.

"Milord, I'm told it's your turn on watch," the soldier whispered in the darkness, shaking my shoulder gently.

"Right," I mumbled, forcing myself awake.

As I stood carefully in the light of the small lantern the soldier carried, I realized I had fallen asleep almost as soon as I lay down on the cot. I shook my head to clear the cobwebs and headed outside. The soldier followed and shut the door behind him.

In the house, Fenwick was standing there. The few candles we found were long since burned out, but there were two lanterns. Our prisoner was still tied to the chair but was awake. The glow of his red eyes was disconcerting in the dimly lit room. As soon as I saw that, I fished in my money pouch, found my ward, and held it in my palm. I would not allow him to gain control of me again.

"You can see he's awake," Fenwick said. "If he starts to bother you, just tap him with your ward, and you'll knock him out again."

"Right. Has he said anything?" I asked.

"Well, that's why I let him stay awake," Fenwick replied. "It has been interesting. Apparently, when he invaded my mind and took control over me, he learned some things about my life. He's tried bribing me, threatening me, and insulting me. Just remember, the things he says he knows are all because of your memories. The man never left Dunland, so everything he mentions about your life he obtained through connecting with your mind."

"How did things go with the men in town?" I asked.

"Surprisingly well," Fenwick responded. "They were all suffering from the cold once we revived them, but not as much as perhaps they should have. They are all stunned and confused and have the ague, but I think their lives might return to normal. A squad of soldiers is keeping watch on them in the hay loft of the livery."

"Anything else I should know?" I asked.

"Nothing comes to mind," Fenwick replied. "Right. Off to bed."

Fenwick left. I checked the fire and added two logs, giving the whole thing a poke to arrange it better. When I finished, I chose one of the camp stools and sat.

"Well, bastard, here we are," the mage said in a gravelly tone.

"Right," I sighed, rising to my feet. "If that's where you're starting, there is no point in keeping you awake."

"Wait, bastard," he said. "Don't you want to know more about Doctor Flamel?"

I paused. Of all the subjects the mage could have mentioned, Flamel was the most intriguing. Then I remembered what Fenwick said about the mage's lack of first-hand knowledge.

"No," I replied.

I touched my ward to his hand, and he fainted.

A couple of hours later, I heard the soldiers beginning to stir. I hoped part of their activity was making something to eat. Due to my mishap the night before, I missed dinner, and I was ravenous.

The queen was the first to appear. I stood to greet her. Lucy followed a minute later and gave me a kiss.

"Did he wake?" the queen asked.

"He was when I arrived," I said. "Fenwick enjoyed talking with him. I didn't, so I put him to sleep again."

"Probably for the best," Lucy agreed. "You should go eat. Today is going to be taxing, and we will need to get started soon."

Heading outside, I saw soldiers lining up. I joined the line, and Fenwick came out and stood with me after asking the soldiers behind me if they would allow it. We were given a wooden bowl and spoon, and when we reached the head of the line, they filled our bowls with hot porridge with raisins. The two of us ate standing up and then went inside so the ladies could eat.

When they returned, we discussed our plan for the day. Lucy and I would go into town with the soldiers. The queen would get the mage to release his hold on the townspeople, then she would sever his connection to the Lord of the Seven Hells. She did not know exactly what would happen after that, but Fenwick was there to protect and assist her.

Lucy and I would work with the soldiers to restore order. When Fenwick and I first captured the mage and knocked him out, most people in the town were still asleep. Though we had allowed the mage to wake a couple of times, the queen said her wards prevented the mage's influence from escaping the room. I hoped everyone was still where they had been. I thought it would make it easier for them.

We bundled up in our cloaks and saddled our horses. The Castle Shield was nearly ready. A bugle rang out, and we started toward town.

When we arrived at the square in the center of town, I was pleased to see that the soldiers had removed the bodies of the men Fenwick and I dispatched. The soldiers dismounted and began to spread through the town. Their job was to begin hollering when they sensed people moving and tell them to get dressed and gather in the square. Lucy and I would speak to them and tell them what happened.

That would certainly not be the end of it. Lucy, the queen, and Fenwick would stay until they felt the town was functioning again. I would be leaving tomorrow, however, as I needed to return to the March for the annual community meetings and the induction of this year's levy into the militia.

It was slightly more than a half-hour later that Lucy and I began to hear the soldiers shouting instructions. Shortly after that, we saw the first residents appear. All looked confused. Some were frightened and some angry, while others were simply struggling to adjust to being free of the mage's control. Seeing Lucy and me on horseback, they came to ask questions. We politely put them off, assuring them all would be well, and we would share what we knew as soon as more people gathered.

When I judged that most people were there, I stood in my stirrups. The bugler blew a short tantara. Hearing it, the crowd fell silent. I was just about to begin speaking when there was some commotion at the edge of the square closest to the manor. The crowd began to part, and I saw another troop of armored horsemen appear. They were carrying the royal standard, with Prince Albert and Queen Liliana immediately behind it.

Albert stopped about halfway to where Lucy and I were. He gave me a cheeky wave. Lucy and I bowed in our saddle in return. He stood in his stirrups, and the crowd quieted again.

"Good people of Dunland, I am Prince Albert, and this is my mother, Queen Liliana," he announced. "You have just been freed from the spell that bound you to a mage of the Dark Arts. It may seem as though you have been trapped in a disturbing dream. Some of you have been under his control for a year. For most of you, it has been only a few months. Regardless, you are free now."

That news generated a quiet buzz in the crowd. It would have been more significant if so many weren't at the same time trying to regain their hold on sanity. The majority of the people were still mired in confusion, which increased with the arrival of the crown prince and the queen.

"As soon as King Mark learned that there was trouble in Dunland, he sent us to deal with it and set things right," Albert continued. "The mage has been dealt with, never to return. The queen and I, and Lord and Lady Oritur," he gestured at us, "along with the Castle Shield, are here to help you return to life as you knew it. We know it will not be easy and that most of you are feeling quite troubled right now. Return to your homes. Try to put your lives back in order. If you need assistance, come here to the square, and we will do our best to help you."

The crowd dispersed slowly. Albert and Liliana rode over to join Lucy and me. Albert was sporting a grin I could see even from a distance. His appearance was a surprise—a welcome one, to be sure.

"Your Highness," Lucy and I greeted him.

"After you all departed, father and I talked some more," he said. "We felt you might not have enough people to set things in order. Plus, he felt it would be good for me to be seen helping the victims. Given the choice between staying in the castle and poring over reports or leaving to do something useful, I was packed and ready in minutes."

While he was speaking, Fenwick rode up. He drew next to the queen and whispered in her ear. She nodded.

"What happened to the mage?" Lucy asked.

Liliana sighed heavily. "I was able to force him to release everyone," she explained. "I tried to reach his true self once more, but the Dark One would not allow it. When I severed the connection between him and the Lord of the Seven Hells, he died."

Fenwick's face bore an expression that led me to believe what happened was not so simple. I would need to learn from him later what transpired. Glancing at Lucy, I could tell she felt the same.

12

The following morning, I set out alone, heading back to the city first, then to Easton. Queen Liliana gave me a letter to deliver to the king, describing what we found here in Dunland and the current situation. After delivering it and making my own report to him, I returned to the March. I was only two weeks late by the time I arrived.

Andy and I made the trip almost without incident. The weather was normal for mid-winter—we saw snow nearly every day but did not encounter anything more severe. Just inside the walls of Easton, Andy threw a shoe. I dismounted, checked his hoof, and walked him to the manor. Lewiston was manning the gate.

"Welcome back, milord," he said cheerily. "Your father will be happy to see you. He has pestered us daily for any sign of you in the last two weeks."

"Well, I'm back, so he won't bother you about that further," I said. "Andy needs to visit a farrier and get a shoe replaced before we go anywhere, though."

I walked Andy to the stable, and Tom Collinwood, the groom, came out to meet us. He immediately saw Andy was missing a shoe and promised to get him to the farrier first thing in the morning. Tom helped me with the saddlebags, and I let him lead Andy away. While I usually like to take care of my horse personally, I was saddle sore and weary and just wanted to get inside. I didn't even go through the kitchen to torment Laurie, our cook. Instead, I went to the proper rear entrance and announced my presence.

Rose, Hazel, and Gladys appeared quickly and bobbed quick curtsies. Gladys took my cloak and my sword, Rose, the saddlebags, and Hazel went to inform Laurie that there would be one more for dinner. Gladys informed me that my father was in the study, reviewing accounts with Theo.

Before I reached the study, Theo emerged. Trailing him was the terrier, Toby. We'd bought the dog to keep the manor free from rats and not as a pet, but no one told him that. When the dog saw Theo for the first time, he launched himself into Theo's arms. As for Theo, one of the oddest, most aloof people I have ever encountered, it was an instant bond. Toby still performed his duties as long as Theo was there. That meant Theo needed to lead him through the house and stables regularly—not a hardship since Theo was the master of the household, in charge of the entire staff.

Theo passed me without even the faintest sign of recognition. He did not like me. As far as I knew, he claimed to like only two people: my wife and Fenwick. He liked Fenwick because the dog liked Fenwick. The dog was indifferent to me and almost everyone else. I would not like to see what Theo would do if the dog decided he did not like someone.

My father was sitting at the desk with the account ledgers spread out. He held up his finger to delay my speaking until he wrote a set of figures down on a separate piece of paper. Finished, he looked up.

"Welcome back," he said, rising and offering me his hand.

"It's good to be back," I replied. "Though I must warn you that Andy threw a shoe just as we reached Easton and needs to visit the farrier."

"We can't leave tomorrow morning regardless," my father said, resuming his seat. "I will send word out tomorrow. You and I will depart in the afternoon and spend the night. Our first meetings will begin the following day. After dinner, we can go over the map if you'd like."

"I would appreciate that," I said. "If you don't mind, I would like to make some notes. I want to discuss who we will meet and their concerns. If I had not been called away on the king's business, we would have had plenty of time for that. Now I feel like I will be unprepared."

"We will have plenty of time in between stops," he said. "For most of them, the issues about which they are concerned are similar and don't change much from year to year. These meetings will be much more positive this year than the last few. We chased the horsemen back home early with few casualties. The king is sending nearly four hundred families who will repopulate the three towns that were empty. Those people should arrive near the beginning of Einmann. Because we are restoring those towns, every community will present us with a list of second sons who are willing to move. They will have first choice of available lands and dwellings in the three towns, provided they make their claims before the end of Goa. Then there is the project you are pursuing regarding reopening Port Charles and the Pheas. That will excite people."

"The list of second sons," I said. "I'm afraid I don't understand something."

"We have had three towns and the surrounding land sitting idle since the nomads sacked them. We left them empty this past year. When the campaigning season began, we did not have enough men to protect the other communities, let alone these three, which would have been undermanned," my father explained. "This year, we will be able to defend them, so I informed the king there were opportunities for people who wished to move to the March. In addition to those outsiders, there are also families with more than one son who is of age. They face the possibility of needing to split their holding or their tenancy between the sons, or the younger sons need to find another way of making a living. If the younger sons wish to move to these towns, they register their claim with me. They may choose to be either freeholders or tenants, depending on which plots of land they select."

"Tenants?" I asked.

"Yes. We—you and I—own a third of the land in these communities, as we do elsewhere in the March. Often, but not always, it is some of the best land with the richest soil. Tenants pay slightly more in rent than a freeholder will in taxes, but tenants enjoy one significant advantage. We will not let them starve. Farming is not an easy way of life, and the first two or three years are the most difficult. If your extended family can help support you during that time, it would be better to be a freeholder. If they cannot, as is frequently the case, the most secure option is tenancy."

"Wouldn't being a tenant be somewhat limiting?" I asked.

My father smiled. "You'll find that some of our tenants are among the more prosperous people we will meet on this tour of the March," he said. "We have always striven to keep rents as low as possible in the March. All of us are better off when prosperity is general. Our job—yours and mine—is to safeguard that prosperity, both by defending the border and by managing affairs for the benefit of the residents. Your stepmother and half-brothers bever understood that."

Rose came in and announced dinner was served. I followed my father as he headed to the staff dining room. The table was full, with six armsmen in addition to the staff. They were pleased to see me, which I found gratifying, and asked what kept me away.

"My wife and I went to the city for the wedding of some friends," I explained. "While we were there, the king asked me to investigate a disturbance in Dunland—a ride of at least two weeks from here. With a companion, I rode to Dunland and determined what was wrong. It was beyond our ability to put things to rights, so we returned to the castle and obtained reinforcements. With their help, we eliminated the problem. Lady Oritur is still there with them, helping to reestablish order, but I needed to return to the March."

"What sort of disturbance?" Hazel asked.

"I don't mean to be coy," I began, "but it is the king's business, so I am not at liberty to discuss it. I can say that there was no rebellion or anything of that sort, and when we had the proper resources in place, the problem was eliminated swiftly and easily."

"When will Lady Lucy be coming back?" Rose asked.

"Soon, I hope," I replied plaintively.

My response drew some chuckles.

"She should return to the city soon. I know she has a few things to do there, but I hope she is back here within a fortnight."

During the next month, my father and I visited every community in the March. The format of the meetings was the same. The mayor or head man or woman would introduce us. We would swear in the men who were drafted into the militia for the upcoming year. On a couple of occasions, we conducted a brief ceremony if someone from the town died in service the year before—thankfully, there were few of those.

My father would then give a summary of the events in the last year. He noted our success against the nomads, the feast of Andvar, and the harvest fair. I would then mention that we would be repopulating the three towns and that surveyors would begin appearing in the March, exploring the feasibility of reopening Port Charles and clearing the Pheas River.

One of my requests at each town was for information. I asked for a summary of the last ten years of harvests and their estimates of how many bushels of the different types of grain they felt they would be able to sell and at what prices, if we had an improved road leading to the Pheas. This information was critical to determining whether my Port Charles project would be financially possible.

We then took questions. There was a great deal of curiosity about me. Rumors had, of course, spread, but people wanted to learn first-hand. My father was effusive in his praise. Some wished to know more about the Port Charles project. I needed to stress that we were just trying to determine if the idea was worth pursuing, and it might turn out to be too costly. At the first meeting, someone asked if the project would raise taxes or rents, so from that point on, I made sure to mention that it would not.

The tone of the meetings was generally positive. People were pleased that we had demonstrated we could protect the March. Those who attended either the feast of Andvar or the harvest fair later in the year had nothing but praise for the two events. My father and I committed to holding the harvest fair annually. After one final meeting, my father and I set off for Easton on the sixteenth of Goa.

"The difference between last year's meetings and these could not have been more stark," my father commented after we had been riding for an hour or so. "It is all due to you. I know you will not allow me to indulge in melancholy wishing to change the past, so I'll simply state that I am thankful to all the heavenly beings and to King Mark that you are here now. I am extremely proud to claim you as my son, even though I did not raise you."

I did not know how to respond, so kept silent. We had this discussion several times before, and I had nothing new to say. I will admit that it pleased me deeply to know he was proud of me.

As we rode, I could sense spring was near. The only snow that remained was on the shaded banks of ditches or the base of the north side of trees. Here and there, we could see shoots of new growth in the vibrant green of early spring. The days were longer, and when it was not raining, we often did not need to wear our cloaks against the temperature.

The surveyors and engineers would come soon, examining the port and the river, plotting the best routes for roads, and determining where docks should be placed on the Pheas. I fought to keep my hopes in check. There was also the looming problem of the return of the nomads. My nagging suspicion was that they would come in far greater numbers this summer.

We returned to the manor before sunset. I allowed Tom to take Andy since I wanted to see my wife as soon as possible. It had been more than two months since we last shared a bed, and I craved her company and her touch.

Lucy met me at the door, jumping into my arms, wrapping her legs around me, and giving me a fevered kiss. She would not let me go, and I was certainly enjoying her ardor. Finally, she pulled away from me.

"Thank you for my solstice gift," she said, then kissed me passionately once more.

Before we left for the city to attend the weddings, I hired Mr. Pruitt to construct a building specifically for Lucy. Pruitt was the builder who had just finished long-overdue repairs to the manor a few months earlier. While we were away, at my request, he created a working space for Lucy.

Before I married her, Lucy owned a flourishing business as an herbalist. In addition to dried herbs, she also made and sold potions, salves, creams, and balms. Their effectiveness, a result of Lucy's supernatural abilities and training, made Lucy's shop a success. Though residents of the city liked to think such things as magic or witches did not exist, Lucy's shop thrived, and her customers swore by her products.

Pruitt built for her a small, single-story building, catty-corner to the stable. It contained a stove, a long table, and lots of shelves. I also had boxes of glass vials, bottles, and jars in various sizes delivered.

While I did not think Lucy would start a new business, her ability to craft these useful remedies was unmatched in my experience. She also enjoyed creating them. One of her ambitions as Lady Oritur was to spread her knowledge throughout the March. I anticipated she would find eager apprentices before long.

"How are things in Dunland?" I asked, changing the subject.

"On the mend," she replied. "It will take months before life resembles what it was before, but they have made a start."

"Are Lily and Albert still there?"

"By now, they will have returned to the city," Lucy said. "I departed before they did, but I think only by a few days. Fenwick accompanied me as far as Aquileia."

"Did you learn what really happened with the mage?" I asked.

"Fenwick told me," Lucy replied. "When Lily broke his connection to the Lord of the Seven Hells, the mage went mad—violently so, like a rabid dog. Fenwick killed him before he could attack the queen."

Lucy took my hand and led me upstairs to our bedroom. The girls were just finishing filling the bath with hot water. I waited for them to leave, then stripped and eased into the tub. Submerging myself completely, it was blissful, made only better when Lucy slipped in to join me.

"What comes next?" she asked.

"Around the beginning of Einmann, two things will begin," I said. "The surveyors will arrive at Port Charles. From there, they plan to work their way up the Pheas. I would like to observe."

"And what else?"

"We are expecting the settlers from elsewhere in the kingdom to start arriving around then to repopulate Alessa, Gambion, and East Norton—the three towns that were sacked the year before last. I will leave that to my father to manage since I cannot be in both places. After that..." I trailed off.

"Yes? After that?"

"After that, I want to ride east," I said, "with some of the armsmen. The nomads will return this summer. I suspect they will come in greater numbers since we routed them last summer. We will scout the terrain and their route of approach. I hope to find a place suitable for an outpost where we can station men who will warn us of their approach. If the gods are kind, we may find a place where we can lie in wait for them and attack them using the terrain to give us an advantage."

"Your father never did this?" Lucy asked.

"No," I replied, shaking my head. "Nor did my grandfather. I suspect I will be the first to attempt something of this nature."

"Why do you think that is?" she asked.

"I hope it is not because there is no place like I have in mind," I chuckled, "though that might be the case. In talking with my father, I suspect it is because I look at things differently. He and my grandfather, and probably the others before, viewed their job of defending the March as beginning at the Patker River since the nomads always make their camp on the far side. I think successful defense of the March means convincing the nomads that it is too costly to continue attacking us and they should stay home—far away."

13

Meeting with engineers was fascinating. The surveyors, on the other hand, were as frustrating as the engineers were interesting. Examining the port and the river was primarily the responsibility of the engineers. They rowed around the harbor, in the places where they could float their small boat, taking depth measurements and dropping weighted lead tubes off the side to determine what sort of material was found on the bottom. There were a couple of areas that were completely silted over where they could not use the boat. The ground was nowhere near firm enough to walk on—anyone who tried would sink to his waist or deeper in the muck. Instead, they broke out ladders and laid them atop the muck and walked on them.

They spoke of cofferdams, dredges, and cubic yards. When I asked them to explain, they did so eagerly. A cofferdam was a set of walls they would construct to block off sections of the harbor. When an area was enclosed, they would pump the water out, and men with shovels would climb in and dig. They planned on using this method for the areas closest to the shore, where stone jetties still stood. For the more open parts of the harbor and the mouth of the river, they would use special boats that had scoops on the sides. One of them drew me a picture and explained the concept was similar to the waterwheel that powers a mill, only these would collect the silt from the floor of the harbor and dump it into a trailing barge.

I spent three days with the engineers and learned enough to understand they were cautiously optimistic, at least as far as clearing the harbor. They would be heading up the river when they finished here. I sensed they were more worried about possible obstructions upstream than the dredging,

After the engineers, I caught up with the surveyors working in what used to be the town and the docks of Port Charles. The wooden structures were largely gone—fallen and rotted away. The stone foundations, piers, and seawall remained. The surveyors spent much of their time looking through eyepieces at measuring sticks, then poring over their maps. My presence and curiosity irritated them much more than it did the engineers. When I asked them to explain things to me, they did so curtly and with an ill-temper. After a day of this treatment, I returned to Easton. I think that made both them and me happier.

It rained all four days of my return journey. Upon my arrival at Easton Manor, Lucy expressed surprise I was back so soon. I growled in response, still cross with the surveyors. The six armsmen living above the stable were the primary beneficiaries of my displeasure. I gave them each a list of items to obtain and asked them to report to me at dinner how long it would take to prepare them.

My visit to Port Charles showed me there was nothing for me to gain by spending more time looking over the shoulders of workers. As a result, I thought we should commence my project—the scouting mission. I owned a portable shelter, but it was made for only one person. There used to be canvas shelters stored at Bannock Hill, the main encampment for the armsmen during campaigning season, but they had all fallen victim to mildew and rot, and I got rid of them last summer. As a result, we needed two shelters that would hold four men each. We also needed bedrolls, rucksacks, a large number of additional water skins, salt beef, dried fruits and vegetables, and anything required to shelter and feed our horses and us for as long as two weeks.

I took on the task of procuring the shelters, rucksacks, and water skins. Based on my experience, I reckoned the most likely tradesman who could make them would be a saddler. The one in Easton quoted a price that seemed outrageous.

"Sorry, milord," he said. "Canvas and oilcloth come from Aquileia. Half the price I pay is to the teamster for carrying it all this way."

This tidbit showed me another way opening the harbor and river would benefit the March. Shipping by water to Port Charles and then upriver to Commerford, the nearest town to Easton on the Pheas, would certainly reduce the cost of transport. In spite of the price the man quoted, I offered a premium if he would deliver them in less than a week. Before he committed to meeting my timetable, he needed to check his storeroom.

"Aye, milord, we can get the work done in four days," he said. "I have just enough canvas and oilcloth. If you want more than these, I'm afraid to tell you it will be at least a month—probably longer. I need to order more supplies, and they come from away, as I said."

At dinner that evening, the men reported that they were successful in obtaining the items on the lists. Most of them would be delivered to the manor the next day. I shared that the saddler would have his materials finished four days hence.

"We will leave five days from now, on Njordday," I told them. "We will be away at least two weeks."

I asked my father if he wished to join us. He declined. I was slightly surprised until he explained.

"While you are gallivanting into the great desert, I will be overseeing the 'second sons' as they arrive in Alessa, Gambion, and East Norton. I also need to make sure that the supplies I ordered have arrived and are kept in good order."

"Supplies?" I asked.

"Some of the cottages were burned by the nomads," he explained. "Part of the resettlement agreement includes materials with which to rebuild. We supply lumber and nails. Without your willingness to shoulder the cost of renovating the manor, we could not have afforded it this year. So, once again, it is thanks to you."

I tried to protest, but he cut me short.

"The March was bankrupt, and you well know it," he said. "We could not have borne even this small expense."

On Njordday, I left the manor with the armsmen, our horses well-laden with extra gear. We reached Bannock Hill near sunset. The following day, we rode to where the nomads were encamped when we attacked them.

It was interesting seeing the area east of Oritur fully green. By midsummer, the grass would be thigh-high and brown—hay. It was currently shin-high and verdant. The weather pattern in the area was such that during the months of Goa and Einmann until the middle of Harpa, these plains would get just enough water to nourish the grass. After mid-Harpa, rain would not fall on these plains for months except on rare occasions. By the middle of Skerpia, the only green one would see came from exceptionally hardy weeds.

Crossing the Patker River was a challenge. It was only ankle-deep and a few yards across when we raided the nomad camp last summer. Now it was dozens of yards wide, chest-high on our horses in the middle, and the current was strong. Andy and I went first and were nearly swept away. Andy ended up angling his body upstream to compensate.

The remains of the nomad camp were as we left it, with one exception. When we dug the huge hole to bury their dead, we put the sod we cut back on top of the mound of dirt when the burial was finished. I was pleased to see the grass growing again. It made it seem less macabre.

After spending the night there, we headed east by south. It was less than an hour in the saddle before we came upon the first body—mostly a skeleton. The men discovered another reason why I insisted we bring shovels. We stopped and buried him. We found seven other corpses that day, all in a similar state. It slowed our progress quite a bit, and we covered less than half the usual distance we would expect from a full day's ride.

As unpleasant as it was to encounter the bodies of men we wounded who later died, at least it indicated we were heading in the right direction. We continued on our heading.

The following day we discovered only three more bodies. We saw these from a distance, as the grass was much thinner and beginning to fail. As the grass gave out, we began seeing rocks jumbled across the landscape. At first, the rocks ranged from fist-sized to no bigger than my head. As we continued, they grew larger, with some as big as one-room huts. Ahead we could see two that were notably larger than those surrounding. We headed for them.

We reached these two landmarks as the light was failing. As we drew closer, we could see the land all around them was a jumble of large boulders, all showing signs of being carved by the wind over centuries. I resolved that we would investigate the terrain in the morning before we departed.

In the morning, I rode to look more closely at the two huge blocks of stone. Upon closer inspection, they seemed to be crags thrust up from the earth. We also saw evidence that there was a track that led between the two, which had been followed many times in the past. As on the nearer side, the further side was cluttered with large stones, but the path seemed to follow the widest gaps and headed east. The scattered rocks did not form an insurmountable barrier by any means. It was just that this trail was the easiest and seemingly most direct path to follow.

I returned to the men and directed them to positions on either side to the west of two huge boulders, then rode through. Within a very short distance, I could not see any of the six men. I returned to the men. They noticed my good spirits.

"What did you see, milord?" the one named Malan asked.

"I saw where we will set a trap for our guests in a few months," I replied with a grin. "Now we keep going until we find a good spot to set a picket."

We rode until midday, noticing the scattered rocks diminishing in size again. Among the landscape of smaller stones, there was one large boulder sitting conspicuously on this dry plain. I dismounted and walked around it, trying to find a spot where I could hoist myself up and climb to the top of it. I gestured to an armsman, Weston, to dismount.

"Can you give me a leg up?" I asked.

He came over and cupped his hands together. I put my foot there and lifted myself. It was just enough that I could grasp a ridge on the boulder and shimmy up. I crawled on all fours to the top of the boulder and looked east. From here, I could see nearly two leagues. I could not keep the grin from my face. This was an almost ideal spot for a lookout. Far to the east, the horizon seemed slightly smudged.

"Do any of you have far-sightedness?" I called down to the men.

Armsman Malan, a lanky young man, raised his hand. "Aye, Cap'n," he replied, "I always had trouble reading because my arms weren't long enough to hold the book at a good distance. Had to read standing up."

"Give him a hand to get up," I requested.

Malan scrabbled his way up next to me and looked where I pointed. "Mountains, Cap'n," he said. "Big 'uns and a long way from here—twenty to thirty leagues. Still snow-covered."

"Thank you, Daniel," I said. "I thought something was different but couldn't quite make out why."

As we slid down the side of the boulder, I thought that a sentinel waiting here would see the approach of the nomads well before they saw him. Our watchman would be able to ride to the two crags to alert us. We would have plenty of time to prepare our ambush. I was pleased. It would have been better if they were closer to the river, but one can't have everything, I suppose.

I told the men we were heading back. We reached the spot where we camped the night before just as night fell. The men were full of questions, and as I answered them, they grew more excited as they understood what I planned to do. I cautioned them from becoming too enthusiastic.

"We still have challenges to overcome," I warned. "There is no food or water here. Posting all our armsmen in wait for the nomads will require supplying them for at least a couple of weeks. We will need to set up a schedule of wagons delivering food, water, and firewood. And even if our trap is successful, we will probably not stop them from advancing. We will reduce their numbers, but they will probably send more men this year because of our success last year."

Along our journey back to Easton, my mind was busy calculating. While the terms the engineers and surveyors used, like accretion, cofferdam, chain, and plumb, and the calculations for determining cubic yards of material and elevations were unknown to me, estimating how much water and food a hundred and ten men and horses would require daily was well within my expertise. By the time we reached Bannock Hill, I had it nearly worked out.

When we returned to Easton the next day, I visited the saddler and placed an order for twenty-five portable shelters. I also called upon the wainwright and ordered five wagons and the cooper for forty water barrels. All of these were needed before the end of Skerpia. The three tradesmen assured me that would be plenty of time.

Returning to the manor, I was eager to see my father and have a bath. I ran into Theo and asked him to have the maids prepare one for me. He informed me in his curt way that Lucy was out, but my father was in the study. I found my father reading, looking quite content in a comfortable chair. He looked up when I entered.

"So, what did you find?" he asked.

"We found a good spot to prepare an ambush and a watch post," I said. "The logistics of feeding and watering the men and horses will be a challenge, but I have already given thought to it. I have some questions for you."

"Such as?"

"I probably should have asked this before I left. Why do all our maps stop at the Patker River?" I asked.

My father paused in thought.

"I don't know," he admitted, finally. "They always have. I never thought to question it until now when you brought it up."

"Would the king have maps that show what is east of the Patker?"

"I don't know," my father replied. "I can write and ask."

"Here's another question—one that I know I have asked before, but since I am not satisfied with the answer, I'll ask again. Why do the nomads attack us every year?" I inquired. "They are clearly not here for conquest. When they sacked those three towns the year before last, they made no effort to hold them. They go through a great deal of trouble to get here. Why do they do it?"

"Your grandfather thought they did it to train young warriors or as a rite of passage," my father replied. "I never really bothered to think about it. They show up, they attack, we defend. No one that I know of has ever tried to talk with them."

"Maybe we should," I said.

My father looked at me as though I had just sprouted a second head atop my neck.

"What for?"

"To convince them to stop," I said.

"But they have always come," he said.

"I know. But why? Why do they come and attack us year after year? With the Rhetians, I know why we are enemies—our religions differ greatly. Both sides feel they have a moral justification for trying to defeat the other. I don't think our state of war with them will ever end because neither side will admit their beliefs are incorrect."

"Why does it matter?" my father asked.

"Try to imagine how much better off the March would be if we did not need to draft a militia every year or did not need to maintain the force of armsmen," I said. "If we convince the nomads not to attack, then we don't need to have a militia or armsmen."

"We have always had a militia and armsmen," my father replied.

I shook my head. "Do you see how the logic of this is chasing its tail? 'The nomads have always come, so we have always needed to defend ourselves.' I want to break this cycle."

"Why didn't you try to speak with them last summer?" my father asked, a sly look of triumph on his face.

"Because when I arrived, things were in a terrible state," I said. "I threw myself into it, and my entire focus was on the next skirmish, the next town they would attack, and winning each encounter. I never took the time to consider the larger situation. In the last few months, though, I have had the opportunity to think about it. Perhaps it is because I was away from the March for so long that I don't want to accept that there is no way to break this pattern."

My father's countenance soured. I held up my hands in a gesture of peace. He clearly misunderstood where I was aiming my argument.

"Father, I don't bring up the past to use it as a club against you. My point is this—being away gave me a different perspective. Your entire life has been focused on the March. Mine was not until recently. I believe the gods often arrange things to happen for a reason—a reason we may only understand after the passage of time. My life has changed dramatically for the better in the last two years, and I can see clearly how my earlier experience prepared me to make the most of the opportunities that presented themselves. That understanding is pushing me to seek a better solution."

"Well, I think you presented a fairly convincing argument to them last summer," he commented.

"I don't think I convinced them of anything," I said. "And, to tell the truth, it bothers me that we rode down men who were sleeping. I'm expecting they will return this summer in greater numbers as a result. Where does that leave us?"

My father sat silently, thinking about what I had asked.

"If the only way to get them to stop is to continue killing them, I will do it. I will seek to make things as unfair for our enemy as possible, even though it may trouble my conscience later. I worry that things will escalate, though. That will lead to more deaths on both sides. If I knew more about why they felt the need to make such a difficult journey, year after year, to attack us—not for the sake of conquest—then perhaps there is a way to end this."

"I think you are doomed to be disappointed," my father said quietly. "But I hope I am wrong. I know the information you seek does not exist here."

"Where should I look?" I asked.

"The only place I can think of is the royal archive," he replied. "You would find your maps of the land east of the Patker there, too, if they exist."

"So, I should write the king?"

"Indeed."

I wrote His Majesty that evening, explaining what I hoped to find. In the morning, I sent my letter off with the Royal Post, paying the premium for express delivery. I heard nothing for three weeks.

The new residents for the towns of Alessa, Gambion, and East Norton arrived, and I helped oversee the claiming of the plots of land. Once that finished, the time for the armsmen to begin training this year's militia was almost upon us. Once spring plantings were complete, the members of the militia would leave home and take up residence in the barracks in the different border towns.

For the three repopulated towns, my father arranged shipments of food. Ordinarily, the residents would feed both themselves and the militia posted there, but they had no stocks of anything. The militia and our tenants would receive the food at no cost. Freeholders would need to pay for it—though the price would be lower than they could find for themselves.

The challenge of orchestrating this kept my father busy. He took care to explain to me what he was doing in terms of the arrangements if I ever needed to do something similar. Having such a complicated problem to resolve kept him in quite high spirits. I have learned that he is happiest when he is fully occupied. I suppose most of us are.

There was plenty of surplus in the March, so costs were reasonable. Arranging a schedule of deliveries was the complicated piece. Grain and dried legumes were stored in bulk. In order to transport them, they needed to be put in sacks. Father needed to order a huge quantity of these.

14

I received a letter with a strange seal I did not recognize. Upon opening it, I learned it was from the Royal Archivist. In his letter, he apologized that he could only provide me with maps. The information regarding the first appearance of the nomads on the eastern border was not to be found.

The maps arrived a few days later. They were not of much help. While they did show land east of the Patker River, the information was scanty and included nothing I did not already know—with one small exception. East of the mountain range we spied in the distance on our scouting mission, the map was labeled, "Sea of Grass." The coverage of the map did not extend to show an eastern shore to the vast continent in which Aquileia was located.

The most challenging problem my father and I faced was restoring the fortifications of Alessa, Gambion, and East Norton. We needed to rebuild the barracks and watchtowers, install skorpios and hold drills with the new residents—particularly those who were new to the March. My father and I made a conscious effort to post only experienced militia members in these towns. The militia did the repair work.

The month of Einmann gave way to the month of Harpa. When I was not out training the militia, I was able to spend time at the manor. During the week, while I was in the field, training soldiers, Lucy was riding from town to town through the March. When I asked her what she was doing, she replied, "Finding students."

I cocked my head in response.

"I told you I want to share my knowledge with the rest of the March, and that I don't plan to sit idle while you are off fighting," she said. "Last year, I did not arrive here until the end of Solmandur. Then we had our hands full getting the manor put to rights. I did not have a chance to do anything."

"Nonsense!" I replied. "You organized the feast of Andvar and the harvest fair. Both were huge successes."

"Yes, but I did not get out, travel to the towns, and meet the people. I should have gone with you and your father, but the queen needed me in Dunland. I have finally been able to travel and visit the towns. I want every community to have a qualified healer or at least someone who has a good stock of medicines and knows how to use them."

"How do you find your students?" I asked.

I regretted the question as soon as it came out of my mouth. Lucy still rolled her eyes at me. With her ability to sense people's auras, it would be incredibly easy.

"Are most of them aware of their affinities?" I asked.

"The first group I've invited is," Lucy replied, "but it is a very small number. As I've told you, there are a great number of people in the world who have no idea that they have a supernatural gift. These few have sensed it and have been dabbling—learning by trial and error."

"So, we will have a school for witches?"

"A workshop for healers and herbalists," Lucy replied, "to learn more about the craft."

On the first day of the month of Skerpia, a letter arrived bearing the royal seal. I returned that afternoon from training. Lucy met me as I came in from the stable with my saddlebags on my shoulder. She was holding the note in her hand. I broke the seal and opened it.

> *Lord Oritur,*
> *We have the reports from the engineers and surveyors regarding the work necessary to reopen Port Charles and the Pheas River. We require your presence at your earliest convenience to discuss their findings.*
> *M.*

I showed the letter to Lucy. She smiled and kissed me briefly. I was not expecting that reaction since, for the king, my "earliest convenience" would require leaving in the morning.

"I'm coming with you," she said in response to my slightly puzzled look.

She linked her arm in mine and guided me into the house. I let her take me up to our bedroom and saw her saddlebags by the door, already packed by their appearance. On the bed were my traveling clothes for a three-day journey. I raised an eyebrow, questioning how she knew to be prepared in advance. She laughed.

"Lily," she answered. "Her note arrived yesterday."

We set off in the morning, and our journey was uneventful. The weather was as pleasant as could be. Arriving in the city, we stopped at the guardhouse at the end of the bridge to the castle and left a note for the seneschal, informing him of our arrival so he could schedule my meeting with the king.

"I want to see Jerry," she said. "It's been forever, and he's such a sweet lad. Can we stop by the inn first? I know you'll need to carry our bags home, but will you humor me?"

"Of course," I agreed.

When we arrived, I whistled, and Jerry slid down the ladder from his room in the stable loft. When he saw Lucy, his eyes widened. In just the few months since my last visit, Jerry seemed to have grown another two inches taller and much more broad in his shoulders. It had been even longer since Lucy had seen him, and she made all the regular comments about what a fine young man he was turning into. Jerry blushed scarlet and did not seem to be able to speak much. His eyes were on Lucy the entire time, drinking in her appearance the same way a desert traveler gulps water. He was so entranced that I was able to ruffle his hair—something he always tried to dodge.

"Cor, Mr. Caz," he complained. "Always picking on a poor boy like me."

"Not a boy any longer," Lucy said with a smile.

Jerry turned even more red in the face and could not lift his eyes. I took both our saddlebags, one over each shoulder. We said our goodbyes to Jerry, who followed Lucy with his eyes.

"Jerry's discovered girls," Lucy said with a giggle after we entered the rear of the inn.

"Poor boy," I commented.

Lucy smacked me on the arm.

The next morning, we had just sat down to breakfast when Roberta announced, "Mr. Fenwick is here."

Fenwick strode right in and took a chair. Roberta followed him in and put a full plate in front of him. I was surprised she was prepared for a guest, but Lucy's smile told me she had anticipated his arrival.

"Come now, Caz," she admonished. "Did you really think Fenwick would *not* invite himself to breakfast, knowing we arrived?"

Thinking of the many times I invited myself to Freddy's for breakfast, I had to smile and replied, "You're right, of course, dear. Fenwick, nice to see you. Make yourself at home."

"Thank you, Your High-and-Mightiness. I don't mind if I do," he replied. "Your Loveliness, your beauty and grace are only exceeded by your kindness to poor lost souls like me."

As Lucy laughed, I said, "Poor Jerry just noticed yesterday how pretty Lucy is."

"Stupefied, was he?" Fenwick remarked. "Not surprising. He's at the age."

Lucy and I both chuckled, remembering Jerry's behavior, as Fenwick added, "You know why I am here?"

"Of course," I said. "You wish to tell me when I am meeting with His Majesty."

"Indeed," Fenwick answered. "You have an appointment with His Majesty and assorted others at nine o'clock. Your Loveliness, you are on Her Majesty's schedule for the same time."

That was a bit of a surprise, then I remembered the queen sent Lucy a note that arrived the day before my summons. Lucy gave me a look that said, *I'll explain later.* I shrugged in acceptance.

While we ate, Fenwick caught us up on the latest gossip in the capital. The treason trials for the conspirators had been held and concluded. All five of the accused were hanged and their families were dispossessed of their lands.

"That creates another problem for His Majesty," Fenwick explained. "The holdings must be managed, and the king needs to decide to whom he will grant them. Beyond the idea of rewarding loyal supporters, the king must also consider fitness for the responsibility. It's no great secret that none of the five ever considered the well-being of their residents as a priority, so almost anyone would be an improvement. To his credit, though, the king wants to ensure that his new lieges are competent and compassionate."

"Any news from Dunland?" I asked.

"Albert just returned a couple of weeks ago," Fenwick said. "He reports that things are as near to normal as they can be, given what happened. He rode to the neighboring communities and explained that the problems in Dunland were over. Trade and traffic have resumed. Count Dunland has been very involved in setting things back in order."

"And how is Miss Traval?" Lucy asked with a twinkle in her eye.

"She is abroad right now," Fenwick said, "traveling to Vanda."

"Don't you worry about her?" Lucy asked.

"That is not permitted," Fenwick said with a sardonic smile. "She has forbidden me to fret. Still, I have been teaching her how to handle a blade, and I am confident she can defend herself against an unskilled ruffian. She has been an eager pupil. Now, much as I would like to stay and chat, you must get moving."

Fenwick had his horse and left, claiming he had other business. Lucy and I went to the market square not far away and found an idle hackney waiting for a fare. We told him our destination, and I helped Lucy inside.

When we were both seated, and the carriage was moving, I asked, "What is the subject of your meeting with the queen?"

"You know my grandmother taught me almost everything I know about my abilities. You also know she was obsessive and mistrustful. Unfortunately, with no other tutor, her warnings and pronouncements still rule my behavior. She has been gone for years now, and I have already seen how her guidance has been in error on several occasions. Lily is as knowledgeable about the supernatural as anyone in Aquileia. I want her guidance, and she wants mine."

"In regard to anything in particular?" I inquired.

"Yes," Lucy replied. "In my travels around the March, I have met a number of people who possess affinity with the gods but are unaware. As you know, I have always been quite close-mouthed about these matters. I am wondering if I should share more. The few people I have met who are aware of their ability are not enough to provide service to the entire March. My worry is that if I apprise someone about his or her affinity, I might upset the natural order of things—my grandmother's biggest fear. What the repercussions of that would be, I don't know. I am hoping that Lily and I can figure it out."

"And if you can't?"

Lucy grinned and said, "We already have a plan in place. The three of us will go on a pilgrimage to the Temple of Njörun."

"I thought you told me Njörun does not have a power that one can summon, like Bellona, or Eir, or Freyja. You said that she attends you or not, according to her whim. So what could we learn at her temple?"

"That is true about her," Lucy agreed. "The queen, however, has made the pilgrimage there and tells me the priests taught her much that pertained to magical ability in general. She feels they might be able to guide us. Since Lily, you, and I share an affinity to Njörun, accompanying her on another pilgrimage is justifiable to the king."

"But—"

"We would leave the day after tomorrow," Lucy said. "You and I will return directly to the March and be back before the end of the month. You never know what you might learn that could be useful."

When we arrived at the guardhouse, pages were waiting for us. Mine took me directly to the seneschal, who escorted me to a meeting room. Lucy was taken in a different direction.

The centerpiece of the meeting room was a gigantic table, on top of which were spread maps, with small weights holding down the corners. Albert and the king were already present, along with two other men. When the seneschal announced me, I entered and bowed to the king and Albert. Albert beckoned me over.

"Look at these, Caz," he said with enthusiasm.

As I drew closer, I could see they were maps of the different sections of the harbor and the Pheas River as they appeared now. Overlaid were bold lines indicating changes to be made. Everywhere were notations. At first, these were incomprehensible but as I studied them, I could figure them out. The king allowed me to satisfy my curiosity for a few minutes, then cleared his throat. I tore my attention away from the maps and looked to him, nodded, and took a seat.

"As you can see, the engineers and surveyors have finished their assessment of the practicality of reopening Port Charles and clearing the Pheas River for commercial traffic," the king said. "Have you brought the estimates I requested?"

I nodded and handed over the packet I had brought. When my father and I visited every community earlier, I asked for them to prepare figures on harvests and make their best guesses as to how much more could be grown if there were a way of getting the grain to market. The numbers surprised and astounded me.

The king opened the packet and looked at the first page. This was the summary of the reports I received. It showed a list of how much grain all the communities estimated they could export.

'Two-and-a-half million modia of wheat," the king read off, "over a million modia of oats, a million modia of beans, and a million and a half modia of rye, half a million modia of peas—is this correct?"

"Yes, Your Majesty," I replied.

"These numbers are nearly double what we expected," he commented.

"Your Majesty, you will find in the other papers the estimates provided to me by the various communities. When I met with the people, I stressed that I wanted a conservative, pessimistic number," I said.

"You will excuse us," the king said as he rose, clutching the packet of papers in his hand. "Albert, please entertain Lord Oritur until I return."

When the king stood, the rest of us jumped to our feet. He departed the room. I gave Albert a sidelong glance. He shrugged, then pointed to the maps. He indicated the other two men should join us.

One of the two men was a surveyor, the other was an engineer. Together, they went over the maps with us. They pointed out what the different markings meant. They started at the furthest point up the Pheas River, just south of the community of Quinn's Ford, near the northern boundary of the March.

The surveyor showed where landings and piers remained. From the landings, he traced the lines of roads that had been present over a hundred years before. I could see how the roads connected every community in the March to the river.

The engineer pointed out obstacles in the river that needed to be cleared in order to restore navigation. They were rockfalls and beaver dams mostly. Some of these created other problems with silting or erosion of the riverbanks. I did my best to follow along, but by the time we reached the mouth of the river, I was becoming overwhelmed. It seemed like it would take an enormous amount of work and money to fix things. Albert noticed my earlier interest had gone silent.

"What's troubling you, Caz?" he asked. "You know I can't read your expression, but you *have* gone quiet."

"So much needs to be fixed," I said softly.

"Eh?" the engineer interrupted. "What's that?"

"It seems like an incredible amount of repair work needs to be done," I said. "It will be too expensive to make it worthwhile."

"This?" the engineer retorted, sweeping his hand over the maps. "Clearing the river and dredging the harbor will not be hard or take long. The only truly difficult task we uncovered will be pulling the stumps of the trees that took root in the roadbed, then restoring the foundation. Where it has not been overgrown by forest, the road still exists, and little needs to be done."

15

The king's entrance forestalled further questions from me. He swept in, ignoring our polite bows in reaction to his presence, and sat down. He placed a sheet of paper on the table and waited for us to sit.

"Lord Oritur," he began, "the numbers you shared with us in the summary are actually lower than the estimates your people provided."

"I thought to err on the side of caution, Your Majesty," I said.

He waved his hand dismissively, saying, "Your estimates have guided us in a different direction from what we were considering before our meeting. The estimates provided by your people are more than double what we anticipated. As a result, we will suggest a different way to get the necessary work done."

"Please pardon me, Your Majesty, but I was under the assumption that I would be responsible for the costs of restoring the river and harbor," I said.

"That is correct," the king replied. "Though we were planning to offer you a loan to cover the cost, so you would not need to liquidate your current holdings. You would then repay the loan from the port fees you would charge. That is no longer in our best interest. Instead, we will pay for the restoration of the harbor and river and retain the right to collect port fees, as we do in Aquileia, Newcastle, and Aurora."

"That sounds incredibly generous, Your Majesty," I replied, slightly stunned. "Thank you."

"Do not thank me, Lord Oritur," he replied with a sly grin. "We are doing this out of selfishness. Based on the harvest numbers you brought, even setting the schedule of port fees at the low end compared to the other ports will still generate tremendous revenue. Quite simply, it will be too large of an income stream for us to allow any single noble family to hold it. It will be better for the stability of the realm in the future for the crown to control it."

I confess I did not know how to react. In almost the same breath, the king informed me the idea I had of reopening the port would be a tremendous success and then would not allow me and my family to reap the full benefit. That, I realized quickly, was poisonous thinking since it was not my intention that we would get rich from the restoration. What has driven the idea is creating new markets for our farmers and increasing their prosperity, which would, in turn, benefit us. I could well understand the king's thinking about the revenue. A noble family with too much wealth could be a source of instability in the future.

"You truly are difficult to read, Lord Oritur," the king commented. "We would like to know what you are thinking."

"Your Majesty, my pursuit of this project came from a desire to help the people of the March. What you have told me is that the signs point to it being a success. Since I was not considering it as an opportunity for direct financial gain, I can hardly be disappointed," I stated.

'Yet you would not be human," the king remarked, "if you were not at least slightly upset at learning of a large revenue stream that you will not be allowed to retain."

I shrugged and smiled, saying, "As you say, Your Majesty."

"All is not lost, Lord Oritur," the king replied. "Hanson, show him the map with the jute."

Hanson was the surveyor. He sifted through the maps and found the one he sought, then pulled it over in front of me. The only feature I recognized was the coast of the Surrounded Sea to the south. There was a large rectangular area marked. As I looked closer, I saw smaller rectangles within.

"This was a jute plantation," Hanson said, pointing to the large rectangle. "The deed to the land indicates it is the property of the Earl of the March. These," he indicated with his finger, "are the foundations of the buildings that stood on the property. The smaller ones were worker cottages, we believe. The largest was the house. The others were related to the treatment of the plant after harvest. There are large sunken structures that I think were used to soak the plants after harvesting. This seems to be the foundation of the manufactory where they made the material into cloth and the cloth into sacks."

From Hanson's expression, this was good news. It meant nothing to me. I had no idea what jute was and confessed my ignorance.

The king reacted with incredulity, saying, "Excuse me, Lord Oritur? I cannot understand how someone so ignorant could be a peer of the realm! How could you not know of the wonderous jute plant?"

"His Majesty jests, Caz," Albert whispered, making sure his father overheard. "He had no more idea what jute was until a few days ago."

Betrayed in his attempt to rib me, the king added, "As His Highness said, we just learned about jute. It is the fibrous plant used to make the sacks in which grain is transported. It will be essential for this venture to succeed. Since this plantation and mill ceased operating, we have imported all our jute from Mooresa on the southern continent. Having our own source of jute, and a mill where it can be made into cloth and the cloth into sacks, located exactly where it is most useful, should prove useful and profitable, Lord Oritur. Unlike the harbor and the river, you will be entirely responsible for the restoration of the plantation and mill, as they belong to you, and will reap the benefits of ownership without the crown's involvement."

Even without understanding a thing about jute, I could see the potential. Though we would not gain from access to port fees, being the local source for the sacks that would hold and carry the grain to be shipped from Port Charles was undoubtedly going to be a profitable venture. I immediately thought of two obstacles to my success, though. One was my complete lack of knowledge. The other was time.

"I am exceedingly grateful to Your Majesty for bringing this to my attention," I said. "It is doubtful I would have learned of it otherwise. My father never mentioned anything regarding a plantation or a mill, and I suspect he knows as little about it as I did until just now. Is there anyone in the kingdom— at the university, perhaps—who knows more about how to grow this plant and then how to take the harvested material and make it into the finished product?"

"No," the king answered flatly. "You will need to travel to Mooresa to find someone. When the time comes, we will allow you to take Fenwick along. He is fluent in Mooren, we understand."

"There is one other issue, Your Majesty," I said. "The nomads. It will be difficult for me to manage this project when my primary duty is to defend the border. I must confess, the problem of my lack of availability has been on my mind, though I was thinking more in terms of needing to supervise the clearing of the river and harbor than of restoring a plantation and mill. I have already taken some steps to prepare for the upcoming campaigning season, but I have concerns."

"Hanson, Thatcher," the king said to the surveyor and engineer, "you will not be needed for this part of the discussion. Please wait outside."

The two men stood and left. While they did, I tried to gather my thoughts. I wanted to make certain the king did not think I was complaining about my duty. After the two left the room, the king and Albert looked at me expectantly.

I explained what I did and did not know about the nomads and my belief that they would return in slightly greater numbers this year. I told them about my scouting mission and the spot we found that seemed ideal for an ambush. The king then interrupted me.

"You believe they will arrive in greater numbers this year?" the king asked.

"A reasonable guess, given the success Caz enjoyed," Albert said.

"What sort of numbers?" the king asked.

"They normally bring between four and five hundred men," I explained. "Their journey is long, however, through inhospitable terrain. The logistics of providing water for the people and animals would probably limit them to no more than six or seven hundred men."

"Albert, this is an opportunity for you to exercise the men," the king stated. "Take a full squadron with you and assist Lord Oritur. Make sure these nomads understand they are not welcome. If we attend to them properly, that should free Lord Oritur to consider other projects."

"It would be my pleasure," Albert said with a smile.

"Lord Oritur, work on the harbor and the river will begin quickly," the king stated, returning to the other topic of discussion. "The engineers tell us everything will be ready before the harvest. Your plantation will not, so we will need to import the necessary materials from Mooresa. If possible, try to get the mill rebuilt first. Buying raw materials is always less expensive than finished products, and it will give your people an opportunity to learn more about how to work with jute. As we suggested, take Fenwick with you."

With that, the king rose. Albert and I hastily stood. When he left the room, Albert turned to me.

"Caz, the last time we took the field together, I was a different man," he said.

Albert was referring to the time while he was my commanding officer in the Rangers. In those days, he was an incredible snob. Because of my illegitimate birth, he refused to speak with me, even when I stood right in front of him.

He would address someone else and say, "Tell FitzDuncan this."

A couple of years ago, in the first of my adventures that I committed to paper, Albert was almost cheated out of his right of succession by his younger brother. I was the person who ruined that scheme. Though I was only trying to save my own hide, I also safeguarded Albert's birthright and spared him what would have been massive public humiliation. Albert possessed enough self-awareness to understand how his supercilious behavior contributed to the difficulties in which he was mired and changed his ways. It did not take long for anyone to see he was a changed man. Since then, we have become friends—as much as anyone can be a friend to the crown prince. Albert had served as one of my seconds in a duel against a former friend of his and had been one of my bridesmen at my wedding.

"Albert, if you had not mentioned it, that thought would not have crossed my mind," I said.

"Yes, it would," Albert said with a wry smile.

"Perhaps eventually," I admitted, "but I was certainly not thinking about it now."

"I also want to thank you for your work in Dunland," Albert said. "Father should have, but anything to do with the supernatural makes him uncomfortable. I learned from my mother and your wife how dangerous the situation was—that you and Fenwick nearly killed one another. I'm dreadfully sorry about that. As for me, I suspect you wondered why I showed up. I will admit to having only a hazy idea of how I could help when I headed off, but I can now say I am glad I did. My men and I were busy helping the residents get their lives back to normal. It was nice to be useful. I spend too much time here in the castle, going over accounts and reports. It's necessary, I know, but it gets dull."

"That is my least favorite side of my new role as well," I said.

"Regarding our upcoming bit of adventure," he said, changing the subject, "from what you mentioned before, will you have the logistical end under control?" he asked.

"It would help if you could bring wagons and water barrels," I said. "Enough to keep your men and horses from getting thirsty. I will have a hundred and ten men and their mounts and have made arrangements for five wagons and forty barrels. If you can bring the same, along with food and shelters for your men, we should be prepared."

"I will make sure we do," he said.

There was a knock on the door. At Albert's response, the seneschal opened it.

"Will you need Mr. Hanson and Mr. Thatcher?" he asked.

"Yes, please," I responded.

The two men returned. I sifted through the maps to find the one which included the plantation. It was difficult to tell from a largely empty map, but Hanson shared that the land belonging to the estate was quite large. Hanson found a map with a scale that showed where the land was in relation to Port Charles.

"May I have copies of these?" I asked.

"Certainly, milord. It will take a day or two," Thatcher replied.

"I will be traveling, unfortunately," I said. "Would you please have them sent to Easton Manor when they are finished? I would also appreciate if there are any notes your people made about landmarks and such that will make it easier for me to find the place."

We were interrupted when Lucy and the queen arrived. Both of them seemed in good spirits. Albert introduced Hanson and Thatcher to the ladies before the two men excused themselves.

"We decided," the queen said after the door shut, "that your presence on our trip to the Temple of Njörun is unnecessary, Caz. You will not be joining us."

While I was curious about what I might learn from the pilgrimage, I was also relieved. I needed to be in the March, making sure everything was ready for the arrival of the nomads. This might also give me the chance to detour on my way back and see the remains of the old jute farmstead.

"I can almost hear the gears turning in your head, my love," Lucy said with a laugh. "You want to be in Easton where you can fret and fiddle before you take the men to meet the nomads. Her Majesty and I decided you would be poor company as a result. Plus, I understand we just learned of some property to which we hold the deed, and I am willing to wager you will find a way to visit it."

I will admit I blushed at this. My wife knew me all too well. Albert noticed my cheeks coloring and started to chuckle.

"I am glad to know there is one person in the world who can make you betray your thoughts," he said. "I thought it could not be done, but it seems Lucy has the key."

"What is distressing is that she is correct," I admitted, "on both counts."

"I will instruct Hanson to copy the maps more speedily than originally planned," Albert said, "and have them brought to your house here in the city before you depart."

The seneschal interrupted us a few minutes later, informing both Albert and the queen of appointments. Lucy and I took our leave. The guards on the city side of the bridge summoned a hackney for us, and we returned to the house.

"How was your meeting?" I asked once the hackney began to move.

"Fah! We just gossiped for the most part," Lucy said. "We decided early on that we would leave you behind. That was our only pressing business. It's just nice to have someone to talk to who understands things."

Realizing immediately how I could take offense, Lucy gasped, "Majors and Minors! That came out wrong. Caz, you are as wonderful, understanding, loving, and supportive as any woman could ask for in a husband. I meant only about those other things, about which you freely admit you are far from an expert."

I knew what she meant the first time and was not upset. Still, it was nice to hear my wife say such nice things. The truth is that it was no burden at all for me.

"It is never a chore for me to pay attention to you, my love," I said, lifting her hand and kissing the back of it. "You are as pretty on the inside as you are beautiful on the outside, and as brilliant as you are beautiful."

"Silver-tongued devil," she whispered as she tilted her head to kiss me.

16

That evening we had Freddy and Greta for dinner. It was a delight to see them and hear the news of our other friends. I realized during dinner that I quite missed Freddy. He had been right beside me through some of my greatest challenges and most difficult periods.

"This will be one of the last times you will be able to simply show up and find us down the street," Freddy commented.

"Time to go home?" Lucy asked.

"Yes," Freddy replied. "Father is feeling his age and wants us there so I can begin taking over."

"When do you leave?" I asked.

"At the end of the month," Greta answered. "I have to say, I am looking forward to it. Susannah has a full schedule planned for me. It will be a nice change of pace."

"It will," Freddy agreed. "I hate to say it, since it might give you a big head, Caz, but things have been dull since you left."

"Not for me," I said.

"Oh, we know," Greta replied. "Lucy is an excellent correspondent and has been keeping us up-to-date on all your doings."

We spent the rest of the evening in cheerful conversation. When it was time for them to leave, I gave Greta a kiss and clasped Freddy in a hug. I was not normally prone to that, but it seemed correct.

After Lucy and I retired upstairs and undressed for bed, she noticed my melancholy and commented, "Things change, dear. You and I are living proof. It is only logical life would move on her for Freddy and Greta."

"I forget that if the king did not intervene, our lives would be as they were before," I said. "And I was perfectly content, as you were with your shop. With everything that has happened since we moved to the March, I could not imagine being satisfied with the tempo of life as it was. I have become accustomed to the hectic pace, though I will confess I did enjoy things being slightly slower the last few months."

"Well, if events unfold properly, perhaps you can one day merely be Earl of the March and not need to worry about nomads every summer. Just take care of your people and fret about your jute crop like a gentleman farmer," Lucy teased.

"Somehow, dearest, I suspect the gods have other things in store for the two of us," I said, "if our first year of marriage is any indication."

In the morning, I shared breakfast with Lucy, then carried her bags to the Foaming Boar. Jerry slid down from the loft and saddled Bella quickly. Lucy rewarded him with a kiss on the cheek, and I thought the poor boy's face might ignite he turned so red.

After Lucy departed, I turned to Jerry and asked, "Have you and Mr. Carl had *the talk* yet?"

Jerry's blush, which was fading, stormed back as he replied, "Aye, if you mean the one about girls, Mr. Caz."

"That's the one," I said, clapping him on the back.

When I returned home, Roberta alerted me to a leather tube that was just delivered. Opening it, I saw copies of the maps I requested. I immediately charged upstairs and threw some clothes in my saddlebags, along with my toiletries. When I returned downstairs, I notified Roberta that I was leaving and returned to the Foaming Boar.

After settling my bill with Carl, I went back to the stable. Jerry was surprised to see me so quickly. I explained that I had a change of plans and would be leaving. Together we saddled Andy, then I rode out of the city.

The journey to Port Charles took seven days. The first three, I traveled east, almost reaching Easton. The last four days, I worked my way south and east, parallel to the Pheas River. Since I had not brought my portable shelter, I stopped in the last community upriver from Port Charles, Hillstead. From Hillstead, the road deteriorated and was completely overgrown in a number of places.

Ordinarily, it would be a ride of only a few hours, but my earlier trip taught me it would take half the day.

After spending the night in Hillstead, I woke before sunup and started off. I figured I would have time to find the ruins of the plantation and return by sunset or shortly after. One thing was different from my earlier visit. With the warmer weather now, when we traveled through woods, insects were abundant, and they all wanted to suck our blood or bite us. I kept Andy moving as fast as the terrain allowed, but we still provided a feast for the bugs.

When we left the woods at the edge of the ruins of the town, I was pleased to see the surveyors had left a number of stakes as markers. I pulled out the maps to see if I could figure out how the stakes corresponded to the marks on the maps. It did not take me long, but then I determined we were on the wrong side of the river.

I debated with myself briefly about whether to bring Andy across but decided against it. From my interpretation of the maps, if I swam across, I would have a walk of roughly two miles. I stripped down and waded in, holding the map case out of the water. The bottom was muddy and unpleasant.

After my swim and slogging up the other bank, I was distressed to see leeches clinging to me. I'd encountered leeches before while in the Rangers. As disgusting as they were, the best way to avoid getting an infection was to simply leave them alone. They would drop off when they had their fill, usually about twenty minutes.

I set off in the direction indicated by the map. There had been a road that went west, and the surveyors had marked it with stakes. When I judged I covered two miles, I kept my eyes open for other stakes.

They were easy to spot when I reached them. I opened the map again to get my bearings. Setting off through the tall grass, I quickly found the ruins of the old house. It had collapsed in a heap—obviously built from wood, not stone. Since I was barefoot, I approached carefully, hoping to avoid stepping on a nail.

Under the remnants of the house, I could spy the foundation stones. Its footprint was much larger than I thought. This must have been a stately residence. Working my way around, I looked for the other buildings. I found what appeared to be two large foundations but with no building debris.

Remembering Hanson's explanation, these were where the plants were soaked to separate the fibers.

Across the remains of the road, I could now see the manufactory. The first story was built of stone and was mostly still standing. The upper story had collapsed. This building was also larger than I guessed.

Retracing my steps, I tried to get a feel for how much land there was. It seemed like quite a bit. The best thing was the only trees in what would be the fields were small and stunted. We would need to remove them but pulling smaller stumps like these would be relatively easy.

I decided to go back across the river and return to Hillstead. What I saw was exciting, but my excitement was tempered by a number of things. If I could not make the nomads retreat, I would not have the time to attend to any of this. Even if I had the time, I knew nothing about jute—either how to grow it or how to turn the plants into cloth sacks. I would need to rebuild everything and find people to work the property.

These ideas were turning over in my head while I strode back to the river. Reaching the bank, I will admit I cringed slightly. The leeches had fallen off while I was walking to the old farmstead, but I was about to attract a new group. It's not that they hurt—they didn't—it was simply that they looked so disgusting, and knowing they were sucking my blood was disturbing.

I waded into the river and swam across with the map case held high. My legs sank shin-deep in the mud as I climbed out. Looking down, I could see more leeches and shuddered. I walked back to where I left Andy and my clothes. I suppose I should have been surprised to see Fenwick waiting there, but he had shown up unexpectedly so many times now it did not startle me.

"Hello, Fenwick," I said.

"Greetings, O Lord of the Leeches," he responded, standing and sweeping his hat off in a bow with an exaggerated flourish.

"Do you have experience with them?" I asked.

"More than I care to remember," he replied.

"Good. Then you can help get them off me," I said.

Other than waiting for them to drop off, the only other safe way to remove leeches is to use a thin, sharp edge to convince them to release their mouth from the skin. Using heat or fire, or trying to pluck them off, often results in nasty infections. Fenwick stooped and withdrew the knife from his boot, and handed it to me. I used it to remove the leeches I could see, then returned it to him and allowed him to clear my back.

"Thank you, good sir," I said when he finished.

I dressed, except for my stockings and boots. The mud on my lower legs was not quite dry. When it dried completely, it would be easy to remove, so I would wait.

"I doubt you are here with another summons from His Majesty since I just met with him, so what brings you by?" I asked.

"Idle curiosity," he stated. "This little project," he waved his arms to indicate all of Port Charles and the river, "will be commanding a large amount of time, attention, and money from the crown in the next few months. That interested me enough to want to come see. If you had waited another day in Aquileia, I would have ridden with you. As it was, I've been chasing you—well, not chasing. That gives the wrong impression…following."

"Fenwick, you are one of the most skilled liars I have ever known," I said. "Perhaps it is because we have spent too much time together, but I think I am beginning to recognize when you are smudging the edges of the truth. What really has you intrigued about this?"

"Our future journey to Mooresa," he admitted.

"Why? Is Mooresa better or worse than Scaramouche?" I asked.

"Ordinarily, I would say it is less corrupt," Fenwick offered. "But they have been the only producer of jute for over a hundred years. Finding someone willing to teach you what you need to know, or—even better—someone to bring back who can run the operation, will not be easy. If the government catches wind of what we are trying to do, it could get ugly."

"As ugly as when the sub-vizier's secretary tried to kill us?" I asked.

"At least that bad," Fenwick said. "The king had no idea what he was asking."

'Have you illuminated him regarding the difficulty?"

"One does not second-guess His Majesty," Fenwick replied. "I did let him know I would need to prepare a number of things in advance. He shared with me that you would be busy with your nomad friends until sometime in Solmandur, so I will get started on those preparations soon. I do know this is a critical piece of the larger puzzle, though. And I wasn't fibbing when I said this entire project is significant to His Majesty."

By now, the mud had dried on my feet and lower legs. I was able to brush it off and put my stockings and boots back on my feet. Standing up, I buckled on my sword and looked to Fenwick to see if he was ready to leave. He responded by mounting his horse. I untied Andy and did the same, and we began heading back to Hillstead.

As we rode, Fenwick mentioned, "I did promise to tell you my life story. You made me stop because you felt I wasn't really ready to share it. You were right. I do want to tell you now. Something about us almost killing one another up in Dunland changed my perspective."

"If you're certain, then I'm interested in hearing it," I said.

"I believe I told you my father died while in militia service," he stated.

"You did."

"We got the harvest in," he continued, "with the assistance of our neighbors. When someone is drafted into the militia, the neighbors pitch in and help. My mother was shattered, though. From the moment she heard, she withdrew into herself. I had to take care of both of us. After the harvest, the neighbors stopped coming by. From that point, my mother would not get out of bed. Then, she stopped eating. I begged and pleaded with her, but she would not move, lying curled into a ball, hugging her knees. It was seventeen years ago that she died."

"I'm sorry," I replied. "That must have been difficult to watch, on top of the loss of your father, at your age."

"It was. I buried her behind the shed. The ground was frozen, so it was difficult to dig a grave. I suppose I should have asked the neighbors for help, but I was so broken myself by my father's death and now hers that I didn't know what to do," Fenwick said. "That spring, they caught me stealing bread. Soon, everyone in Northrup knew what had happened. The town decided I would go live with a childless couple, the Banfields. They treated me like a slave, so I ran away."

"Who could blame you?" I offered. "Where did you go?"

"I went to Newcastle," he said. "I found work at the docks, loading and unloading ships, always hired by the day. During that time, I got my growth, and the work made me fit. Every wheat head I earned went to my belly or to keep a roof over my head. I lived in a hovel of a boarding house, sharing a bed with two others. The end of the shipping season was drawing near, and I was worried about how I would live through the winter. The foreman for whom I'd worked most often approached me and asked if I wanted to make some extra money."

"I think I know where this is going," I said.

"Of course, I wanted extra money. After work, the foreman had a couple of us meet him. He asked if we had weapons. I didn't, so he gave me a knife. A foreman at the third dock down had lost a bet to my guy and refused to pay. We were going to make a show of force to shake the money loose," Fenwick explained.

"The other guy was expecting us and had his own people gathered and waiting. I'd never been in any sort of a fight before—not even a schoolyard brawl. I was so scared—I wasn't sure how to hold a knife for fighting. I do remember feeling that having a knife in my hand in the midst of this dangerous setting also felt *right*, in a way that nothing before ever had. Things turned ugly fast. When it was over, after only a few minutes, my foreman and I were the only two still standing. I was covered in blood, and my foreman looked at me with an expression of amazement mixed with horror. I killed four men that day. It happened so quickly. I remember feeling so powerful, so fast—I guess that was the first time Bellona's influence affected me."

"It was much later for me," I said. "Less than two years ago. I fought Bergeron duPais in an old shrine to Fortuna below the castle."

"My boss told me to collect the money pouches from the dead men and meet him in the shack at the end of the dock. When I got there, he'd found the other foreman's stash. He told me to use the sturdiest of the money pouches I collected and put the contents of the other ones in it. Then he gave me twenty ducats and told me I should leave Newcastle before sunrise so the constables would not find me. He gave me the name of someone in Aquileia I should contact."

He looked at me, assessing my expression. "That's how it started. I came to the city and found the man whose name I had. He wasn't a foreman at the docks. He controlled the dock area, though, as far as criminal activities were concerned.

He took me on as an errand boy. One day after making my collections, three men tried to rob me. I killed all three, armed with only a knife. Later I learned my boss set it up to test me. After watching me in action, he came up with a new idea. He had me join a salle d'armes and paid instructors to teach me fencing, fisticuffs, and wrestling. A year later, he gave me my first assignment."

"That's when you started killing people for a living," I commented.

"It was. When I learned how much he was charging for my services, I demanded that he pay me ninety percent, or I would leave. He refused. I left. Just after that, Donald Farquahr absorbed his operation, and I was on my own."

"How did a farm boy turned stevedore become the Fenwick we know today?" I asked. "You're cultured, seem well-read and intelligent—as sophisticated as anyone I know—how did that come about?"

"My former employer had been charging hundreds of ducats for my services, eliminating people who were completely unimportant. I reckoned that rich people probably had just as many enemies—perhaps even more. If I could swim in those waters, I could charge a much higher fee—many times higher. I decided to educate myself so I could pass as a gentleman. With almost five hundred ducats to my name at this point, I could afford to devote some time to self-improvement."

He paused for a drink of water. He squirted some from a skin into his mouth. After replacing the cork and wiping his mouth, he resumed.

"I was extremely fortunate. A couple of days after I decided on this course, I was on my way to buy some lunch and saw an older woman being harassed by some young toughs. She was obviously well-to-do, and I wondered what brought her to this part of town. Before things got ugly, I went to her assistance. I learned her name was Madam Andrés, and she was trying to deliver some money to an employee who was sick. She thanked me for my protection, and when I finished escorting her to her house, she invited me in for tea," Fenwick recounted.

"*The* Madam Andrés?" I asked. "She is a legend."

"An incredible woman," Fenwick agreed. "In her younger days, she was the mistress of Thatcher Coombs, the merchant. When Coombs died, she decided to start a business related to what she knew best. She bought her house, in one of the nicer neighborhoods in the city, and established a high-class brothel. Her rates were high, her girls were beautiful, and she guaranteed discretion. Now, I did not learn all that immediately. In that first meeting, I merely sensed there was something that was not adding up. I took a leap of faith and explained how I wished to better myself—without explaining why. Something about the way I said it intrigued her, and she invited me to return the next afternoon for further discussion. I moved into the house days later and stayed there for most of the next three years. She taught me everything."

"That explains how you learned to dance so well," I remarked.

Fenwick laughed. "I dare say I had the most beautiful dance partners in the kingdom," he agreed. "Among other things, Madam Andrés insisted I become well-read. She gave me a list of over a hundred books and instructed me to go to the university library, pretend I was a student, and do my reading there. When I finished a book, we would discuss it for hours."

"Did you ever tell her what you planned to do with your new-found skills?" I asked.

"She figured it out on her own," Fenwick said. "She was a clever lady. It was she who suggested I maintain my contacts on the docks. She pointed out that people looking for my type of service—even wealthy people—would start their search in a rough area like that. She was right. It was only later, as word of mouth grew slowly and quietly, that I began to get work from referrals."

We rode in silence for a time. I thought I understood why Fenwick decided to tell me this, but I didn't know quite how to respond. After a few minutes, I was about to open my mouth, but Fenwick spoke first.

"I've always been very reticent about my past," he said. "You, on the other hand, have been an open book. It is one of the things about you that I admire. You are not ashamed of who you are or your path through life."

17

Fenwick and I parted ways the following day. I returned to Easton, and he was off to an unknown destination. He told me he was going to begin preparing things for our trip to Mooresa later in the summer.

What he shared with me regarding our trip to Mooresa added that journey to my list of concerns. In pondering the situation while I rode, I assessed that it would be best if we could lure someone away and have him or her return with us. If we could, that person could supervise the restoration of the farmstead and manufactory.

When I returned to Easton, I needed to put those thoughts aside. There were now just under three weeks until the solstice. The armsmen would gather a week before it at Bannock Hill.

My father and I spent quite a bit of time going over the preparations he made for the campaigning season. He informed me the portable shelters, wagons, and barrels I ordered had all been delivered to Bannock Hill already. I share with him that Albert and a full squadron of the Castle Shield would be joining us to meet the nomads between the two huge crags.

I rode to Bannock Hill to check on everything. My father assured me it was unnecessary. I knew it was and told him so. The main reason I went was that I was restless.

Roughly two hours into my ride, I had the strangest experience. It was as though I had left my body and was looking down upon myself. Even though my perspective seemed to be at a distance, I could see myself clearly. I also appeared much more colorful than I knew I was.

Despite the oddness of this feeling, I raised my left hand and waved it above my head. My peculiar vision showed me doing the same. I gave Andy a small tug to get him to stop and nudged him to turn. As we rotated around, the bizarre experience stopped suddenly, and I saw with my own eyes again. I tried to figure out the angle to determine from where I was seeing myself, and the only thing I could spy was the top of a tall fir tree. As strange as it was, it did not make me uncomfortable.

When I reached Bannock Hill, I found everything in perfect order. The five new wagons were there, covered by tarps. I checked the small storage building, and it was packed with the new barrels. The new portable shelters were stacked in neat bundles. The small kitchen and the sleeping platforms seemed to have survived the winter weather with no damage.

On my journey back to Easton, I wondered whether I would have the same strange experience. It did not recur. When I reached the manor and rounded the house to the stable, I was delighted to see Chauncey sitting on the roof peak. I did not see her horse, Bella, but Chauncey's presence meant Lucy was not far away.

After handing Andy to our groom, Tom, I hurried inside the house and up into our bedroom. Once there, I opened the windows. A moment later, Chauncey lit on the windowsill. Usually, he would immediately hop to his perch and go to sleep. I waited for him to do that so I could pull the windows closed. He stared at me, not moving.

Chauncey and I could not communicate any better than a human and an owl could. Even so, Chauncey had helped me on a couple of occasions—once by leading people to where Lucy and I were being held captive. I felt he approved of me, even though we did not share the deep connection he and Lucy had.

He did not seem upset, so I was not worried about Lucy. Rather than continue to stare at one another, I turned to leave. I heard the whoosh of wings, then felt him land on my right shoulder, his left wing brushing the back of my head as he tucked them away. Chauncey was taking care not to hurt me—his talons could easily have gouged my flesh. I tried tilting my head away and trying to turn it so I could see him from the corner of my eye. It startled me slightly to see he had bent forward and turned his head to me—we were nearly eye-to-eye.

It was unnerving, so I straightened my neck and resumed looking ahead. Chauncey shuffled closer to my head, then settled. He leaned against my head with a gentle touch. Lucy had explained to me that this was a gesture of affection and trust.

"Thank you, Chauncey," I said. "I'm happy to see you since it means our mistress is not far."

Chauncey made a sound like he was laughing at me, then hopped off my shoulder and went to his perch. Puzzled at this interaction, I followed him with my eyes. When he landed, he turned himself around to face me, then shut his eyes. I laughed silently to myself, having no idea what had just transpired.

Lucy arrived within the hour. I greeted her at the stable and brought her saddlebags in. When I came inside, I could see Rose using the hoist, lifting two buckets of hot water upstairs. I had warned the maids that Lucy was on her way home after seeing Chauncey and asked them to prepare a bath. By the time I was upstairs, Hazel had withdrawn the two buckets. She followed me into the bedroom, then headed to pour them into the tub in the lavatory. Lucy was not far behind us and saw Hazel putting the two now-empty buckets back on the hoist.

"Oh, wonderful!" Lucy sighed, throwing her arms around my neck and kissing me softly. "I did want a bath but thought I would need to wait until after dinner."

"Chauncey alerted us to your imminent appearance, so I had them get started," I explained.

It took only a few minutes before the tub was full. Lucy wasted no time and was already down to her underthings by the time Hazel poured the last two buckets in. Lucy shut the door behind her, then took my finger and began pulling me with her.

"Join me," she said. "I've missed you."

My clothing flew off as I hurried to obey. I slid into the tub behind my wife. She leaned back against me, resting her wet head on my left shoulder and pulling my arms around her, and holding them to her.

"How was the pilgrimage?" I asked.

"Informative," she replied. "I learned what I wanted to know and more besides. Lily even admitted she learned some new things."

"What was the most interesting thing?"

Lucy paused before answering, finally saying, "I can't pick just one. There were several. For instance, I learned that my grandmother's warnings—about sharing the glimpses of the future I receive—are valid. Apparently, my clairvoyance is a gift from Njörun—not a common one, but not rare. Lily has no clairvoyance, even though she has affinity with Njörun."

"What else?"

"My dilemma over recruiting people who don't know they have an affinity to Eir to serve in my group of healers is not such a big problem," she said. "While I don't think our society would welcome me flitting about and telling everyone, the issue should resolve itself."

"How so?"

"Do you remember that you had no idea you possessed any supernatural affinities before we met? And that your link to Bellona only manifested itself after that?" she asked.

"Yes, of course," I answered. "I always figured you had something to do with it."

"That's true, though it was nothing I did," she explained. "It was my affinity to Njörun—my awakened affinity—that woke yours, just from spending time together. So, I can invite these people who have dormant affinity with Eir to come learn from me, and their links should become active."

"That does solve your problem," I remarked.

"It also solves a problem for Lily," she said.

"In what way?"

"Lily is eager to find someone in the kingdom who also has Ceridwen Sospita as a dominant. If she does, she plans to take that person on as a disciple. Lily's own link to Njörun should awaken that person's abilities if they spend any amount of time together," Lucy explained. "Think how much more difficult it would have been to deal with the mage without her. There is no one else in the kingdom who can do what she does."

'I can see how important it is," I said. "What else?"

"Those were the biggest revelations," Lucy said. "What about your trip to Port Charles?"

"I saw the farmstead they told me about," I said. "It's large. Fenwick showed up. I was glad to see him."

"Oh, come now! You enjoy his company," Lucy said, smacking my arm.

"Well, he usually comes bringing orders from His Majesty that require me to drop everything," I said. "But he was most helpful this time."

"In what way?"

"He helped get leeches off my back after swimming across the river," I said. Lucy shuddered.

"My feelings, too," I said. "He had no orders, saying he was just curious. He indicated our trip to Mooresa would be trickier than the king has any reason to believe. On the way back to Hillstead, the next town north, he also told me more of his life story. Did you know he lived with Madam Andrés for three years?"

"Will you be mad at me if I told you I did?" Lucy replied.

I processed my feelings before answering, "Not mad. Puzzled, perhaps."

"I think for men like you and Fenwick it is often easier for you to talk about certain things with a woman than another man. Particularly about feelings."

"You may be right," I admitted after pondering it. "I talk about my feelings with you, but I never would with Freddy."

"Precisely," Lucy stated. "Fenwick feels more emotional about his past than you do. You possess a remarkable objectivity about your life—something that is a gift of Njörun, by the way—that allows you to view your past dispassionately when you choose to. Fenwick is learning that skill from you. He admires you for it."

"He mentioned something like that," I admitted.

I was enjoying being with my lovely wife and completely forgot to ask her about the strange experience I had when riding to Bannock Hill. When I remembered, I was in the field with the men. I would not see Lucy for a few weeks.

It was only a few days more until Albert arrived with his squadron of troopers on the day before the solstice. On the solstice itself (our anniversary), everyone would have the day off for the holiday. Albert was staying with us while his squadron bivouacked on a fallow field outside the town walls.

For the evening of Albert's arrival, we invited the mayors of the fifteen largest towns in the March to come to dinner with their spouses. Lucy took care to make sure all of them had rooms at one of the inns in Easton. Albert accepted his fate as the guest of honor with good grace and was friendly and sociable—a far cry from his former haughty personality. Our guests were thrilled to be included.

For me, it was a welcome distraction. As the time of our departure grew closer, I became more anxious. Lucy and my father both noticed it in the days leading up to our departure. There was so much I wanted to do to improve the lives of everyone in the March, and all of it started with these damned nomads.

On the solstice itself, Lucy, Albert, and I wandered into Easton. There were hundreds of people in the streets and food vendors of every type. One of my great weaknesses is food carts. Meat and vegetables cooked on skewers, dough cooked by dropping it into bubbling oil then drizzled with honey, sausages in a bread roll, muffins with the first berries of the season—all of it irresistible. It was a new experience for Albert. Lucy and I made him try some of our favorites.

As we ambled along, a fair number of people recognized Lucy, greeting her with calls of, "hullo, Lady Lucy!" A few remembered me from the Feast of Andvar or the harvest fair. No one knew who Albert was until after midday when someone figured it out. At that point, a crowd began to follow us. The three of us decided we enjoyed ourselves enough for one day and returned to the manor.

For the first time since Lucy and I moved in, we sat on the veranda at the front of the manor, overlooking the town. It was a gorgeous day, with blue skies and not too warm. As we sat, Albert let out a satisfied sigh. It made Lucy giggle.

"I've never done that before," Albert said with a slightly wistful tone. "Just wandered around like anybody. It was nice. I hope I can do it again before long."

"You are always welcome here," Lucy said. "And if you come more often, people will get used to seeing you and won't make a fuss after a while."

Albert's comment reminded me of some similarities we shared. Growing up, I was not allowed to mix with the local children. Even though I was a bastard, I was still the son of the earl.

Albert likely had no playmates except his younger brother—who ended up betraying him. When Albert went to school—the same boarding school to which I was sent—he was quickly surrounded by toadies and sycophants trying to curry favor with the crown prince. It was easy to imagine how that would warp a person.

After the shock of his brother's treachery, Albert was humbled. It must have wounded him to his core. He rebuilt himself, and though he was still a bit heavy-handed at times, he had worked hard to earn the trust of everyone. It was certainly not my place to have an opinion, but I was proud of him.

Later, my father joined us. Our conversation eventually turned to the Port Charles and Pheas River project. Albert explained why his father was so keen on pursuing it.

"Peace and prosperity have enabled the population of the kingdom to grow," he said. "Unfortunately, agricultural production has not. Roughly a generation ago, most of the nobility maximized their land use. That meant expanding production into areas where crop yields were mediocre in the very best years. Production from those lands has been falling steadily since—they are simply played out."

"Is there a food shortage in the kingdom?" my father asked.

"Not yet," Albert said, "but reserves have fallen to the lowest point since records have been kept—over a hundred years. The kingdom is one drought away from emptying them. That's why opening the harbor and the river is important. The March used to ship food to the rest of the kingdom hundreds of years ago, but as people spread out, new areas were put into cultivation, and local production was ample enough that there was no longer a market for the March. The cost of keeping Port Charles open probably exceeded the port fees gathered."

"I looked to see if we had any records or correspondence regarding that," my father said. "There wasn't any. It was over a hundred and fifty years ago, after all. What is the cause of the shortage? Did something happen?"

"Nothing sudden," Albert answered. "The population of the kingdom simply continued to increase and—again, about a generation ago—some areas were no longer self-sufficient. About six years ago, the kingdom faced the first deficit—where agricultural yield fell short, and His Majesty needed to tap into the reserves. That has happened four times since, with last year being alarming."

"And the March can fill the gap?" Lucy inquired.

"Based on the estimates Caz provided, yes," Albert said. "And perhaps even be able to export abroad. Even better, land use in the March is well under one hundred percent, and fertility of the soil has never been a problem."

"When do you expect the project to be finished?" I asked.

"Ideally, His Majesty would like to be able to ship grain from Port Charles this fall," Albert replied.

"That's not much time," Lucy said.

"No, it's not," Albert agreed. "It's one of the reasons why the king has decided to take over the project. He is less concerned with the budget and more interested in completion. The one obstacle is rebuilding the roads from the different communities to the Pheas. We think we might encounter a labor shortage."

Considering that issue, some pieces of a puzzle fell into place in my mind. Faced with a labor shortage and the need to clear roads, our hundred armsmen and the far greater number of our militia would make a difference. Perhaps that was why the king was so quick to offer the assistance of a squadron of heavy cavalry in meeting the nomads. I met Albert's glance, and he betrayed a look of understanding.

Mentioning this in front of my father would probably not be a good idea. Father was so set in his ways he would resist allowing the armsmen or militia to do anything other than what they have always done. I was more pragmatic. If we sent the nomads home, the armsmen and militia would still draw their wages—why not put them to work?

"Do you really think it can be finished in time to ship this year's harvest?" my father asked.

"The engineers estimate that dredging the harbor enough to make it usable will take three months. Clearing the obstacles in the river will require much less time," Albert replied. "Rebuilding the piers in the harbor and the landings on the river properly will need more time, but temporary wooden structures can be put in place for this year."

"But the roads..." my father mentioned.

"We may have a solution for that," Albert stated. "Of all the tasks, clearing the roads is the least sophisticated. If we can find the men to do the work, we should have them passable in time, then do a complete job of restoring the roadbeds and drainage next year."

"I'm trying to remember if there has been a bigger project that I know of," my father said.

'This is not actually one of the bigger projects the crown has taken on in my lifetime," Albert said. "Building the dam on the Boreal River was much larger. In terms of significance, though, it has unique importance. Caz's idea of reopening Port Charles could not have been presented at a better time. None of us were thinking of the March as a possible solution to the grain shortages before, and after he made his inquiry, a number of people were embarrassed they had not thought of it themselves."

18

The following morning, Albert and I departed for Bannock Hill. My father decided he was too old to enjoy sleeping on rocky ground and decided to stay behind. Albert was leading his squadron of the Castle Shield, while I had only the six armsmen who spent the winter living in the quarters above the stable. The remainder of the armsmen would make their own way, but all were due to arrive before sunset.

"Am I right in guessing that a possible source of the laborers needed to unblock the roads might be our armsmen and the militia?" I asked.

"You are," he replied. "I have to tell you that my father is vexed. He has never paid much attention to the eastern March. In terms of being a threat to the security of the realm, a few hundred horsemen cannot compare to the threat of an invasion by the Rhetians—and, quite frankly, we are probably overdue for one of those. Plus, your father and grandfather kept the situation under control until the year before last."

"They did," I admitted.

"Father was quite pleased with himself for arranging to return you to the March and how quickly and decisively you restored order," Albert continued. "He likes nothing better than to see one of his pronouncements validated so emphatically. As far as the grain problem, he was not thinking of the March as a possible solution. He was hoping that better management of the Braintree holdings would result in enough of an increase in agricultural production to lessen his concern, but…"

"But he has not even named new lieges yet, so any improvement is still a year away," I suggested.

"Even then, it won't make a significant difference," Albert said. "Then you came to us with your idea. What is irritating to my father is that a few hundred nomads, who attack us every year for no known reason, might interfere with an immediate and long-lasting resolution. His view was that the nomads were a local annoyance that needed to be kept in check—"

"Which they are," I said.

"Which they are," Albert agreed, "except he never before realized how much keeping them under control drained the eastern March's resources. He is embarrassed that neither he nor any of his predecessors thought to put an end to the problem before now—either diplomatically or militarily."

"If my father and the previous earls were less competent—"

"It would have been dealt with long ago," Albert concluded. "But the eastern March has been managed so ably for so long, and he and the others before him had more pressing concerns, so it was overlooked until it became a problem."

"With my stepmother."

"Exactly."

"All of this explains why you are here now," I said. "it was not merely an idle fancy on your father's part to give you an opportunity to shine."

"Correct," Albert confirmed. "If you had not developed your idea of setting a trap for the horsemen, I probably would have been joined by a much larger group of soldiers later this summer to 'assist' you. Father wants to end this annual annoyance permanently. I must tell you that he is impressed with how you have embraced your responsibilities—not only on the military side but also as the one who will be his liege lord."

"Some of that is Lucy's doing," I pointed out.

"We know," Albert said with a smile. "The two of you are a formidable combination."

It was then that the strange sensation of viewing myself from above returned. As before, the colors I saw were much more vivid than anything I had ever observed with my own eyes. This time, my perspective was not from a fixed spot. I was looking down on our column from above but keeping pace with us.

Tree branches occasionally blocked the sight of me, but my viewpoint was from directly overhead.

"Albert," I asked quietly but urgently, "is there something in the sky directly overhead?"

"Can't you see for yourself?" he asked.

"Not at the moment," I replied. "I'll explain in a minute. Just please look."

From my vantage point, I could see Albert look up as he and I rode out from under a tree. He seemed to be looking directly at where my vision originated. Immediately, my normal sight returned.

"It was a sparrow hawk," he said, "but it just turned away. Now, what's going on, Caz?"

I searched for the right words before I answered, "You know about Lucy."

Albert gave me a look of mixed understanding.

"And your mother," I added.

Albert's understanding solidified.

"And you and Fenwick," he said.

"Right. Well, Lucy has an owl, Chauncey," I explained. "He's not a pet, and she doesn't 'own' him in that way. They're—"

"The owl is her familiar," Albert stated.

I looked at him, surprised he knew.

Albert laughed.

"That might be the first time I've been able to elicit a blatant reaction from you, Caz, old stone-face," he chortled.

"I thought I would need to explain—"

"A couple of months ago, you would have," Albert admitted. "I met Chauncey in Dunland. My mother explained to me about him while we were there, along with many other things. I learned so much on that trip and am extremely glad I went."

"What sort of things?"

"It's no secret that any mention of the supernatural makes my father uncomfortable," Albert said. "And since the whole thing with duPais, me as well—though I was fascinated in a childish way before that."

"Go on."

"While we were in Dunland, helping those poor people put their lives back together, mother took it upon herself to educate me," he explained. "I was unaware of my own mother's special talents until your mission to Eatonford the year before. Because father is so leery of it, I did not ask her about her abilities afterward. She decided while we were in Dunland that I needed to know—for the good of the realm."

I nodded in agreement.

"In the evenings, she and Lucy explained as much as I could understand, though I have come up with more questions since," he said. "One of the things they taught me about was familiars, like Chauncey."

"Does your mother have one?"

"She did," Albert said. "The family dog, Luke, was her familiar until he died three years ago. She still misses him terribly and has not yet encountered another. None of us ever knew that she and Luke were connected that way. It explains a lot, though, about how she always knew what mischief Wim and I were getting into when we were young. We were convinced there were secret spy holes everywhere in the castle and hidden servants watching us. It was Luke."

"I tried to get Lucy to tell me about her relationship with Chauncey, but she said it was difficult," I said. "It was something she felt but that she could not describe."

"Mother said the same thing," Albert stated. "The way she put it, once she and Luke bonded, she could experience the world through his senses but at the same time, still be herself. She called it a 'third eye.' Mother said that Luke did not see color, but he could smell people's emotions. Lucy told me that Chauncey sees much more color in the world than she does. So... about that sparrow hawk?"

"Just now, I saw us from his point of view," I admitted. "And as Lucy said, the view was more colorful than what I could see. It happened to me before, not long ago, and in this same general area. I could only see what the bird saw, though—I could not see from my own eyes."

"Perhaps you and the bird will bond," Albert suggested.

When we arrived at Bannock Hill, Albert's men quickly set up camp. My armsmen were arriving throughout the day. Our cooks met with their counterparts in Albert's men and collaborated on dinner. The last of the armsmen arrived shortly before it was ready.

After dinner, I had Gus Polever, one of my kersants (in the rest of the kingdom, the term is sergeant), whistle to get everyone's attention. Gus was one of those people who could stick two fingers in his mouth and generate an ear-splitting blast of sound. I stood on the table to tell everyone what our mission was.

By the time I finished, I could tell both groups were excited. I met with my kersants and asked them to develop a schedule, rotating which unit would be in charge of water each day and which unit would make the journey to the southern forest for firewood. They quickly worked it out.

We left after breakfast, early in the morning. We reached the Patker River before noon and pressed on until we judged it to be a couple of hours before dinner. The cooks got to work while the rest set up the portable shelters.

The next day, we reached the two crags where we would lay our trap. While the men were setting up camp, Albert and I rode the kersants and Albert's officers to the other side so we would determine the best plan of attack. One of Albert's officers asked if there was a way to get some archers on top of the two huge rocks.

We examined both and found no way to climb when the same officer suggested that the next group to collect firewood bring back a couple of saplings—as big as they could drag back. The men could then use the trees to reach the part of the crags where they began to slope inward. We decided each of the two could hold ten men and that the armsmen were more experienced bowmen.

The following morning, I took the officers and a group of three armsmen out to the lookout boulder I spotted on my earlier visit. We made sure the armsmen had enough food and water to last until the next day. One of their questions was whether we expected them to keep watch all night. Albert looked to me for the answer.

"Yes," I replied after considering it. "As far as we can tell, the land between here and the mountains is desert. The nomads will want to cross it as quickly as possible to get to the river. Undoubtedly, they will travel at night. Fortunately, we are coming up on the full moon, so you should be able to see them at a distance. As soon as you do, leave and ride to the camp as fast as you can and spread the alarm. Don't count on being able to hear them since the wind usually comes from the wrong direction and could prevent the noise from reaching you."

When we returned to camp, the officers, Albert, and I, hashed out our order of battle. The Castle Shield were heavy cavalry, meaning the men and horses had more armor than my armsmen. They also had longer lances. They would go first. The armsmen would follow, using bows at the beginning, firing over the heads of the Castle Shield into the enemy ranks. Our archers on the two crags would rain down flanking fire.

Our goal was to wait until as much of the enemy was between the two rocks as possible. After discussion, the group convinced me, against my will, to be the one who climbed the crag and gave the signal to attack. I wanted to be with the men, but I permitted them to persuade me otherwise. One of the things I learned when I made my pilgrimage to the Temple of Bellona is that my ability from her would also provide insights into strategy. From the higher vantage point, I might see something that could give us an even greater advantage.

We held our first 'rehearsal' that afternoon. We arranged the soldiers of both groups out of sight behind the two crags. From the end of each formation, I looked to the opposite wall to see where our enemy would catch his first glimpse of us. I made a mental note of where those spots were, so I could trigger the attack when the nomads reached those locations.

On my signal, the armsmen would fire a blind volley over the two huge rocks. The Castle Shield would ride from either side, meeting in the middle and charging down the small canyon. When the enemy retreated, it was possible some would try to scatter amid the smaller boulders on the other side. We made the decision to have the Castle Shield continue to pursue the bulk of what remained of the enemy force while the armsmen would weave their way through the broken landscape looking for any of the nomads who split from the main group.

We practiced forming up three times each day, at random times. We interrupted meals and even conducted a drill in the middle of the night. Beyond that, we settled into the routine of camp life.

I was pleased to see Albert in no way resembled the man who was my commanding officer in the Rangers. Since he was the crown prince, there would always be deference to him, but he now tried to minimize it. He spent time wandering through both sides of our camp and learned the names of many of the armsmen. One night, when it was just the two of us sitting by one of the fires, I told him so.

"Thank you, Caz," he said. "I told you I was going to change my ways almost two years ago. It was difficult at first, but now the person I used to be is a stranger to me. I find it hard to believe I was such an ass, but … I was. Majors and Minors! It's a good thing the Gods don't always give us what we deserve, or I would not be here right now."

"I can certainly understand, Albert," I agreed. "They've given me blessings I could never have imagined, even in my wildest flights of fancy."

"Perhaps, but what impresses me, and my mother and father too, is that you are never content to rest on what you have received," he said. "You and Lucy both want to improve the lives of everyone in the March. Together, you both look for ways to do that. In watching you, I understand my father better than I ever did before. He has the same goal, except for the entire realm. Now I do too."

19

On the seventh day after we set up camp, our pickets came galloping back from the lookout point. It was just past midday. They were three members of Doug Campbell's group of armsmen.

"Milord," the one named McSweeney said breathlessly, "I'm pleased to report that we have spotted the nomads. They were about a league and a half away."

"Very good, McSweeney. Did you get an idea of how many they were?" I asked.

"No, milord. It was too far away. They're moving at a normal pace, though," he said. "No dust cloud."

"Good to know," I said. "And McSweeney, don't forget to check in after we're all done here."

"Aye, milord. I'll try to remember this time."

After our nighttime raid on the nomads last summer, the kersants took roll. In his excitement, McSweeney forgot to give his name. We had teased him gently about it ever since.

I found Albert quickly and told him the nomads were on the way. His officers and my kersants had seen the lookouts return, so were ready for me. All my officers had grins on their faces.

Unlike our drills, there was nothing frantic about our preparations for battle. All the men knew what to do and realized we possessed enough time to be thorough and not rush. I strapped on my breastplate and donned my helmet. Making sure I had an extra bowstring, I slung my bow and quiver over my shoulder and headed to the crag on the right.

Reaching the slender tree propped up against it, I began to shinny up. When the trunk was small enough that I could wrap my fingers around it, I put my boots against the rock and continued climbing, hand-over-hand and step-by-step. I reached the point where the rock slanted. This was the trickiest part—if no one was bracing the bottom of the tree, it would be impossible.

Looking down, I made sure someone was doing just that, then rotated around the trunk, so my back was to the rock face. In practicing, I copied this method from one of the armsmen. It looked ungainly, but I didn't care. I eased myself back until my butt made contact, then let go of the tree and leaned back. From this point, I scooted backward on hands and feet like a crab until the rock face changed to a slightly shallower angle. Then I rolled over and crept up on hands and knees until I nearly reached the top.

Three armsmen were already there. Their bows were strung, and they were lying on their backs, with their heads below the crest. I greeted them, and they answered with grins. I took my helmet off and handed it to the nearest one, then crept up to look over the top. Albert had been the one to caution me to remove my helmet, warning that a reflection of sunlight off the metal could give us away.

It did not take a moment to spy the horsemen. At their current pace, they were less than ten minutes away from our trap. They were riding in a long column of generally four abreast. Following the horsemen were a dozen and a half large two-wheeled carts. After the carts came cattle with a handful of riders at the rear, keeping the animals together. I ducked my head back down.

While I thought the nomads would return in greater numbers this year, I was wrong—unless there was a second group following this one. Since we had never before attempted to meet them until they reached the river, I did not know whether that might be the case. I cursed myself for not thinking of that.

This group was not many more than three hundred riders, I reckoned. Since I had thought they would bring double that number, my worry that there was a second group rose. Before I panicked, I also considered that the losses we inflicted on them the previous summer might not have been easily replaced. I clutched at that sliver of hope.

I summoned a tendril of my power in preparation for the battle. As soon as I did, my worry faded away like fog in bright sunlight. Regardless of whether there was a second group, we were poised to annihilate this one. Three hundred tired and thirsty riders against the well-laid trap and our experienced men would be no contest.

Creeping up again and peering over, the first of the nomads was about to enter the passage between the two crags. I lowered myself down and took my helmet back, and shoved it on my head. Taking my bow, I looped the string on the notch at the bottom end, then jammed it against a crack in the rock face. I forced the bow down until I could attach the bowstring to the upper notch. Then I crabbed sideways to where I could see the reference point I noted earlier and pulled an arrow from my quiver.

I caught myself holding my breath while I was waiting. It seemed to take much longer than it should. Finally, a rider reached the mark. I stood carefully and hollered at the top of my lungs, "Attack!"

I nocked my arrow. In an instant, I judged the elevation, distance, and windspeed, then released at my target. As I did, I heard the sound of over three dozen arrows flying not far over my head.

The man I was aiming for fell—whether from my shot or one of the many from the armsmen, I didn't know or care. I looked for another target. The horsemen at the front of the column were desperately trying to turn back. Those behind them were still pressing forward, as yet unaware of the disaster about to roll upon them. I chose another target and let fly and heard the thundering sound of the Castle Shield beginning their advance.

On hands and feet, I clambered up to the top of my crag to be able to see. The front of the nomad column was chaos, while the rear was confused. I watched as the Castle Shield crashed into the nomads, their long lances lowered, their armor gleaming. It was a slaughter, with men screaming and horses squealing in terror.

The Castle Shield advanced in a relentless wave. When lances stuck through our enemies and were irretrievable, they drew their long, heavy swords. The men in the front forced their way forward to allow their fellows behind them a chance. A group of no more than fifty nomads broke and tried to run away. Before my armsmen even cleared the small canyon, the Castle Shield ran all the nomads down when they were slowed by the cattle that were following them.

The handful of nomads who were behind the herd of cattle bolted. The cattle were confused by the noise and commotion and began to scatter, working their way in between the large rocks on either side of the main trail. The carts stood abandoned on the path. My armsmen rode up, and Rissolo's unit wove their way through the carts and frightened cattle and set off in pursuit of the few nomads trying to escape. Our men and horses were fresh—the nomads' were not. It would only be a matter of time.

Bill Martin started shouting to his men. I could not hear what he was telling them, but it soon became clear. The armsmen were trying to collect the cattle and return them to the trail. It would take some time to clear the entrance between the two crags of the bodies of horses and nomads, so the armsmen would need to find another way around.

I had seen enough. I returned the tendril of Bellona's energy to the place within myself. After unstringing my bow, I started scooting down on my butt until I reached the tree. There was no one there to brace it, but an armsman was nearby. I got his attention, and when he was in position, I grabbed hold of the trunk and worked my way down.

Jogging over to where Andy was tied, I unstrapped my breastplate and dropped my helmet, bow, and quiver, then mounted and rode to inspect the carnage. The floor of the narrow passage between the rocks was a carpet of corpses, human and animal, with lances, some broken, sticking out at crazy angles. Here in the front, the bodies were piled atop one another, three and four high. The smell was horrid—the coppery odor of blood mixed with the stench of bowels loosened by death. It would only get worse.

Looking past the gruesome scene, it seemed not a single one of the nomads remained alive. Many of their horses were dead. Beyond, I could see some of their riderless mounts wandering injured. We would need to see if they could be saved. Quite a few followed the example of the cattle and scattered themselves among the boulders.

One thing that struck me was the youth of the nomads. The faces I saw seemed to be less than twenty years old. Only a very few appeared to be older.

On the far side of the passageway, the bodies were more spread out and not stacked up, but the tiny amount of ground I could see was soaked with blood. Andy had no desire to try to climb over the heap of flesh in front of us and refused to go further. I couldn't blame him. Albert appeared on the other side, and I called to him.

"Your Highness, we need to get some men to clear a path," I said.

Albert nodded and turned to give the necessary orders. Almost all the soldiers were on the other side of the small canyon. I turned Andy and went to the twenty armsmen on my side.

"Men, we need to move some bodies so we can get through to the other side. The quicker, the better," I said.

Noticing their unhappy grimaces, I added, "Better to be the ones still standing…"

None of the men looked too happy, but they understood. Dealing with the aftermath of bloody conflict was horrible, but it was better than being one of the victims. The men approached the pile and coordinated with the men on the other side about where to begin. They started picking up bodies and heaving them to one side or the other. Others tied ropes around the dead horses and used their own mounts to drag them out of the way.

It took over an hour before a way was cleared. Albert was one of the first to ride through. His horse was none too pleased, and he needed to calm him after he dismounted. I crossed over to him while he was soothing the frightened animal.

"Your plan was brilliant, Caz," he commented. "We caught them completely unaware. It could hardly have turned out better."

His tone was positive but lacked energy. I felt much the same. After the adrenalin rush of the battle faded, it was normal to feel a bit low.

"What should we do with the bodies?" I asked. "Burn or bury?"

Albert paused before responding, "If we were in a normal landscape, I would say burning would be best. Our problem is we would need to send all our wagons to the Southern Forest to obtain the wood, and that would take days. We'll need to bury them. Horses, too."

"I suppose we should look for a good spot, then," I said.

We walked away from the camp in search of a large enough patch of soil amid all the rocks. There was one not too far away from the mouth of the passage between the crags. We scuffed our feet on the way back to leave marks since it was not a straight line.

"How many of them were there?" I asked.

"Near as I could tell, three hundred," Albert said. "Your people said they had about a hundred and fifty cattle and ten dozen horses that were sound. Going to celebrate another Feast Day?"

"We might," I replied with a smile. "What's the next one?"

"Freyja," he replied with a grin, "on the last day of the month."

Freyja, who was Lucy's dominant supernatural influence, was the goddess responsible for romance and sexual pleasure. Her feast day was widely celebrated in the smaller villages and towns in the countryside. Most larger towns and the cities in the kingdom no longer held official celebrations, though neighborhoods often did.

As you might imagine, when groups of people gathered to celebrate a goddess with her qualities, licentious behavior often ensued. Given that her day came on what was usually one of the warmest days of the year, people tended to wear as little clothing as possible, using Freyja as an excuse to dress immodestly. There was also the belief that blatant flirting and teasing behavior that would be frowned upon normally was perfectly acceptable on Freyja's day. Add alcohol to the mix, and misunderstandings quickly escalate.

The idea of celebrating Freyja and dressing Lucy up as a human representation of her captured my fancy. Of course, with Freyja as her dominant, who knows what could happen? All of Easton might fall into a riotous orgy. That would be a disaster, though it was amusing to contemplate for a moment.

"I'll have to think about that," I said with a smirk.

We returned to the camp and found most of our officers and men had returned. Albert and I issued orders to begin digging a mass grave. When the soldiers retrieved the shovels we brought, Albert and I took them back to the spot we found.

We learned quickly that we would not be able to bury the dead. The shovels hit solid rock underneath the thin layer of soil. We asked the men with shovels to fan out in all directions to see if there was an area where digging was possible. No one met with success.

In the meantime, Bill Martin reappeared with his unit, moving the captured cattle and horses through a different, more difficult route. I instructed him to keep going. The cattle seemed weak, and I reckoned it was due to a lack of water.

"Take them to the river, then keep going to Easton," I said. "Take them to Williamson's stockyard and tell him to wait for my instructions before he does anything with them other than keeping them healthy."

"We will need to burn the dead," Albert said quietly after he crossed to me.

"Right," I agreed. "I want to keep one unit behind to continue to man the lookout in case there is another group and to fetch water from the river. Take everyone else and all the other wagons and the carts we captured to the Southern Forest for wood in the morning. If you have that many people, will you be able to gather enough wood for a pyre?"

"It will take two trips," Albert said.

I groaned. The corpses were already getting ripe from exposure to the midsummer sun and heat. Adding two more days would make the stench worse. At least the wind generally came from the west. Moving dead bodies was never pleasant, but touching ones that had been in the hot sun for three days was an invitation to mutiny.

"I'm going to send one of my officers to Oritur," I said. "It's the nearest town of any size. I'll have him bring the militia, as many tarps, and as much peppermint oil as they can find."

"I understand the peppermint oil," Albert commented. "It's to mask the smell. What do we need tarps for?"

"To make it easier to move the bodies," I said. "Better to heave them onto a tarp and then drag the tarp. No one wants to touch a corpse any more than he needs to. With the militia added to our men, it will reduce everyone's workload to a more tolerable level. Otherwise, I worry that some of the men might be tempted to refuse—it's such a distasteful job."

"Some of them are already talking about just leaving the corpses," Albert shared.

"We can't. Even though I am not the most religious person, I can see how the gods would take offense to that. For whatever reason, they granted us great success today. We scorn them at our peril," I warned. "In addition, leaving the bodies might enflame our enemies' hearts for revenge even more than they are now. We do not know how many of them live across the mountains. If they decided to return in the thousands, they would lay waste to the March, and all our hopes would be destroyed."

"Good points—both of them," Albert agreed, "though the enemy would need no more reason for vengeance than what happened today."

"Still, we could make it worse," I said.

Kersant Rissolo rode up then. He reported that they dispatched the remaining nomads. Behind him, I saw five riderless horses and the carts the enemy brought with them. Three appeared to be laden with food, one with wood, two carried large iron kettles, and three held barrels, presumably of water.

"Did you see any sign of a second group following this one?" I asked.

Rissolo shook his head.

Albert and I called the men together, getting Gus Polever to whistle for their attention. As the men shuffled over, Albert and I climbed onto one of the wagons. Once everyone was assembled, Albert began to speak.

"Men, you performed brilliantly today and did the Eastern March and the entire kingdom of Aquileia a great service," Albert called out, so everyone would hear. "If those nomads have half the sense their horses do, they will never bother us again."

The men cheered. Albert waited for the noise to subside. It took some time.

"Unfortunately, our job is not finished," he announced.

A groan rose from some.

"Lord Oritur told me, 'The Gods granted us great success today. We scorn them at our peril.' He is correct."

Murmurs of assent came from the soldiers, at least as many as those who groaned.

"Taking care of the dead is the responsibility of every soldier—whether the bodies are ours or theirs, so our job is only half finished. Tomorrow, and the following day, most of you will ride with me to the Southern Forest. We will gather as much wood as we can carry in order to dispose of the bodies properly. Lord Oritur is summoning the militia from Oritur, who will help us with this task. None of us think this is pleasant, but it is our duty. When the job is complete, we will go back across the river."

Polite applause followed. Albert looked to me as if to ask whether I wanted to say anything. I shook my head. We climbed down from the wagon, and I found Mike Dorne, one of my kersants.

"Mike, your unit will stay behind tomorrow," I instructed. "Pick three men to keep watch at the lookout. The rest will have water duty. You yourself will ride to Oritur and bring back three things: the militia, as much peppermint oil as you can lay hands on, and as many tarps as they have in the town."

On the afternoon of the second day after the battle—if you could call something so one-sided that—I sent a rider to collect the pickets. With the help of the militia, we built twenty-five pyres and dragged the rotting corpses of men and animals to them and heaped them on top of the wood. I had not thought to instruct Albert in this, but he brought back only fir and pine. Other types of wood, fresh-cut, would not burn as well. As sunset neared, we lit the first fire. Soon, all of them were blazing, throwing inky spoke into the sky.

The next morning, just after sunrise, I went to inspect the results. Some of the fires were still warm, but no flesh remained. Only the bones were left. That was acceptable to the Gods, so our job was done.

When Albert appeared, I informed him our work was finished. He instructed his officers to break camp, and I did the same with my kersants. In less than two hours, we were heading west.

20

As we rode back, Albert and I quietly discussed what would happen next. For the rest of this month, Solmandur, we would leave the militia and the armsmen in place. There was a possibility that a second group of nomads might follow the first. We both agreed they would probably arrive sooner than later.

If a second group did not appear, we would begin work on the roads. Albert said he would have a schedule prepared and sent to me, listing the different sections of road and their length. It would be up to me to assign my men to the various locations.

"I'll send you the schedule shortly after I return to the city," he said, "along with the contract."

"Contract?" I repeated with a puzzled expression.

"Of course, a contract," he said. "Did you think we wanted you to do this work at no charge? The crown will pay for the work as we will all the other pieces of the project. If we did not pay you, we would be paying someone else. I told father you would never think of charging us, but we both insist that you and your people be compensated like every other contractor we employ."

"Um, actually, you are correct. I never thought we would charge you," I stammered, "but I can see your logic. It will certainly help keep the men happy if we are able to pay them for this in addition to their normal wages."

"Don't pass it all along to them," Albert suggested. "We will expect you and your father to manage them and their progress, so you should draw wages as well."

In between Bannock Hill and Easton, it happened again. Without warning, I saw myself from above, riding next to Albert. Remembering what Albert mentioned about his mother telling him she could see through her familiar's eye and her own at the same time, I tried to do the same. Nothing—no matter how hard I strained. Then I thought to search within myself for that place that doesn't really exist in the physical world. I hoped I might find *something* that might give me a clue.

There, where I link with Bellona and Eir, I sensed a reddish-brown entity that was different. I touched it with my mind, the way I learned to touch my other connections. As soon as I did, my own sight returned, but at the same time, if I chose, I could see myself from above. I looked up and saw a sparrow hawk gliding above us. As I did, thoughts other than my own came into my head.

If you have read my other attempts at committing my adventures to paper, you will know that my ability to describe the supernatural plane is deficient. I keep trying since these involve matters that are important to who I am, but I always feel my skill as a writer is inadequate. In this case, I sensed thoughts. My brain converted these thoughts into words, but that is not how I received them.

Well, you're a bit thick, aren't you? The owl warned me you weren't very skilled. Powerful, I already knew for certain, but somewhat inept.

Suddenly, I realized I had stopped riding, and men were passing me on either side. Albert was looking at me to see what was wrong. He told me later I had an extremely odd expression on my face. I concentrated on my own senses for a moment and nudged Andy forward to rejoin Albert.

"Something wonderful is happening, Albert," I whispered. "I need to concentrate on it, but I promise I will tell you as soon as I am able."

Something wonderful indeed. I was beginning to worry that you were unwilling to mate with me.

"I apologize," I thought, attempting to respond to this communication of a strange type. "I admit I am unskilled, but I am honored and excited that you have chosen to communicate with me. Are you also choosing to bond with me?"

Mate, the bird corrected. *We are one but separate for the rest of our lives.*

I understood her meaning. She believed our connection was permanent and only death would end it. She had chosen me, and we would share knowledge, thoughts, and experience. It was a commitment of the most intimate type, and *mate* was a better descriptor.

"Why did you choose me?"

You are very powerful, like a bolt of lightning on a dark night. I became aware of you a year ago. It was too soon for me—I was too young, just hatched. When you departed, I was able to follow. I met the owl. His aura showed he was joined to a female human in the same household. He explained that you and she are human mates. When I saw her aura, I could understand why. My aura is the same. The owl's aura matches yours. It is fated.

"Did you choose me?"

There was no choice. It is compulsion. Having experienced your power and your aura, I needed to join you.

"Are all animals like this?"

Are all humans like you?

"Are all animals capable of this type of connection?"

No. Most are not. Of those who are, most are unaware. My senses awoke not long after you arrived at the watchtower place. When they woke, the compulsion came.

"I'm sorry. I do not wish to compel anyone to be with me."

There is no blame. It is the world. It is fated.

"Do we share like this all the time?"

No. We are one but separate.

"We share like this when we choose to?"

Choose—yes. Or need. If you want me, I am always where you found me.

"And you can communicate with me when you choose?"

Or need. Yes. Even when we are distant. You are amazed and grateful. I am happy. This is good. It is fated.

"Will you teach me?"

We will share. The owl shared his knowledge with me, and I have shared with you.

"Would you like to live with us the way Chauncey does?"

Perhaps later. Not now. I am young.

"Is Chauncey old?"

The owl likes to be comfortable.

"Do you have a name, like Chauncey?"

Name? I am I.

"If I wanted to tell my wife—my human mate—about you, it would help if I could give you a name instead of just referring to you as a sparrow hawk. Humans have names."

I need no name for you. You are my human.

"As you are now apparently my sparrow hawk, but what would I call you that is different from any other sparrow hawk? We humans have names so we can communicate without being joined the way you and I are."

Ah. I understand. You may call me ShaSha.

The sound she made was not exactly that. It was the sound of two beats of her wings. The closest approximation I could think of was "Shasha."

I said aloud, "Shasha."

Albert gaped at me. I waved him off with my hand.

Close enough. What is your human name?

"Caz," I said aloud.

From above me where she was gliding, I heard a high-pitched squawk that sounded a bit like "Caz."

"Close enough."

You are amused. I am amused. I am glad you wished to join, Caz.

I heard the squawk from above and smiled.

"I am happy you did not give up on me," I thought, then said aloud, "Shasha."

With that, I sensed our conversation, if you could call it that, was ended for now. I no longer saw what she was seeing. Realizing I owed Albert an explanation, I took a moment to try to compose my thoughts.

"Albert," I whispered, keeping my voice low and leaning toward him so I would not be overheard, "I just bonded with the sparrow hawk."

"I wondered," he said. "What did he have to say?"

"She," I corrected. "She is a year old and felt my presence last summer, but she was too young to bond. When I left Bannock Hill, she followed me home and communicated with Lucy's owl. She has been trying to connect with me, but I only figured out how to do it just now."

"So, what does this mean?" he asked.

"I have no idea," I replied, shaking my head slowly. "I need to talk with Lucy about it when we get back. She knows much more about this than I do."

I was bursting to tell Lucy about Shasha, so naturally, she was away when I arrived at the manor. Albert was getting his men settled just outside of town. My father heard my voice as I spoke with Rose just after I entered, and he came to learn what had happened. We went to the veranda, and I told him all about it.

"I suppose I should go to Bannock Hill then, and make sure the lads don't get up to mischief," he said once I finished.

"They have a list of things to do that should last them through the week," I said, "so there's no rush."

I wanted to discuss the plan to put the armsmen and militia to work on the roads, but I wanted Albert and Lucy present when I did. My father's first reaction would undoubtedly be negative. Albert's involvement added the weight of royal authority. Lucy's inclusion in the conversation would soften my father's temper.

We saw Lucy and Albert arrive at the gate. A few minutes later, they joined us. When I returned to my seat after rising to greet them, Lucy slid onto my lap as she was accustomed to doing. After being apart for nearly two weeks, I appreciated being close to her.

Lucy wanted to hear about our encounter with the nomads. Albert helped in telling the tale. My father seemed to enjoy listening to it again. After spending his entire adult life keeping them at bay, hearing how badly we defeated them must have been like hearing the sweetest music.

When Albert wrapped up the description, Lucy (may all the heavenly beings bless her) asked with feigned innocence, "What will the armsmen and militia do if there are no nomads to fight this year?"

Albert and I cleared our throats at the same time. Lucy laughed. My father looked from one to the other of us.

"We will keep them in place until the end of the month," I said. "But then, Albert and I have a plan for how to keep them busy."

My father's eyes narrowed, and his expression came as close to a glower as he dared, given that the crown prince was there. Albert restated the key points of the port and river project we discussed in this very spot before we left to deal with the invaders. My father's expression hardened, and I could tell he was impatient for us to get to the point.

"Together, the armsmen and the militia add up to the better part of a thousand men—men whose wages we will be paying to do nothing," I said.

"Unlike the harbor and river, clearing roads does not involve skilled labor. It merely requires brute strength, and lots of it."

"The crown would consider it a very great service to the realm if we could employ these men to make the old roads passable by the time the harvest comes in," Albert said.

Albert continued, mentioning the things we discussed on our ride back—particularly payment and developing a schedule. I could tell my father was not listening. He was choking back his temper, waiting for Albert to finish so he could respond negatively.

"Absolutely not," he declared flatly when he finally had the chance to speak. "There is nobility to service in arms. I will not have my people digging ditches. They would never stand for it."

"Sir, I believe you underestimate them," I said quietly and carefully. "This project, of which the roads are a critical piece, benefits everyone in the March. Every freeholder and all of our tenants will enjoy increased prosperity. Other businesses will reap rewards as a result. If we explain to the men—both armsmen and militia—how important this work is, and the fact that they will be paid an additional wage on top of what they are already earning, I know they will want to do it."

"How? Have you already spoken to them?" my father asked querulously.

"Of course not!" I stated firmly. "You are the Earl of the March. I cannot mention this to them without your approval."

"Unless you wish to step down," Albert added in a steely voice.

That comment, with the unspoken threat that the king could replace my father at any time, surprised me. In Albert's deadly serious tone, I recognized he was his father's son. It also underscored for me how important this project was to the king.

I watched different emotions wash over my father's face. There was indignation and anger at Albert, which he wisely suppressed. I saw a sense of betrayal, aimed at me. There was an element of fear, as he knew Albert could fulfill the threat he made.

"Or you could be remembered as the earl who brought everlasting prosperity to the March, and who assisted his sovereign with this looming crisis," Albert added.

Oh, well played, Albert, I thought.

"What guarantee is there the nomads do not return?" my father finally objected. "If they come, who will stop them? They would rampage through the March."

"Lord Easton," Albert said, "we left none alive. Chances are the nomads will know nothing of what happened for months—when no one comes back."

"Father," Lucy said, leaning forward and placing her hand on his arm gently, "think of how much your people will benefit from reopening the river and the port. Everything you do, you weigh in terms of the benefit to the March. In your late wife's malfeasance, the deepest wound was not what she did to you but how her actions jeopardized your people's safety and well-being. The king would never propose anything that would put your people at risk."

From the moment Lucy touched his arm, I could see my father's expression soften. I had never heard her address him as "father" before this, but it obviously affected him. Watching my father now was like watching a bellows collapse.

"What else can you share with me to reassure me the nomads will not return?" he asked.

"Because of how effectively we dealt with them last summer, I fully expected them to return in greater numbers this summer," I said, after I pondered what sort of information would help ease his worries. "They did not. There were only three hundred, compared to roughly four hundred and fifty last year. That indicates to me that they could not replace the men they lost. I suspect their population is not great."

"Go on," he said.

"Before our final raid last summer, we reduced their force by a substantial amount," I stated. "They did not receive any reinforcements, leading me to think they had no people to send. Or there was no communication back to their home. If that is the case, then as Albert stated, I do not believe they will know of the destruction of their force until none of their people return at the beginning of the winter. Also, as we have discussed many times, I am more convinced now that their annual expeditions against us are a rite of passage or coming-of-age tradition. The bodies of the dead were almost all under the age of twenty. Only a handful looked older. That relates back to the population number."

"One other thing I have not mentioned, Lord Easton," Albert said. "If Caz had not developed his plan of intercepting them, which worked so well, father would have sent me with a much larger force after the nomads arrived. Our entire purpose would be to deal with them so harshly that they might never return. He is chagrined that he never paid much attention to the internal affairs of the March and did not understand how the nomads stressed your resources. That is a credit to how well you and your father, and your forebears, managed your affairs. Events in the last two years have forced him to learn more, and he is resolved to find a permanent solution to end their annual incursion.

"They have been coming for hundreds of years," my father said. "It is hardly your father's fault."

"I think the nomads were never seen to be as much of a threat as the Rhetians on the western border," I suggested. "Your family—"

"Our family," my father corrected.

"Our family has managed the territory competently since Robert Gau installed Douglas Barry as the earl. There have always been other problems elsewhere in the kingdom that were more demanding of the sovereign's attention. It is only the events of the last couple of years that have attracted any need to focus on our affairs."

"So, you are saying that if the family had produced an incompetent boob before now, the nomads would have been dealt with permanently?" my father asked.

Albert laughed darkly and said, "That's an interesting way of phrasing it, but uncomfortably close to the truth."

"Well, you almost had that happen. Thank all the heavenly beings it didn't," my father remarked in a quiet voice. "A permanent end to the annual campaigning season? I've never considered it. This is the only life I've known."

"But, father—" Lucy said.

He patted her hand gently, saying, "I'm not saying I'll miss it. Majors and Minors! This is a lot to digest. My misgivings still remain, but I will not stand in the way of His Majesty's wishes."

21

It was not until we retired to our bedroom that evening that I finally had Lucy alone. Well, not quite alone. Chauncey was there when we entered. Lucy opened the window, and he departed.

When Lucy turned back to me, I crossed to her and folded my arms around her, whispering, "Something wonderful happened today."

Lucy pulled her head back to look me in the eyes and asked, "What?"

"A sparrow hawk—"

"Oh!" Lucy exclaimed. "It happened! That's marvelous! Tell me all about it!"

We sat down on the edge of the bed together, and I shared what took place and how my conversation with Albert helped. Lucy had many questions. Some I could not answer for lack of knowledge. I had just as many to ask her.

"You acted as though you knew about it," I said.

"Chauncey let me know last summer that the sparrow hawk came looking for you," Lucy replied. "She was only a few months old at the time—too young to join with you. I hoped she would remain interested."

"She might have lost interest?"

"It has been known to happen."

"Can all animals converse with one another?" I asked.

"My understanding of this is limited," Lucy said. "I've never asked Chauncey about it. Your sparrow hawk was probably able to interact with Chauncey because both of them have active abilities. Otherwise, it would probably have been difficult, like people who speak different languages."

"Do you and Chauncey communicate the same way as I described?"

"We do," Lucy admitted. "It would have been so difficult to explain unless you experienced it yourself. Now that you've felt it, I hope you understand. I was not withholding information from you about something I saw in one of my premonitions—it is just so difficult to describe having this other being in your mind. You would have thought I was crazy."

"You were crazy enough to marry me, so …" I teased.

Lucy kissed me briefly and said, "And I would do it again."

"Have you ever asked Chauncey to help me?" I asked.

"No. The times he has helped have all been of his own accord," she said. "When Pedersen kidnapped us, Chauncey was following me when they snatched me. He was hunting the night you first met Fenwick. Chauncey smelled you and checked on you because he knew you were important to me. He saw you fall and came to get us because of all the blood. In Eatonford, he saw Esme and was interested in her aura because he had never seen an aura linked to the Lord of the Seven Hells. He was watching when you encountered her and saw your aura change when she pulled the ward off your neck. Figuring it was important, he decided to help you find it."

"Can you ask Chauncey to do things for you?" I asked.

"There is no need," Lucy replied. "He is in my mind. But he does only what he chooses to do, if that makes sense. If I were to ask him to follow someone, he might or might not do it. He probably would if he sensed I believed that person was dangerous to me."

"So if I asked Shasha to fly out over where we met the nomads to see if another group was coming, she might if I could let her know why it is critical for me to know?" I asked.

"Since it is such a big concern, I would guess she might do it without your asking," Lucy said. "You will need to communicate with her about it."

"How does Chauncey feel about me?" I asked.

'He studied you carefully when we first met and while we were getting to know one another. You and he have the same aura, and he understood that you could be his human counterpart in terms of linking with me," Lucy explained. "Since then, you have earned his respect, and he is fond of you because he knows how important you are to me."

"He thinks I'm a bit dull-witted, though," I suggested.

"No," Lucy replied, laughing. "He knows you do not have the training that my grandmother gave me and that your abilities woke recently. He does not think you're stupid."

"Are you going to tell him that I have bonded with Shasha?" I asked.

"I already did," Lucy said. "He is glad. She has the same aura as I do, so he thinks he will like her, even though they will have little interaction."

"How often do you communicate with him?" I asked.

"Well, he depends on me to open the window," Lucy said. "So, daily. There can be stretches of weeks where that is our only interaction."

From here, I changed the topic to discuss what Lucy was doing while I was away. She spent most of the time away, revisiting some of the people she met on her earlier tour through the March and inviting them to come to her workshop. The latest people she called upon were unaware of their affinities. From what she learned at the Temple of Njörun, if they came to learn from her, there was a good chance their affinities would awaken. All of them were women except one.

The following morning, Albert departed immediately after breakfast. As soon as we bid him farewell, my father asked to speak with me. I followed him to the study. He chose one of the armchairs instead of sitting behind the desk.

"Did you and His Highness discuss replacing me?" he asked.

"No, sir. Not in any of our discussions," I answered immediately. "The first mention of it was when he brought it up yesterday afternoon."

He considered me for a moment or two before responding, "I believe you. It seems clear that his father has mentioned it, or His Highness would not have had that arrow in his quiver. Do you agree and want me out of the way?"

"No, sir," I said as firmly as I could. "There will come a time when we both know it's right, and I am content to wait until then. In the meantime, there is a great deal I need to learn from you."

He nodded slowly, then added, "If you are successful in convincing the damned nomads to stay away, we should have plenty of time for that."

I nodded briefly in acknowledgment.

"There have been so many things I have wanted to do over the years," he sighed, "and I never had time to take them on. Eight months of every year, I was busy on the border or training the militia. One month was devoted to visiting the communities. The other three months would see me buried in the account books. There was never time for planning further ahead than the next campaigning season. We held no feasts or fairs. I rarely traveled outside of the March. Your wedding was the first time I had seen some of my oldest friends in two decades. You will pardon me if I sound bitter, but it has occurred to me that if I worked less diligently, the crown might have helped end the problem with the nomads years ago."

"It might also have jeopardized your position," I advised. "If His Majesty had other matters he felt were more pressing, he might have simply replaced you."

"There is that, I suppose," he admitted with a slight smile. "Though worse incompetents remain in place, year after year."

"You should consider it a compliment that the way you, and grandfather, and the Barrys before, carried out your duties, you never drew the attention of the crown in a negative way," I said. "Just as you said that there are many things you put off doing because of your workload, I imagine His Majesty faces the same shortage of time. His Highness mentioned his father regrets not seeing the extent of the problem before. He had no need to say anything like that, so I believe there is genuine remorse."

"I have not had the opportunity to have a civil discussion with His Majesty since your grandfather stepped aside," my father said. "We used to be friends— as much the king can be friends with anyone. Perhaps for my own peace of mind, I should call upon him."

"I think the last year has been difficult for him as well, and being able to talk to an old friend might be something he would welcome," I said.

"In the meantime, I promised I would not obstruct His Majesty's plans," he said. "Seven Hells! I'm no fool. The potential benefits for the March are enormous. We need to inform the armsmen and the militia. Do you want to do that?"

"I would prefer it if we did that together, sir," I replied.

"So they can blame me, I suppose," he muttered.

"No, so they know to give you credit for always seeking the best life for the people in your care, sir," I said. "I do not think any of the men will complain.

They will still be drawing their pay from the March and be paid wages for the work on the roads. This will be a year of bounty for them. Even better if we can free the militia in time for the harvest, as we did last year. In every meeting we attended this winter, they were grateful."

"That was your doing, not mine," he said.

"You are the Earl of the March, father. They see you as being responsible for that good fortune," I countered.

"In agreeing to this, what are we taking on?" he asked.

"His Highness will be sending a schedule listing the work to be done and a contract," I said. "I think it will be for us to assign the proper number of men to each job and supervise their progress. Fortunately, the armsmen and the militia already have officers to whom we can delegate responsibility."

"What else?" he asked.

"Oh, Seven Hells!" I muttered. "Wait right here."

I had completely forgotten to tell my father about the jute plantation. When I returned home, I was so focused on dealing with the nomads, I was not even thinking about it. I charged upstairs and retrieved the map case where I had left it, propped in my armoire.

"Did you know," I said, a bit out of breath, as I was pulling the maps from the case, "that we own a jute plantation just west of Port Charles?"

"A *what* plantation?"

"Jute," I repeated. "It's the plant that produces the fiber used to make the kind of sacks that hold grain and seed. When the March begins exporting produce this fall, we will need millions of these sacks. At the present time, Mooresa is the only place that makes them. Sometime soon, Fenwick and I will need to travel to Mooresa to buy enough of these sacks to hold the surplus we expect this fall and try to find someone who will come with us and help us resume growing our own jute and manufacturing our own sacks."

"And we own land that used to be a farmstead for this jute?" he asked.

"Yes. And a manufactory," I said. "I visited it on my return from the city. Unfortunately, by the time I reached Easton, my mind was entirely focused on the nomads, and I completely forgot to tell you. I apologize."

"How on earth did you learn of this?"

"His Majesty informed me of this at the same time he told me that the crown would fund the restoration projects but also collect the port fees in Port Charles," I said, then recounted the entire discussion I had with the king on the topic.

"How big is this property?" he asked.

I showed him the map. It took him a moment to find the scale in the lower corner. He then took a ruler and began measuring. His eyes widened as he did.

"It's an enormous chunk of land," he said. "And we own it?"

'The surveyors researched the deed," I said. "We own it."

"Tell me what you saw when you visited," he insisted.

I described the ruins of the buildings, pointing out their locations on the map, then said, "Unfortunately, only the foundations remain, and I have no idea whether they are still sound. From the buildings, I could also guess how the operation was managed. The workers were not tenants—they were employees."

"We can examine both," he said, "and decide which makes more sense. Having tenants generally increases production. Using employees keeps costs down."

"Then, from what little I know, I'm going to guess that they used employees in the last years of operation," I suggested. "With traffic through Port Charles declining, the need for the sacks probably dropped as well."

"Who will manage this property?" he asked.

"From the size of the foundation of the house, someone important," I joked. "It was a residence not much smaller than the manor."

"Huh," my father grunted, straightening his posture. "Well, this will need to wait until you and Fenwick return from Mooresa, I suppose. In the meantime, we should make plans to visit the armsmen and the militia units and tell them what is coming. When would you like to start?"

"The sooner, the better, I suppose," I replied.

"Day after tomorrow," he said. "We'll start at Quinn's Ford and work our way south. What about the other communities?"

"We should probably let them know what is being planned," I said. "I don't know if I will have time to do another tour with you. Fenwick will come to collect me at some point."

"We should probably draft a letter," he said, "and send it to the mayors and head men and women. You, Lucy, and I will need to copy them all out tomorrow and put them in the post. That way, everyone will learn the same thing at roughly the same time—except the towns with the first militia units we visit. Oh well, I can't think of another way."

"I certainly don't wish to upset anyone," I said. "This is good news, after all."

"Some people will be disgruntled because it represents change, just like me," my father said with a smile. "Though I will admit, my attitude has come a long way since breakfast. I will even confess I'm beginning to feel somewhat excited."

Lucy found us then. She came in and settled onto my lap. After giving me a brief kiss, she turned to my father.

"You look to be in a better frame of mind, father," she said.

A tinge of color washed onto his cheeks at this, and he responded, "You have no idea how it pleases me to hear you call me 'father.' And, yes, I am much improved after speaking further with your lesser half."

"Ow," I said, pretending to be wounded by his quip.

If my father's sense of humor, limited though it was, showed itself, then he had come to grips with the change that was coming. It led me to think of how much he needed to deal with in the last year. Too often, my life is so full I have difficulty thinking beyond myself and Lucy, but he went through the same turmoil, and he must have been emotionally drained at the beginning.

"While I have you both," I said, "there is another topic I would like to discuss. From the nomads, we took roughly a hundred and fifty cattle and ten dozen horses. They should be at Williamson's. I would like to trade the horses for oxen since we will need them for the road-clearing work. With the cattle, I thought to celebrate the next feast day."

"Which is whose day?" my father asked.

"Freyja's," I said.

"Why are you asking? We should do it," he said.

"Father, most cities no longer have official celebrations on Freyja's day because behavior tends to spiral out of control," I cautioned.

"Easton barely qualifies as a city, son," he said. "Plus, as you have pointed out, our armsmen will still be drawing wages and will have no enemies to fight.

Their presence, in addition to the constabulary, should keep a lid on things. Lucy, what do you think?"

"We just won a significant victory," Lucy said. "Plans are in motion that will improve life for everyone in the March. We should celebrate both."

"Then it's settled," my father announced. "I'll have someone to fetch the head priest. Now, I need you two to leave me alone for a bit. I need to draft the letter we will send to the communities. The two of you will assist me in copying it out later, so plan on spending a good portion of the day with quill in hand."

Lucy rose gracefully from my lap and kissed my father on the cheek as she went past. I followed closely behind her. When we were outside of the study, I grasped her by the hips and pulled her back to me.

"If we do this, I want to dress you as Freyja, my goddess," I whispered in her ear.

Lucy spun around, hopped up, and wrapped her body around me while attacking my mouth with a soul-devouring kiss. I staggered up the stairs to our bedroom, with Lucy attached to me like a barnacle, never ceasing her kiss. Fortunately, the door was open. I kicked it shut behind us with my heel. We did not emerge for quite some time.

22

I learned later from Lucy that my whisper in her ear was a sign of another of her "hinge points" that marked the opening event in one of her clairvoyant visions. When something happened in reality that matched exactly what she saw in one of her divinations, then what she had seen would happen. She once explained to me that her glimpses of the future were not a narrative—she equated it to a fence. She did not see the entire line of the fence; she saw the fenceposts.

Regardless, whatever she knew of what was to come, it put her in the best of moods. After our passionate interlude, for the rest of the day and all the next, she didn't move through the house as much as dance. A beautiful smile graced her lips, and I caught her humming happily to herself. That afternoon, while copying out letters (ordinarily a task of deadly dullness that nonetheless required careful attention), her happy presence was infectious, and I found myself wearing a silly grin for no reason. When I glanced at my father, he bore a similar expression. Even Theo seemed affected by her, as I could have sworn I later saw what passed for a smile on his face.

The next morning, the head priest from the Temple of the Three Major Gods in Easton called upon us. We became acquainted with him the year before when we organized a festival in honor of the Feast of Andvar. He arrived in good spirits. The news of our victory over the nomads was spreading, and I think he was hoping we wished to conduct another celebration.

"Excellent," he gushed when we told him, rubbing his hands together happily.

"Surely it means a great deal of work for you and the other priests?" I suggested.

"Oh, it does," he replied. "But the festival in honor of Andvar did wonders in terms of bolstering people's faith. Attendance in the temple has been higher, and donations have never been more generous."

Our meeting was brief. He promised this celebration would be far easier, having held the one before. When we finished, I walked with him to the gate.

"Hroth," I said, using the formal title for priests, "there is one thing I would like to ask."

"Of course," he replied.

"You probably know, or at least suspect, that Lady Oritur has supernatural abilities," I began.

"I did not know for certain, but you are correct. I had a strong suspicion," he said.

"Her dominant is Freyja. Would it be sacrilegious to dress her like the Goddess? I wish to honor the Goddess, not anger her, and I also wish to honor my wife," I explained.

"In the countryside, it is common practice at most major feast days for someone to dress as the Minor God or Goddess honored," he replied. "It is only forbidden to appear as one of the Three Major Gods. Personally, I think Freyja would be quite pleased to have someone as lovely as Lady Oritur as a human representation."

"Thank you, Hroth. I was hoping it would be something like that and not viewed as vain or prideful," I said.

"Milord, as far as the people of Easton are concerned, and I would venture to say the entire March, Lady Oritur is regarded quite highly. I suspect everyone would enjoy her appearing in that role," he said.

I almost skipped back to the manor. It took a moment to find Lucy, but when I did, I shared what I had discussed with the priest. She smiled a naughty smile.

"Be careful what you wish for, Casimir FitzDuncan," she teased.

I heard the clicking of claws on the wood floor and sensed the hulking mass of Theo behind me. Releasing Lucy from my embrace, I turned to face him. As always, he looked at me impassively.

"Your father wants you," he said. "At the stable."

When I found my father, both our horses were saddled.

"We're going to Williamson's to instruct him what to do with the animals you brought back," he said. "Then to see Bruce Kinchen about trading those horses for oxen."

Our meeting with the stockyard was short. He would continue to feed the cattle and send us a bill later. Our discussion with Kinchen took considerably longer. He kept straying from the point of our discussion. We finally hammered out the basics of an agreement. He would trade the hundred and twenty-two horses currently at Williamson's, along with their tack, for at least two hundred oxen. He balked briefly when we told him we wanted the oxen by the end of the month but ultimately agreed he would do it.

"You know the man's a cheat, father," I said as we rode back to the manor.

My father laughed before saying, "Of course he is. All livestock traders are. It's not a profession for an honest man. Kinchen is the least larcenous of them, though. At least with him, we won't have to worry about him providing diseased animals or surprising us with a 'delivery fee' at the end. The horses are worth more than what we agreed, and we could probably have struck a better bargain, but this way, he'll make a tidy profit and will do everything he can to make sure we are satisfied. In return, we'll get serviceable animals, he will deliver them on time, and we won't need to worry."

That evening, just as we were about to sit down for dinner, our maid Gladys entered the dining room, stopping to say, "Milord, there's a gentleman—"

"Thank you, Gladys, but they know better," Fenwick said as he came in.

"Hello, Fenwick," my father greeted him.

"Milord," Fenwick responded with a slight bow, "Your Loveliness," he said to Lucy, taking her hand and kissing the back of it, "Your Leechiness," he addressed to me with a wave of his hand.

"Please join us for dinner," my father invited.

"Thank you. I would be delighted," Fenwick replied.

"Laurie!" my father hollered, "One more for dinner!"

"What brings you by, Fenwick," my father asked in a normal tone.

"I need to steal your son away for a few weeks," Fenwick said. "We're going on a fabulous journey to the cesspool of morality known as Mooresa."

"When?"

"We must leave in the morning," Fenwick stated. "I apologize for the lack of notice, but I just finalized our arrangements. If I sent a letter, it would arrive after we need to leave."

My father and I were planning on leaving in the morning to begin meeting the armsmen and militia to inform them of the work they would be doing and the additional pay they would receive. I glanced over at my father. He had a wry smile and was shaking his head. Fenwick noticed, so I explained what he was interrupting.

"It will be fine, son," my father assured me. "As you pointed out, I will be the one to communicate that they will be paid twice for the same job. I think even I can do that without too much difficulty."

"I apologize," I said.

"For not being two people, so you can accomplish both tasks?" my father said. "We knew Fenwick was arranging this trip—we just did not know when. It's a critical part of the project, and if His Majesty and Fenwick need you to go, you should go. Fenwick, I am curious … why did you address him the way you did?"

"I was waiting for him when he swam back across the river from visiting your property near Port Charles," Fenwick explained. "He was covered in the things—must have been at least three dozen. I removed the ones on his back. The trickiest one was in the crack of his a—"

"Thank you again, Fenwick," I interrupted.

Lucy and my father were roaring with laughter at my embarrassment. Fenwick soaked it in with a satisfied smile. One day I hope to get the better of him, but it was not today.

"What do you need to accomplish in Mooresa?" Lucy asked.

"First, we need to negotiate a price for ten million sacks, each capable of holding one modium," Fenwick said.

"Ten million?" my father exclaimed. "Who is paying for them?"

"The Lord of Leeches over there," Fenwick replied.

"I am?" I sputtered.

"The crown is lending you the funds, don't worry," Fenwick said. "It will all be in the contract. We will buy the bags using the crown's money. We have a letter of credit to spend up to thirty thousand ducats. We should be able to keep the cost to that—even with Lord Compote involved. You will then sell them—"

"Lord Compote? You are bringing Freddy along?" I asked.

"And his two saucy maids, plus his trusty factotum to carry all the baggage," Fenwick said. "Guess which part you play?"

Lucy started to laugh. My father looked perplexed. I was confused.

"You need to start at the beginning, Fenwick," Lucy advised. "Caz is about to burst a blood vessel in his forehead."

"Right," Fenwick said. "I've explained this to different people a few times already, so I forget I haven't spoken with you about it at all. Caz and Freddy, along with Julienne and Greta, are traveling to Mooresa aboard a Traval ship. Lord Compote and his maids will enjoy the best accommodation the ship has to offer. Caz will sleep in a serpentin along with the crew. I have made other arrangements and will arrive separately."

"You are not joining us?" I asked.

"I'm not," Fenwick replied. "I have a different objective."

"Which is?"

"Luring someone away who knows how to grow and process jute and turn it into sacks," he said. "I believe I mentioned to you that Mooresa is the only supplier of jute in the area bordering the Surrounded Sea, and they are zealous about protecting that status. If I were to go with the rest of you, I would fail in my assignment. Your group is there to buy the bags and attract as much attention as possible. Lord Compote is excellent at commanding the interest of everyone nearby, as you know."

"But Freddy knows even less about jute than I do," I protested.

"True," Fenwick agreed, "but Julienne knows far more than all of us added together and doubled, *and* she understands Mooren, the local language."

"When did she learn that?" Lucy asked.

"Professor Aloysius has been teaching her," Fenwick answered with a bit of pride, referring to himself by his first name. "And I have had her spend the last two weeks helping in an inn by the docks that is owned by some Mooren I know. They have only communicated with her in Mooren the entire time. Her accent is Aquileian, but her command of the language is good. Julienne will advise Freddy during the negotiations."

"But—" I tried to protest.

"Julienne advises me that the usual cost to buy that many sacks would be between twenty-seven and twenty-eight thousand ducats," Fenwick stated. "Lord Compote may not be able to get as sharp a price, as you have guessed. Even if he does so poorly that the price climbs to thirty thousand, you do not need to worry. The standard charge to the grower for that bag is roughly a copper each. You will still make a profit of over a thousand ducats."

"Are you serious?" my father asked.

Fenwick frowned, saying, "Milord—"

My father threw his hands up as if withdrawing the question. Lucy laughed. I was still trying to wrap my head around this plan.

"Oh, I almost forgot," Fenwick said, reaching into his jacket. "This is a letter for you from His Majesty."

He handed it to my father. My father cracked the seal with his finger and opened it. The rest of us waited for him to finish reading.

"The king suggests we make arrangements with one of the trading houses," he explained. "He says Fenwick can tell us why."

"That was the entire letter?" Lucy asked.

"There is more, but it is of a personal nature," my father said. "Go ahead, Fenwick, educate us on why we need to engage one of the trading houses."

"Right," Fenwick began, rubbing his hands together. "Farmer Jones has grain to sell. He obtains sacks made from jute to hold the grain, then loads his wagon with the full sacks and takes it along the newly cleared road to the nearest landing on the river. What happens then? The grain does no one any good sitting on the landing. Someone needs to take it downriver. Once it reaches port, it needs to get on a ship and be delivered to someone, and so on and so forth. Who will pay farmer Jones for his grain and when?"

I understood what Fenwick was trying to explain now better than his plan for Mooresa.

"If we hire a trading house, they supply farmer Jones with the sacks and deduct the cost of them from what they pay for the grain. The trading company has someone at the river landing, so farmer Jones gets cash upon delivery. The trading agent arranges for the grain of farmer Jones, farmer Brown, and others, to get on a boat where it goes to Port Charles. Once in Port Charles, they load the grain on a ship. The ship sails to another port, where the trading company has arranged for someone to buy it. Is that about right?" I asked.

"Close enough," Fenwick admitted. "There are other wrinkles, like warehousing, port fees and so on, but you have the general idea."

"Should we engage more than one trading house?" my father asked.

"That would be my choice if I were Earl of the March," Fenwick said. "I would try to meet with Coombs, Hawkins, and Traval at least. They are the biggest. If one of the smaller houses inquires, invite them to bid as well."

"Bid?" my father asked. "What are they bidding?"

"The price they will pay to farmer Jones," Fenwick replied. "In Aquileia, there is a place where speculators and the trading houses buy and sell grain and other food products, but it is all done on paper. All the transactions are done in the open, so if Coombs is willing to sell a modium of rye for a certain price, the other houses can match that price if they wish. That activity and that group of people establish the price per modium, though it fluctuates from one year to the next. Where the trading houses make a profit is the difference between what they pay farmer Jones, along with all the shipping expenses, and what they sell the grain for. The bid you would receive from a trading house would be an agreement to pay a certain fixed percentage of their selling price."

"We do not collect or pay any money—is that correct?" my father asked.

"That is correct," Fenwick confirmed. "Your goal is to convince the trading houses to pay farmer Jones the highest number possible. Of course, the bigger trading houses will probably offer rates that are nearly identical since they compete with one another."

"Did you have any idea it would be so complicated when you came up with this idea?" my father asked me.

"No," I replied and laughed.

"Well, at least I understand the rest of His Majesty's letter," my father said. "He offered to meet with me for a 'wide-ranging discussion.' I am hoping he has advisors he will lend me to make sure we get the best prices for our people."

"I believe that is his intent, Lord Easton," Fenwick said.

"When will the two of you return?" Lucy asked.

"If we leave here tomorrow, I believe I can have Caz back in your arms by the end of the month," Fenwick answered.

"You'd better," Lucy warned. "We are holding a festival on Freyja's Feast Day, the last day of Solmandur, and he must be here by then."

"Am I invited?" Fenwick asked.

"As if we could prevent you from coming," I retorted.

23

Three days later, after arriving in the capital two hours before, I was dressed in my "factotum" clothing and wrestling with the trunk containing "Lord Compote's" things, as well as the belongings of his saucy maids, Greta and Julienne Traval. I dragged it onto the deck of the *Morning Star*, a ship belonging to Traval & Company. My friend Freddy, Lord Rawlinsford, was playing the role of Lord Compote, a dull-witted, crude-mannered aristocrat. His portrayal had started as an imitation of a former schoolmate who displayed those qualities, but Freddy had expanded the character to new depths of stupidity and boorishness. The most difficult thing about the operation was preventing myself from laughing.

Lord Compote had already berated a member of the crew for the size of his cabin. The poor sailor showed Lord Compote that his cabin was the same size as the captain's. Compote then complained about the size of the bunks.

Greta and Julienne stood with blank expressions as though they were just as dull-witted as their employer. It would be difficult to decide whose costume was more immodest. Both were wearing their hair up under frilly white caps. Their dresses bared a near-obscene amount of décolletage. Their hems, in the front, showed nearly the entire length of their legs, revealing even the garters holding up their translucent black stockings.

"Poppet, they must mean for us to lay stacked on top of one another," he leered. "Lots of fun, to be sure, but not good for sleeping."

Greta and Julienne both blushed. I looked around, and every sailor on the ship was ogling the two women while pretending to work. The sailors suddenly tore their eyes from the women and began to act busy. I turned and saw the captain striding up the gangway.

Seeing the gold braid on the man's shoulder, Freddy immediately scurried to him and started his complaints anew. The captain listened impassively, with his arms folded across his chest. The sailors were watching the scene from the corners of their eyes, anticipating the captain's reaction.

"If you don't like it, Mr.—" the captain began.

"Lord," Freddy said peevishly. "Lord Compote."

"If you don't like it, *milord*, you are free to leave the ship and find passage on another," the captain said.

"That just won't do," Freddy said. "We have an appointment, you know. Can't you get a bigger ship?"

"No," was all the captain said as he shouldered past Freddy, ending the discussion.

We set sail an hour later, just before sunset. I daubed some ginger oil on my upper lip to help stave off seasickness. As soon as the sun went down, I went below, found my serpentin, and fell asleep.

We arrived at the port of Acrius near midday on the third day of our journey. Mooresa was the closest country on the southern continent to Aquileia. When we docked, I wrestled the trunk to shore. As Fenwick had warned me, Mooresa was even hotter than Scaramouche. The temperature was similar, but Mooresa was noticeably more humid

"Ashe," Freddy called, using my fake name of Reginald Ashe. "Get us one of those hats. See if they have anything for the girls while you're at it."

I knuckled my forelock and jogged off. At the end of the pier, there was a stall with a money changer. I stopped briefly and exchanged five ducats for local coins. Due to my inability with the language, I was sure I was cheated but could do nothing about it.

Not far away, a man was selling straw hats. I pointed at one style and held up two fingers. Scanning the others he had hanging there, I found two that seemed to be for women and pointed at them. The man gave them to me and then, presumably, asked for payment. Since I could not understand, I held out my hand with a small collection of the copper coins I received from the money changer. It appeared as though the vendor was going to demand more, but he changed his mind and contented himself with scooping all the money from my hand. By the time I returned, Freddy and the women were sitting in an open carriage with a man dressed in loose-fitting white clothing.

"There you are, Ashe," Freddy exclaimed. "Dawdle on your own time, please. Give us those hats and fetch the trunk."

I handed over the hats and put on my own. Then I fastened the trunk to the back of the carriage. When it was secure, I climbed up on the bench next to the driver.

I reckoned the man in white was the person we were supposed to meet about buying the sacks. According to the plans Fenwick and Julienne made, his name was Autrey Ruiz. He would take us to a hotel and later would have dinner with Lord Compote and the ladies. The women would stay in Freddy's room at the hotel while I was banished to a dormitory for servants.

The hotel was on top of a hill overlooking Acrius. Ruiz explained that was done to take advantage of the breezes. Of course, there wasn't even a puff of air I could sense.

In the time it took me to carry the trunk from the carriage, I overheard Lord Compote casually insult Mooren customs three times. He mocked their language, made fun of their manner of dress (which looked quite comfortable), and asked Ruiz about a hand gesture he saw a man make during our ride here.

The gesture was obscene enough that Ruiz had difficulty answering. Lord Compote, being quite thick-headed, did not understand the more polite way Ruiz was trying to explain. When Lord Compote finally understood, he began laughing like a schoolboy who had just learned a naughty word and started repeating the gesture at others in the hotel, ignoring Ruiz's profound embarrassment at his inappropriate behavior.

It took every bit of self-control to refrain from laughing out loud. I did not dare make eye contact with Greta or Julienne for fear of breaking character. From the corner of my eye, I could tell they were looking at the floor.

Finally, the arrangements were made, and I was able to follow them to the room. Ruiz was kind enough to inform me where the dormitory for servants was located and tell me that dinner was provided, but servants would be fed much earlier—in just over an hour. He left me before we reached the room. I would have bet a wheat head against a florin that he was shaking his head in dismay as he walked away.

When I entered the room, Greta was collapsed on a sofa, holding her sides and shaking as tears rolled down her red cheeks. Julienne had put a small pillow over her mouth and was laughing just as hard as Greta. I would have escaped without cracking, except Freddy turned and gave me an innocent look, as if to say, "What?"

I clapped my hand over my mouth to try to keep the sound from leaking. Unfortunately, the spasms of my chest muscles from the suppressed laughter caused me to lose my balance, and I fell on my rear to the floor. This added to the hilarity, and it took us several minutes to recover.

When I finally felt I regained control, I picked myself up. I headed for the door. Then I made one more error.

"Will that be all, milord?" I asked, my voice choked from trying not to laugh.

Upon hearing that, Greta and Julienne both started up again. That set me off, and I buried my face in the crook of my elbow, leaning against the wall. Upon recovering, I quickly scooted through the door before anything else happened.

I found where I was to stay. A bath would have felt wonderful, but that was not a luxury provided for servants. I was able to wash my face, though, and that helped.

At the appointed time, I followed some of the other servants, none of whom spoke Aquileian, to the area where we would be served dinner. At least they were kind enough to get my attention and make motions like eating, so I figured it out. We were served outside, and the dishes seemed similar to what I enjoyed in Scaramouche.

There were no utensils—we would eat with our hands. I quickly learned the food was spicier than what I ate in Scaramouche, and I seized a cup of water and began to gulp it down. One of the other servants wagged a finger at me and handed me a chunk of bread, indicating I should eat it. The bread did a much better job of neutralizing the burning sensation in my mouth, and I nodded my head in thanks.

Though servants were supposed to eat now, I did not expect to see Greta or Julienne. Lord Compote would insist they eat with the other guests. It would make everyone feel uncomfortable, but Lord Compote would never notice. I hoped there was somewhere where I could watch. Freddy was sure to give a virtuoso performance.

Once I adjusted to the spiciness of the food, I found it delicious. I kept my appetite under control, however, worrying that too much would make for a restless night. My fellow servants tried to speak with me, and I am sad to say, I remained in character and responded like a typical Aquileian. I spoke loudly and slowly, as though they were simple-minded (which I knew they were not).

When everyone was finished, we returned to the dormitory area. One of them brought out a deck of cards, and three began to play. I quickly recognized it as a version of plafond, a game at which I was quite good. The game is normally played in pairs, so one player had a dummy as his partner. I quickly let them know I wanted to play. They argued among themselves as to who would get me as a partner—thinking I would be horrible.

I quickly learned the Mooren names for the different suits and how to say, "no trump." That I understood the concept altered their thinking, and they assigned me a different partner than originally planned. We played two games, consisting of ten deals each. My partner and I won both, then I bowed out. I indicated I would return, but I wanted to observe Freddy's antics.

I was able to find a seat in the lobby where I could see Freddy and the women. Dinner was over, and Ruiz was looking fatigued. I took that to mean Freddy had been busy.

For dessert, they served whole peaches, providing a small knife with which to cut them open. I almost started to laugh, thinking of the fun Freddy could have. He did not disappoint me.

He cut his in half and removed the pit, saying, "Mmm, peaches. We know I love to eat peaches, don't we, Poppet?"

Greta said nothing but turned bright red at her table. Julienne may have been relieved that Freddy did not target her, but that relief was short-lived. Freddy picked up half the peach and extended his tongue into the hole where the pit had been.

"What do you think, Bunny? Is this how I eat a peach?" he called over, then waggled his tongue in the hole.

I stayed just long enough to see Julienne's cheeks turn an even brighter shade of scarlet than Greta's. Before I laughed out loud, I rose quietly and made my retreat. Once I rounded the corner, I buried my face in my elbow again and waited until I regained my composure. When I returned to the dormitory, the others were waiting for me to rejoin the game.

I gestured to let them know I was grateful for their kindness, and we resumed play. I had a different partner for the first game, and we switched again for the second, so I played with all three that evening. My partner and I won every game, but not by such huge amounts that it would make anyone feel uncomfortable.

I thought about visiting the room where they were but decided it might cause us to fall into hilarity again. Certainly, I would never think of eating peaches in the same way in the future. Stretching out on the narrow cot provided, I fell asleep quickly.

The stirring of the other residents woke me. From the light coming through the window, I could see it was near daybreak. One of them indicated it was time to eat. I imagined servants would again be fed much earlier than their employers.

They served us fresh-baked bread and fresh fruit, including peaches. They also had qava. When I ordered mine, I made sure he added a lot of sugar. Qava on the southern continent was brewed to be very strong. I also had a peach, thinking of the scene last night and grinning like a fool.

When I was finished, I took an extra peach and headed to the room. I knocked gently. Julienne opened the door a few moments later. She was clad in a robe, and her hair was sleep-disheveled, but she was still a very pretty woman.

I gave her the peach, saying, "This is for you," and strode into the room.

Her bark of laughter came a second later. Greta came in, also wearing a robe, to see what the noise was. Julienne had shoved her forearm in her mouth to keep quiet. She held the peach out to Greta. Greta tried not to laugh but the sound escaped through her nose, like a strangled sneeze. That made things even funnier.

Freddy strolled in to find us all in spasms. He looked us over, shaking his head. Seeing the peach next to Julienne, he crossed over and picked it up.

"Oh, yummy! A peach," he said, and lifted it to his mouth and took a large bite with a devilish look in his eye.

"You're mean," Julienne said to me after we recovered, and Freddy finished the peach. "That was not fair."

"You wanted to come along on this adventure," I replied. "There is a price to be paid for be allowed to bask in the presence of Lord Compote."

"Fenwick warned me," Julienne said. "But he severely understated what the reality is."

"And you're surprised?" I asked. "You know his sense of humor."

"Grr. You're right," Julienne admitted. "Now I'll need to plan how to get my revenge."

"Good luck with that," I said. "I owe him about ten times over, and I haven't come up with a good idea yet."

'That's because you aren't devious enough, Caz," Greta commented.

24

In the negotiations that took place later that morning, Lord Compote proved to be surprisingly effective. It was a triumph of obtuseness. Whenever Ruiz presented an offer that was unacceptable, Lord Compote pretended not to understand. He would then ask question after question, some of them completely unrelated to the matter at hand. It did not seem to matter if he had asked the same question earlier, after a previous round. Lord Compote insisted on receiving the full explanation again. Watching Ruiz and his compatriots, I could tell Freddy was wearing them down.

The end result was agreement on a price of just under twenty-eight thousand ducats for ten million sacks sized to fit one modium of produce. Ruiz and the two other Mooren in the room appeared to be emotionally drained by the time we struck our bargain. Ruiz prepared a contract—in Aquileian—while we waited. Julienne, who was sitting hip to jowl with Freddy the entire time, read it over without appearing to and nudged Freddy that it was acceptable for him to sign. Freddy then produced the letter of credit, crossed out the amount of thirty thousand ducats, and noted it with the agreed-upon price. The bank would release the funds to the Mooren when they received confirmation we received the sacks.

Ruiz apologized, saying he had other pressing business that would prevent him from accompanying us back to the hotel. His driver would deliver us and return to collect us in time to board our ship, which was leaving on the morning tide. He thanked us for the opportunity and bade us farewell.

We waited until we were back in the hotel room before talking business. Even then, we kept our voices low. We could crow in triumph after we reached home.

"That went far better than I would ever have expected," Julienne said once we sat down. "Who knew that unrelenting stupidity was an effective bargaining tactic? You were brilliant, Freddy."

"I don't know," Greta complained with a whine. "The last trip was more fun."

She quickly smiled to let us know she was joking. Greta had a valid point, though. When we went to Scaramouche, we knew they were going to try to cheat us. We tricked them instead. What we just finished was a business transaction where a fair price was reached. Freddy playing the fool was the full extent of our deception.

"Julienne—Bunny—you make a marvelous saucy maid," I said. "Though Poppet over there sets a high standard, I think you performed just as well."

"It has been great fun," Julienne said. "Thank you for letting me play with you. That said, I'm ready to go back to being me."

"We will be leaving the city for Manton when we return," Greta said. "This was probably our last adventure with you, Caz."

"Don't say that Poppet," Freddy replied in his Lord Compote voice. "It's only the last until the next."

I arrived back in Easton with a day to spare and desperately in need of a bath. The closest I'd come to bathing was a saltwater dousing I took on the ship home and then being caught in a summer rain on the middle day of the journey from the city to Easton. I encountered Theo first upon entering the manor and asked him to get the maids to prepare one for me. Lucy's horse was in the stable. Theo informed me she was not in the house, but my father was in and requested my attention.

"If you don't mind, sir, can we meet on the veranda?" I asked my father. "I'm a bit ripe."

Certainly," he agreed. "How did you fare on your trip?"

"Well. We struck a deal for the sacks at a reasonable price. It's a funny story, so if you don't mind, I'd like to share it later when Lucy can hear," I said. "How did the men take the news?"

"I'm happy to admit I was wrong thinking they might resist the idea," he said. "With no threat of attack, the armsmen and the militia have been growing bored, and that generally leads to trouble. Having something worthwhile to do and being paid doubly seemed pretty popular. The armsmen will be arriving in Easton tomorrow to assist in keeping order during the festival. I stressed to them that this is work and not a holiday."

"I expect they will still indulge," I said.

"So do I, but not like the last time when they were all nearly incapacitated. They will depart the day after the festival and ensure the oxen are delivered to the proper locations. I also received the contract from His Majesty with a schedule of the different road projects. In your absence, I had my solicitor review the contract, signed, and returned it. I have also assigned the different units of armsmen and militia to the various tasks on the schedule. You will need to take over managing the project since I will be heading to the city after the festival."

"Are you meeting with His Majesty?" I asked.

"And some advisors," he said. "His Majesty offered their assistance in working with the trading houses. You and I will have the chance to go over the schedule later this evening and all day tomorrow. Now go dunk yourself in some hot water before your lady wife returns. We can't have her smelling you the way you are."

By the time I reached the upstairs, the bath was ready. I wasted no time stripping off my clothes and sliding into the hot water all the way until my head submerged. When I surfaced, I reached for the soap and started to scrub away two weeks of accumulated crust.

Dinner that evening was fun, as I shared Freddy's antics as Lord Compote with Lucy and my father. After dinner, I began reviewing the materials relating to the road work. It was far more than a mere schedule. The information included maps and detailed descriptions of the work to be done, even including the number and type of trees to be removed from sections that were overgrown by neighboring woods. In addition to all the information provided in the materials, there would be an engineer and a surveyor assigned to each section of the roads.

My father did an impressive amount of organizing. He assigned specific units to each portion of the work and figured out where the oxen would be needed and how many. He designated which officer from the armsmen or militia was in overall "command" of each team of workers. He ordered tools—hundreds of picks and shovels, miles of rope, and scores of pulleys. He even organized how the men would be fed. Section by section, I reviewed his plans to see if there might be something he overlooked. If there was, I could not find it. He came into the study while I was reviewing the last section.

"You did an amazing job," I said.

"Eh. It was fun," he replied. "It's like planning for a campaign but not against an invader. We will probably need to make adjustments as we get further along, but I hope this will get things off to a productive start."

"The tools you ordered—where are they being delivered?" I asked.

"To the job sites," he replied. "I went through our local people, even though they needed to get them from Aquileia. The money for this needs to stay in the March as much as possible.

"I agree. What do you see as our role in this?" I asked. "With a surveyor and an engineer at every site, they will be the ones to provide direction."

"I think you and I simply go from site to site and make sure things are running smoothly."

My father turned around just as Theo's large frame filled the door of the study. I was a bit surprised, as I did not hear the usual clacking of Toby's claws on the floor, which was the best way to learn of Theo's approach. Theo moved with incredible silence for such a large man.

"Mr. Fenwick is here with guests," Theo announced.

My father and I left the study and crossed the entrance hall to the large receiving room. Fenwick was indeed there with a man and a woman whose backs were turned, but they did not seem familiar. Fenwick was kneeling on the floor, giving Toby a rub on the belly. Toby had all four paws in the air and looked to be in a state of bliss. Julienne Traval was standing next to Fenwick and gave him a nudge. Fenwick looked up, noticed our entrance, and stood.

"Milords, may I present Victor Balboa and Madame Ariana Hernandez," he said. "Lord Easton, this is Julienne Traval. Your son has met her, but you have not. Mr. Balboa and Madame Hernandez, Lord Easton and Lord Oritur. Julienne, Lord Easton. Mr. Balboa has graciously accepted your offer of employment and will help you manage the farmstead near Port Charles. Unfortunately, he currently speaks no Aquileian, which is why Madame Hernandez is here. She will serve as his translator and tutor until you no longer need her services."

Fenwick spoke to them both in Mooren, and we exchanged greetings. I took a closer look. Balboa was short but powerfully built, with broad shoulders and a barrel chest. Madame Hernandez was not a small woman. She was tall and broad-shouldered but also beautiful, with tanned skin, a slender figure, straight black hair, and dark brown eyes. Both of them seemed to be somewhere in age between my father and me. I would guess Balboa was around fifty years old. Madame Hernandez appeared to be a handful of years younger.

"Lord Easton, I also have a note for you from His Majesty," Fenwick said as he handed it to my father. "I can tell you that it is requesting that you postpone your meeting for four days in order that you can show Mr. Balboa the property."

"I would like to see it myself. Will you join us for dinner?" my father asked, his gaze firmly fixed upon Madame Hernandez.

"If you would be so kind," Fenwick answered.

"You are welcome to stay with us," I offered.

"Again, that is very gracious of you," Fenwick said. "Especially since there are no rooms available at any of the inns due to the celebration of the Feast Day of Freyja tomorrow. How fortunate that we arrived in time."

Theo was standing by the door, waiting for Toby. Toby was leaning against Fenwick's leg, hoping for more attention. I crossed to Theo.

"Please bring their luggage in," I said quietly. "Put Mr. Balboa and Madame Hernandez in separate rooms unless Fenwick tells you otherwise. Put Miss Traval in Fenwick's room. Ask Fenwick if they would like to bathe before dinner and if they do, see to it. Tell Laurie we will have four more for dinner and ask one of the maids to prepare some refreshments and deliver them to us on the veranda."

Theo's expression did not change. He moved from the wall to Fenwick and whispered in his ear. Fenwick nodded at Theo's questions. Theo then strode out of the room. Toby, realizing that Fenwick was not going to pet him more, skittered after Theo.

"While your luggage is being brought in and your baths prepared, please come sit," I said, gesturing to the front door.

I heard Madame Hernandez repeating my invitation in Mooren quietly to Balboa. I opened the door, and my father went through first, leading the way. Once everyone was outside, I followed.

"Please tell us about yourself, Mr. Balboa," my father asked.

Madame Hernandez translated. Balboa began to answer, and as he did, his speech grew quicker and more heated. Madame Hernandez held up her hand to get him to stop so she could cover what he said.

"I was the manager ("Foreman," Fenwick interrupted) of the second largest jute plantation in Mooresa," Hernandez recounted to us. "It is about the same size as Mr. Fenwick said your plantation will be. I have spent my entire adult life growing and processing jute. There is nothing about the care of the plant or how to process it that I do not know. Though our property was smaller than our biggest competitor, the size of our crop was equal. My wife died three years ago. Our son is grown and works on a ship for Traval and Company, so I am alone. The son of the owner of my plantation told his father that he thinks they pay me too much—that an idiot could run the operation. He tells his father to cut my wages, and if I don't like it, I can leave, and the son will do my job."

"Go ahead," my father requested.

"Then Mr. Fenwick arrived," Madame Hernandez translated. "He asked if I would like to manage a plantation in Aquileia that had been abandoned many years ago. He said the father and the son knew nothing about jute and would be honored if such a knowledgeable expert would help them. They would give me a house and pay me a hundred ducats a year. Mr. Fenwick said I could not tell anyone I was leaving, and he would come to get me, and he did."

My father excused himself, saying he would return in a moment. I did not know what to say. We waited for my father to return. When he did, he had the surveyor's maps of the property. He unfurled them and bent over to show Balboa.

"How much jute can you grow on a property this size?" father asked.

Madame Hernandez translated. Balboa looked at the map, trying to see the size of the property. He shook his head and spoke in Mooren.

"He wants to know how big? How much land?" Hernandez said.

"How many acres?" Fenwick asked.

"Over two thousand," my father answered.

Fenwick converted acreage into whatever unit of measure they used in Mooresa and gave the information to Balboa. Balboa was clearly doing math in his head. Finally, he responded to Fenwick. Then it was Fenwick's turn to do some figuring.

"In Mooresa, Balboa says he would produce around two and a half tons of usable fiber per acre," Fenwick reported. "That is enough to make ten thousand bags. With a farm the size you mentioned, he would produce enough for twenty million bags."

Balboa added to his earlier comment. Fenwick questioned him, and Balboa responded. Fenwick did some more quick arithmetic in his head.

"Balboa does not know whether the soil here will be as good as Mooresa," Fenwick said. "If it is not, the yield will be smaller. He also does not know whether he will be able to plant two crops or only one. It will depend on the growing season."

"He could harvest two crops each summer?" my father asked.

Hernandez translated and gave the response, "Yes."

Balboa started speaking again. Madame Hernandez obviously did not know what he was talking about, so Balboa turned to Fenwick. Fenwick listened, then asked a question. It was a lengthy explanation.

After Balboa responded, Fenwick said, "I am supposed to tell you about legumes, like peas. Balboa says that after the plants are harvested, they are soaked in enormous tubs or tanks to separate the fiber from the plant. He says that if you save that water and spread it on the fields, it is a wonderful fertilizer for legumes. Apparently, legumes do good things for soil also, so there is a two-crop rotation. That is why it is best to have two growing seasons."

Lucy joined us then. We introduced her to Balboa and Madame Hernandez. When she finished greeting them and Julienne, she slid onto my lap.

"So, we will leave the day after tomorrow," my father said, addressing Fenwick, "and head south until we reach Hillstead?"

"Correct. Then we will go to Port Charles, cross the river and view the property," Fenwick said. "The engineers have already begun work on the harbor, so a boat should be available to take us across."

"Good. I've always hated leeches," my father commented.

"Then you will head to the capital, and Mr. Balboa will return here and begin writing down what he believes you will need to do to restore the plantation to full production," Fenwick said. "By the time you return from the city, he should have that figured out, and you can go find people to do the work."

25

I will admit it was disconcerting to hear Madame Hernandez translating for Balboa. She was not loud, and her voice was pleasant. Plus, it was only polite to include him in the general conversation, but it was not something I was accustomed to hearing.

Theo appeared and informed us that baths were ready for Mr. Balboa and Madame Hernandez. We asked Theo to take them to their rooms. We waited for them to depart.

As soon as they did, Lucy pounced, asking, "Tell us where things stand with the Travals."

Fenwick sighed dramatically, "Fine, Lady Nosey."

"We want to know about your mother and father, Julienne," Lucy added.

"Her mother was initially put off since I have no family background I can claim," Fenwick said. "Her lack of enthusiasm for my candidacy as a suitor faded quickly when Julienne told her I was a Privy Advisor to His Majesty."

"A what?" my father asked.

"Privy Advisor to His Majesty," Fenwick repeated.

"I don't believe such a thing exists," my father stated.

"Probably not," Fenwick agreed. "Julienne made it up."

"Her father?" Lucy asked.

"My father's primary concern is for my happiness," Julienne related. "Beyond that, he wants to make sure I do not end up with some bounder who is only after money. In addition, father would like his business to continue. He is convinced that I am enjoying Fenwick's attention, as I am, so the first condition is met."

"When I realized I was serious about pursuing the matter further," Fenwick added, "I allowed her father to discuss my financial situation with the man who manages my accounts. That resolved the second point. Julienne herself is addressing the third item—continuing the business. Much to her father's great delight, she has shown she possesses an intuitive understanding and has thrown herself into it. Because of her gender, Herbert never considered that Julienne would follow in his footsteps. Once he gave her an opportunity, however, she quickly proved her mettle. He is thrilled that Julienne will probably become the first woman to lead a major trading house in Aquileia."

"Is that true?" Lucy asked.

"We've discussed it," Julienne replied.

"It did not escape my notice that Fenwick probably learned of Mr. Balboa's circumstances from you or someone in your company," my father commented. "Thank you."

"My father feels indebted to Caz for a number of reasons," Julienne replied. "This is a very small thing. It helps that Fenwick has let His Majesty know of our part in restoring jute production to Aquileia. It sounds from what Balboa said that the March would never need to buy from Mooresa again, plus you might be able to reduce the amount of jute Aquileia imports from Mooresa for other market areas. That helps the overall balance of trade which is always a good thing."

"I had not even considered that," my father said.

"Lord Easton, are you aware I was captured by Rhetian pirates last fall and that my father asked Caz to deliver the ransom?" Julienne asked.

"Yes. Fenwick told me about it," he said.

"When we returned, Caz suggested to my father that he keep the ransom money handy and mentioned the possibility of investing in the Port Charles project. Even though the circumstances are different now with the crown's involvement, we still see an opportunity. Father plans to begin construction of a significant warehouse and wharf in Port Charles as soon as the port is passable. Because of Caz's suggestion, we are ready to act. Hawkins might be able to move as quickly because of Greta's knowledge of the project, except I don't believe her father has allowed her near their business and probably does not listen to her. Her brother Ratty might have some influence, but he is junior in their ranks. Coombs is definitely not going to be swift to take advantage."

"You know that we will probably split the trade concessions along the river between the three firms," my father advised.

"That is in your best interest," Julienne agreed. "But, when the goods come downriver, they will need warehouse space while waiting for shipment. If Traval & Company has the only warehouse in Port Charles, the other two will need to pay us for its use. They might decide they are better off renting space from us than building their own facility."

"On whose land will you build?" my father inquired.

Julienne smiled and said, "Our own. Two traders that Traval & Company purchased many years ago held deeds to adjacent pieces of waterfront property in the harbor. Father's people found those documents and have already been to court to ensure they are still valid. We have plenty of room to build. As far as the other land in Port Charles, once the port is declared open, the crown intends to publish a list of the property owners. Heirs and assigns have a certain period to assert their rights. If no legitimate claims are presented, the land is subject to escheatment, in which case the crown holds two-thirds ownership interest, and the local liege lord holds one-third."

"Just from your knowledge of this situation, it seems like Traval & Company have a significant head start compared to the others," I said.

"It was my primary focus during the winter months," she replied.

Rose came and informed Julienne and Fenwick that their bath was ready. Julienne blushed prettily, and they departed. Father looked at Lucy and me with an eyebrow raised.

"She's sharp," he commented.

That evening, as we were getting into bed, Lucy said, "Your father is quite taken with Madame Hernandez."

I laughed, replying, "He was not too subtle about it, was he? I would like to know more about her before anything happens. The last thing he needs is another bad relationship. We heard Mr. Balboa's life story, but Madame Hernandez has said nothing about herself."

"Ask Fenwick tomorrow. He is the one who engaged her services, so he will know," Lucy said.

"Speaking of tomorrow…" I started.

"Your father and I have everything arranged," Lucy said. "I have something for you to wear. You will need to arrive at the temple just after ten o'clock, and you should ride. We will need Andy later. I will be coming separately."

"Am I allowed to ask what you have planned?"

"You're allowed to ask, but I probably won't give you the answers you really want to know," Lucy teased. "Just try to maintain a state of happy anticipation—I think you will enjoy it."

"You said my father has been involved? When has he had the time? He did all that planning for the work we will be doing," I asked.

"His role in the planning was small but significant," Lucy answered. "He actually offered a suggestion that we are using, and that's all I will say for now."

The next morning, after everyone had breakfast and spent some time in idle conversation, Lucy instructed me that it was time for me to get dressed. I went up to our bedroom and saw what she had prepared for me. Upon seeing it, I nearly refused.

My breastplate and helmet were there, but Lucy had attached two wings of feathers on either side of the helmet, making it look like something from a myth. There was a linen undershirt that was cut so it would not be seen under my breastplate. For my lower half, there was a leather skirt that would only reach the middle of my thighs and leather sandals with long thongs that I guessed I was supposed to entwine around my calves.

I hollered downstairs for Lucy. By the time she came to the bedroom, I was dressed in a shirt, skirt, and breastplate. I still had my underclothes on, and the legs extended below the bottom of the skirt.

Lucy took one look and wagged her finger, saying, "No underthings. You would look ridiculous with them."

I tried to protest, but she put her finger on my lips to silence me, telling me, "You are a mythic warrior from Freyja's hall of slain heroes. You will be my escort today and need to look the part. Freyja is also a war goddess, remember? It's just not her main responsibility."

Bellona was the Goddess of War, but part of the lore regarding Freyja included her hall in the afterlife where she welcomed fallen heroes—especially anyone who died bravely to protect his lover. Realizing I was defeated before I started, I allowed my underclothes to drop to the floor. Lucy kicked them aside. She giggled but gave me a brief kiss as a reward for complying.

"How do I wear the sandals?" I asked.

Lucy knelt down and quickly began to crisscross the long leather thongs around my ankles and up over my shins. She tied the thongs just under and behind my knee, atop my calf muscles. Lucy then buckled my sword belt.

"It's not the right type of sword, but it will have to do," she said. "Put on the helmet and let me have a look."

Sheepishly, I put the helmet on. I knew I must look ridiculous. Lucy dragged me to the mirror and stood behind me on tip-toes, looking over my shoulder with her hands around my chest.

"My brave warrior," she said, then growled sensuously. "I may make you wear this some other time, just for me. One more thing."

She dashed into the lavatory and returned with a small bottle. Uncorking it, she poured some oil into her hands. She then began to rub my shoulders, arms, and legs.

"What's that for?" I asked.

"To make you gleam," she said. "It will show the definition of your muscles, and then everyone will see that you are worthy of being my escort today."

When I looked in the mirror again, there was a difference. Though I didn't feel anything other than oil on my skin, it did make the shape and size of my muscles much more apparent. It made me look more like a figure from a myth, though I still had misgivings. Still, it was what Lucy wanted, and her ideas had always turned out well, so I set my ill humor aside and resolved to enjoy myself in this role.

"Now, scoot," she said, smacking me on the rear. "I need to get dressed, and I don't want you to see until I arrive in front of the temple."

She did plant an extremely passionate kiss on my lips as she guided me to the door, so maybe this costume had some merit. I went down to the stable and found Andy was already saddled. His mane was braided with a white ribbon with gold trim, and his tail was wrapped with the same. Fenwick and Julienne came from the rear of the house, saw me, and gave a low whistle.

"One smart remark out of you…" I threatened.

Fenwick held his hands up in a gesture of peace and was on the verge of uttering some clever insult, but Julienne smacked him on the arm and said, "He looks amazing, Fenwick, so shut your mouth. Caz, you look like someone from one of the old stories of ancient heroes. I half want you to scoop me up and ride away with me."

"Only half?" Fenwick commented, rubbing his arm where she hit him.

"Only half because he's totally in love with his wife," she said. "If you dressed up like that for me, I would absolutely welcome it if you stole me away and ravished me."

"I'll need to keep that in mind," Fenwick said.

I mounted Andy carefully, so I would not expose myself. As I rode out the gate of the manor toward the temple, I saw a group of eight armsmen heading in the opposite direction. They gave me a wave. I wondered why they were going to the manor.

When I arrived at the temple, I dismounted just as carefully, mindful of my lack of underthings. After tying Andy to a post, I climbed the steps to where the chief priest was waiting. He turned to me with a broad smile.

"Quite impressive, Lord Oritur," he said. "This is going to be so much fun—something that everyone present will remember for the rest of their lives."

"Can you tell me what to expect?" I asked.

"I'm afraid not, milord," he replied. "Lady Lucy swore me to secrecy and implied dire consequences would befall me if I broke her trust."

"She would never hurt you," I reasoned.

"Lady Lucy is a powerful and extremely skilled witch, milord. Though she is as kind as she is beautiful, one dares not anger someone with her ability," he stated. "Without sharing any details, I think it is safe for me to say that you will be mightily impressed and will enjoy what she has planned."

"We will be making an invocation as we did the last time?" I inquired.

"Lady Lucy will," he said.

"I'm just here as decoration, then," I suggested.

"It *is* Freyja's Feast Day," the priest said.

I shrugged in acceptance.

"You are here rather early. Perhaps you would like to wait inside?" he suggested.

Unlike our enemies on the western border, the Rhetians, whose religion demands they all attend a weekly service honoring their single god, our religion is less structured. Regular attendance at a Temple of the Three Major Gods is encouraged on Soliday (also known as Temple Day), but our worship takes the form of quiet contemplation. A Temple of the Three Major Gods is designed to make that quiet contemplation easy. They are large oblong buildings, basilicas. Worshippers enter, spend time in contemplation, then go to the lamp in front of each of the Three Majors Gods and make a sacrifice. The usual sacrifice is to drop a small pinch of incense into the flame. If you have a specific problem you are wrestling with, you meet with a priest for counsel.

I am a strong believer, but my attendance is sporadic. The priest's suggestion to come inside reminded me of that. I had so much for which to thank the Gods, and I wanted them to know I was grateful for their many blessings.

Sitting on one of the polished stone benches, I reviewed the many wonderful opportunities the Gods granted me. I thanked them for each one, including the addition of Shasha. Most especially, I acknowledged the gift they gave by putting Lucy in my life.

The priest found me and warned me that it was almost time. I rose and added a pinch of incense to the flames burning in front of the statues of each of the Three Major Gods. When I finished, I thanked them again and went outside.

The square in front of the temple was now full of people. Over to the side, on the broad steps covering the entire front of the building, I saw Fenwick, Julienne, Mr. Balboa, Madame Hernandez, and my father. Armsmen in breastplates and helmets cordoned off a path from the corner of the square nearest the manor to the front steps.

A fanfare of bugles sounded from that corner of the square. Moments later, I saw the eight armsmen I noticed approaching the manor earlier carrying a litter covered in brilliant white cloth with gold trim. The armsmen were wearing only leather skirts and sandals like mine and seemed to be covered in the same oil Lucy spread on me.

Lucy was seated on a throne-like chair in the center of the litter. She was wearing a helmet like mine, only hers was of gleaming bronze. Her breastplate seemed to be made of scaled bronze armor and hugged her figure closely. Her hair under the helmet was long, wild, and free, with untamed curls. It was difficult to see from her posture, but she appeared to wear a white linen skirt below her breastplate that was no longer than mine. On her feet were sandals tied with similar crisscross thongs up to her knee. She held a spear in her right hand. I once saw a picture depicting Freyja this way.

When she first appeared, there was a momentary silence, followed by the collective gasp of the thousands present. A thunderous roar of approval immediately followed. You would think by now I would have learned never to doubt my wife. This was a magnificent spectacle. The priest was correct—no one present would ever forget it.

"Go to the bottom of the steps," the priest said in my ear, fighting to make himself heard over the crowd. "You help her from the litter, then follow her up here. On her right side, you will kneel on your left knee. After that, follow her instructions."

I went to wait for her arrival. The armsmen were moving at a stately pace. Lucy was sitting upright, and—Majors and Minors!—I could have sworn she was Freyja herself. There was something ethereal and other-worldly about her.

The armsmen reached the steps and lowered the litter to the ground. I stepped forward and offered my hand to Lucy. Something about her appearance convinced me I was in the presence of the divine and that I should lower my head, so I did. After using my hand to steady herself while stepping off the litter, she released it and began to climb the steps. I followed, keeping my head bowed.

When she reached the top, she stopped and turned. The crowd fell silent. I took my place on my knee to her right, my head still bowed. "Welcome to the Feast Day of Freyja," Lucy announced, her voice ringing out over the square.

The crowd roared approval.

"We have much to celebrate in the Eastern March," she continued when the noise faded. "There has been a great victory over the nomads who have plagued us for so long," she announced, brandishing her spear.

Another roar greeted this announcement.

"It is right for us to give thanks to all the Gods, Major and Minor, for this success," Lucy said, holding her hands up to forestall another reaction from the crowd. "We must also give thanks to all those who died defending the March, and their loved ones, over the centuries. Those are the heroes Freyja welcomes to her hall."

The crowd erupted again.

"There are other blessings to come," Lucy called out. "Thanks to the foresight of Lord Oritur and Lord Easton and the support of our sovereign, King Mark, work has already begun on a project that will bring prosperity to the entire Eastern March. Port Charles is being reopened. The Pheas River is being restored to enable safe navigation from Quinn's Ford to the sea. Roads are being cleared that will make it possible for every farmer in the March to sell all of his excess production—from the upcoming harvest."

This drew perhaps the loudest cheers from the assemblage.

"Finally, remember today is Freyja's Feast Day," Lucy said. "Freyja is the Goddess of Romance and all its pleasures. She is not a Goddess who approves of wicked or immodest behavior. Be sure to honor the Goddess properly or risk her certain wrath."

The crowd did not break out in cheers at this warning. I would not have expected them to do so. There was no grumbling, though.

"Rise, noble warrior," Lucy said, offering me her hand, "and take me to our people."

I took Lucy's hand and stood. The armsmen moved the litter away from the bottom of the steps. My father now stood there, holding Andy's reins. Lucy and I walked down. Lucy handed her spear to my father. Fenwick appeared beside Andy and cupped his hands. Lucy put her left foot in them. He then lifted her while she straightened her leg so she could reach the saddle without exposing herself in her short skirt. I followed, putting my foot in the stirrup. I tried to be as graceful and discrete. My father handed me the reins and Lucy her spear.

"The sacrifice has been made," Lucy announced, "and is ready for your enjoyment. Take pleasure in the Feast Day of Freyja!"

The crowd provided one last burst of applause and began heading to the rear of the temple, where the smell of cooked beef was already tantalizing. As people passed us, most bowed their heads at Lucy. I was seated behind her, so I could not see, but I sensed something different about her, something special, something more. My feeling of being in the presence of the divine lingered.

26

We stayed for about an hour before Lucy turned to me and said urgently, "Take me home. Now."

As we arrived, she said, "Leave Andy for now. I need you."

Lucy ran through the house, pulling me along. She took the stairs two at a time. As soon as we entered the bedroom, she jumped in my arms and wrapped herself around me. We were still wearing our breastplates, and they clanked together. I would have laughed, but Lucy had her mouth on mine and was frantic with passion.

Later, when we were catching our breath, still in our costumes, I noticed she looked as she always did. She was still breathtakingly beautiful, but the special glow that was surrounding her was gone. She saw my inquisitive look.

"Do you remember when Liliana summoned Ceridwen Sospita?" she asked.

"Yes."

"I did the same thing with Freyja, but not to the full extent. I had never before tried to maintain that particular spell for more than a moment, to see if it worked. Using it for as long as I did today brought with it some other consequences. I felt as though I was possessed, which I was. Plus, the oil I spread on you was imbued with a glamor associated with Freyja and made you look amazing."

"Lucy, I was convinced I was in the presence of the actual Goddess," I said.

"You were, through me. The spell I accessed invited Freyja to share my body, but not completely. Keeping her spirit from taking over is why I ended up losing control of myself. It was too much of her essence for too long," she said.

"Now, much as I could spend the whole day in bed with you, we need to dress—in normal clothing—and return to the festival."

After we dressed, we went to the stable. Bella, Lucy's horse, was decorated in the same manner as Andy. We rode to the temple and tied the horses. It was not long before we saw my father with Mr. Balboa and Madame Hernandez.

Moving through the crowd, many recognized us. There were many who muttered "Lady Lucy" or "milord" in greeting as we passed. As time went by and I did more things for the people of the March, I felt less uncomfortable with my title. I hoped I would always feel as though I needed to earn it, having met too many nobles who demanded respect and provided nothing in return.

We said hello to my father and our guests but continued to where they were serving the food and drink. Taking our food, we retreated to the steps of the temple to sit and eat. Fenwick and Julienne found us there.

"Much better than the last one," Fenwick commented.

"I'll say," I agreed. "No one tried to kill me this time."

"That's not it at all," Fenwick countered. "I've simply seen no one as arrestingly beautiful as Her Loveliness this morning. Julienne even gave me permission to say that."

"Thank you, Fenwick," Lucy replied. "And it was wise of you to seek her blessing before saying something like that."

"And Caz looked incredible too. Is there a secret to it?" Julienne asked.

Lucy slid closer to her, and the two of them began speaking quietly to one another. Fenwick and I were not included. I realized this was an opportunity to ask Fenwick about Madame Hernandez.

"Aloysius," I said, using the name he detests because he had just tried to tease me, "tell me about the interpreter."

"Madame Hernandez? Certainly," Fenwick replied. "Her husband was the sailing master of the ship Julienne was on when she was captured, so she is a widow. She is also Mooren, as you may have guessed but has been living in Aquileia for more than a decade. The company compensated her for the death of her husband, so she is far from destitute. Even before her husband's death, though, despite being well off, she was not content to sit at home. She is part owner of the restaurant where Julienne honed her ability to speak and understand

Mooren. We offered her the position as Balboa's interpreter and tutor, and she accepted."

"Are she and Balboa…?"

"No, and I know why you are asking," Fenwick said. "I see the way your father looks at her. Who could blame him? She is a striking-looking woman."

"I certainly have no idea what might happen," I said. "As you know, my father's marriage was horrible. But if he is interested, I wanted to make sure he would not be taken advantage of."

"Caz, I like your father," Fenwick said. "I won't allow anything bad to happen to him if I can prevent it."

"Thank you. One other concern I have is both Balboa and Madame Hernandez are connected to Traval & Company," I said.

"You should be more concerned with the huge benefit Travel will gain as a result of you sharing advance information with Herbert Traval," Fenwick replied. "They already have all their construction materials ready to load aboard a ship as soon as they know Port Charles is open for navigation. There is no way either of their major competitors will be able to respond as quickly."

"Oh," I sighed. "Do you think the others will complain that I played favorites?"

"Coombs might," Fenwick said. "Hawkins cannot. Greta and Ratty have both known about the plans for Port Charles as long as Herbert Traval. I feel sorry for Ratty in a way. He has probably been trying to urge his father to take action, but as the younger son, his father does not listen. This might end up helping his position with the firm in the long run, though."

Lucy and Julienne finished whatever they were discussing and were now looking attentively at us. Now that Lucy and I were done eating, we decided to take a stroll through the streets. Once we climbed back down the steps, we saw my father with Balboa and Madame Hernandez.

"Watch me do a good deed," Fenwick said.

Fenwick split from us briefly and began speaking with the three of them. After a short exchange, he returned with Mr. Balboa. I knew Fenwick had invented some excuse to allow my father an opportunity to spend time alone with Madame Hernandez, and I was not wrong.

"I told Mr. Balboa that you had questions for him regarding which buildings should be erected first and also whether it would be better to have employees work the property or tenants," Fenwick said. "You should also ask about seeds. He managed to bring enough of the highest quality seeds for a first crop—even on such a large estate."

We strolled through the streets of Easton for the next couple of hours. Balboa had a definite opinion on what should be built first—a barn to store the materials needed to construct the other buildings and later to be used in the operations. He also was unfamiliar with having tenants work the land.

In Mooresa, the land was worked by employees, and he freely admitted the landowners treated them poorly. It was the biggest problem he had as the manager of the plantation he came from. The concept of tenant farmers paying for the use of the land with a share of their harvest excited him.

Balboa was proud of himself for forcing Fenwick to bring the seed stock. It made his departure from Mooresa more complicated, as instead of only two men riding away, they now had a well-loaded wagon. Still, they managed it, and Balboa would be starting with seeds from the best strains of jute.

As we walked through Easton, we could see everyone was enjoying the holiday. It was a beautiful summer day but not too hot. There were no signs of misbehavior, and we saw several of the armsmen strolling along, keeping an eye on things.

We ended our meandering through the town and returned to the temple. My father and Madame Hernandez were not in the vicinity. Fenwick and Julienne told us they would walk Mr. Balboa back to the manor since Lucy and I both had horses.

When Lucy and I rode up to the house, we saw my father and Madame Hernandez sitting on the veranda chatting. Lucy gave me a knowing smile, and I returned it. Who knew what might happen, but it seemed things were off to a good start.

My father left the following morning with Fenwick, Julienne, Mr. Balboa, and Madame Hernandez on their way to Port Charles. According to the plans my father established, I was riding with a group of armsmen as we shepherded a group of oxen from Williamson's yard to the different work sites.

The men were in great spirits. Though my father instructed them not to overindulge and maintain order, they all managed to enjoy the holiday. All of them commented on Lucy's appearance as Freyja. None had ever seen anything like it, and they were amazed.

"So was I," I admitted.

When we reached the first worksite, a team was already gathered and had begun. The surveyor crossed to me and told me he had them start. They were clearing the road surface in open fields and looked to be making progress. None of the farmers had tried to claim the roadbed or plant on it, but it was covered with weeds and grass. The men were pulling up a thin layer of sod and exposing the hard-packed gravel surface of the old road. The engineer came over and explained why no one tried to till it.

"With so much fertile land on either side, why waste time and effort on a bunch of rocks?" he said.

Some deep-rooted weeds were the only things slowing them down. The engineer insisted on digging the roots out since the weeds would return otherwise. Then the men had to dislodge the gravel from the roots and put it back.

My last stop that day was Quinn's Ford, the northernmost community that linked to the Pheas River. Upriver from where the landing was, the river was not navigable by boat. I arrived near sunset, and the men were done with work for the day. They were staying in the militia quarters in the town and at the camp our armsmen used during the campaign season. From what I could see, they cleared almost a half-mile of road.

I took the four oxen to the camp and greeted the men there, then rode into the town. After checking in at the militia barracks, I went to the small inn. I'd missed dinner, but there was enough left over that they were able to feed me.

The innkeeper kept me company while I ate, more for his own reasons than wanting to ease any loneliness I may feel. He had a hundred questions about the project. I answered the ones I could, but there were some I could not (for instance, "Which trading company will have the concession for the Quinn's Ford landing?").

In the morning, after I ate, I started riding back the way I came, spending more time at each site. Everywhere I went, I saw green fields with growing crops. The sight reassured me that this whole endeavor would be rewarding.

On the third day after the festival, I decided to detour to see the resettled communities of Gambion, East Norton, and Alessa. Most of the fields nearby were under cultivation. Only a few remained fallow. I checked in with the head man of Gambion, the head woman of Alessa, and the mayor of East Norton. The town centers were beginning to repopulate as tradesmen saw opportunities and moved to fill them. All three of the local leaders were pleased and reported no problems. They all had questions—many of them similar to what the innkeeper asked in Quinn's Ford.

Not long after I left East Norton, my vision shifted, and I saw myself from above. I searched within myself and found the reddish-brown spot and touched it with my mind. Immediately, I was able to see through my own eyes again and through Shasha's at the same time.

"Hello, Shasha," I thought, but instead of my pronunciation, I substituted the sound she made when she gave me her name.

Hello, Caz, she answered, but for my name, I heard my own voice. *You catch on quick. Maybe you are not as unskilled as I thought.*

"I do not want to disappoint you," I thought.

The men clearing the stony paths have disturbed prey. Hunting has been easy. I am feeling spoiled.

"Is hunting usually difficult?"

No. I sensed amusement. *I am not hungry now, or I would show you.*

"I think I would like that."

It will happen.

"How have you been?" I thought.

Hungry for knowledge. I am unskilled like you but want to learn. You should be more curious. Lucy will teach, but you must ask. You do not ask.

Shasha was right. I made use of my ability, but overall, I was not comfortable with the supernatural. In Lucy, I accepted it—it was part of who she was. For me, it felt strange and separate from my personality.

Stubborn.

"Perhaps," I thought.

Accept. Embrace.

"Who is teaching you? The owl?"

Yes.

"Is he skilled and powerful like Lucy?"

He is skilled, but our kind lack power. Power is for humans—some humans. You have power. Your mate has more power than you, and more knowledge. You should learn.

"I have had other priorities. My life has been full. I have not had time.

Find time.

"Easy for you to say. I have other responsibilities I must fulfill."

No one is coming.

"What?"

You are worried about the men from over the mountains. No one is coming. I will let you know if they do.

"You have been watching?"

Yes.

I then saw Shasha's memories of a recent flight. She went beyond the Patker River and passed over the two crags. I saw the remains of the five nomads who tried to escape. She flew until she saw a river on the near side of the mountain, and then the vision stopped.

No one is coming.

"When did you do this?"

Yesterday. I have been watching since we became one.

"Thank you."

It is important to you, so it is important to me. It takes little effort. I may not hunt, though.

Shasha shared an image of a larger bird flying over that landscape. I sensed he claimed that territory. If Shasha hunted on his lands, he would attack her.

I am not stupid, Caz.

I laughed out loud. "Good. I hope not to be stupid either."

27

For the rest of the week, I rode between the different sites. The men were productive and seemed in good spirits. Progress was quick through the open fields. Only one of the groups had reached the woods.

With a hundred and fifty years of neglect, mature trees were in the roadbed. I spent almost an entire day watching them cut down trees. After felling one, some of the men would then cut the trunk into smaller sections, and the oxen would drag those away from the road. While that was happening, others were digging out the roots with picks and then hacking at them with flat-bladed axes. Finally, they would secure ropes around the top of the stump, then run the ropes through a series of pulleys attached to the trunks of other trees off the road and have the oxen begin pulling the ropes.

Slowly the stump would be pulled from the ground. When it was at last clear, the men gave a cheer. The oxen would then tug the stump from the road, leaving behind a hole in the roadbed.

"Oaks are the worst," the engineer supervising told me. "They have a heart root, like the tap root certain weeds have. We can only do so much before men need to climb into the hole and chop away at it before the stump will be free."

"What will you do about the holes in the road?" I asked.

"We will fill them for now but will need to rebuild the roadbed next summer," he said. "The tree roots have destroyed the underlying roadbed, and it needs to be replaced properly."

When we reached the end of the week, I returned to the manor. Lucy was saying goodbye to her students. Once they were gone, she came to me and folded me into her embrace.

"How is the work progressing?" she asked.

"Well. There is little for me to do except ride from site to site and try to look important," I replied. "How are your students?"

"Some are quicker than others," Lucy said. "All are eager to learn. I have the more clever ones help the slower ones."

We spent a pleasant two days with one another. Only the staff was there. My father was on his way to the city by now, and Mr. Balboa and Madame Hernandez were likely returning in a day or two. I was planning on heading south to check on those work sites and perhaps see what the engineers were doing on the river and the harbor. Up to this point, the planning my father did got everything off to a smooth start. I wondered about his meeting with the king and hoped things would go well.

Two days later, it was raining, and I was on my way to spend the night in Hillstead. I had not encountered Mr. Balboa and Madame Hernandez yet. Whether Fenwick and Julienne were still with them, I did not know. My vision changed. I saw a view of woods from above. Searching within, I found the reddish-brown spot.

Caz, you must come back. Now. Your Lucy sent the owl to find me. It is important.

"What is wrong?" I thought with alarm. "Is Lucy—"

Lucy is safe. Someone else.

I wheeled Andy around and nudged him to a trot. If Andy and I rode through the night, we could reach Easton after dark tomorrow evening. Andy would be exhausted, though. If I needed to travel after that, I would need to borrow Lucy's horse, Bella.

Yes. Hurry.

"Is there anything else you know?"

The owl did not linger. He is searching for the other man—the clever one, the owl said.

"Fenwick," I thought. "If he is now behind me, his Davy will be more blown out than Andy when he reaches Easton. That's no good."

I'm sorry I cannot help more.

"Shasha, you have done well by letting me know."

In the next town, I grabbed a loaf of bread and some cheese to eat. I let Andy get water and filled a feed bag for him. We would dine on the move.

The rain stopped in the middle of the night, and it was much easier to see afterward. Andy and I continued on, alternating walking and trotting. As dawn arrived, the walking periods grew longer and the trotting shorter. I was trying to make sure Andy was able to make it to Easton.

I caught myself sleeping in the saddle a few times. There were times I was convinced Andy was asleep while he walked. We halted twice more for water and food.

That night I heard the bells of the clock chime ten times as Andy and I entered Easton. We rode to the manor. Jon Sinchak was guarding the gate.

"Jon, what is going on?" I asked.

"I don't know, milord," he replied. "A letter arrived two days ago, and Lady Lucy has been in a state since. I'm glad you're back."

I nodded my thanks. Andy and I went to the stable. Tom Collinwood, holding a torch, came to get Andy.

"We rode day and night to get here, Tom," I said. "Andy needs to recover. Take good care of him."

I unstrapped my saddlebags and threw them over my shoulder, then headed to the house. Before I reached the door, Lucy came flying out. In the light spilling from the open door, I saw a letter in her hand. She came and embraced me.

"Your father has been kidnapped," she said. "Thank all the heavenly beings for Shasha. You need to go to the city now."

"Is that what the letter is?" I asked.

"Yes."

She handed it to me. I could not read it in the dark, so we went inside. Lucy lit a candle and held it close so I could see.

FitzDuncan—

> *Your father owes us twenty thousand ducats for debts incurred by his sons. We have made polite inquiries repeatedly, and your*

father has refused to acknowledge our right to collect this debt. His stubbornness has forced us to attempt an alternative method of collection.

We hold your father. You will deliver the full amount in specie to us no later than the eighteenth of Heyannir, or your father's life is forfeit. When you arrive in the city, one of my associates will contact you and give you instructions on where to deliver the money.

Your friends who live in the castle cannot help you. If you attempt to have me arrested or use force against me or my people, your father will die an untimely death.

Farquahr

Today was the eleventh of Heyannir. Ordinarily, it took three days to reach the capital, stopping overnight. If I rode night and day, as I just did in returning to the manor, I could be in the capital in two days. Unfortunately, I would be exhausted, and I would need to give whatever horse I rode a few days to recover from the journey.

Leaving at this hour of the night seemed foolhardy. Getting some sleep and allowing my brain to chew on the problem while I slept seemed a much better idea. A hot bath would also be a good way to ensure I settled myself so I could sleep rather than toss and turn all night.

"Lucy, this might sound selfish and foolish but have the maids heat some water for a bath. I'm going to soak and think, then sleep. In the morning, I will leave for the city. That will get me there the afternoon of the fourteenth. I should have enough time to either figure things out or obtain the coins from the bank if I fail to develop a better plan."

While I unpacked my saddle bags and loaded them with clean clothing, Lucy started the maids and Theo preparing a bath for me. I sat on the edge of our bed, waiting. My mind was racing.

When I ran afoul of Donald Farquahr's criminal counterpart Nils Pedersen, Sir Oliver West, the principal of the City Watch, and Prince Albert with two troops of horsemen from the Castle Shield, accompanied me to meet with Pedersen. Albert and Sir Oliver instructed Pedersen that any further attacks on me would result in his death and the destruction of his entire operation. Farquahr would certainly have known this, so I wondered why he was so bold now.

For some reason, Farquahr must feel he was protected. Since the crown had shown its support for me with Pedersen, and I felt I was even further in His Majesty's good graces these days, Farquahr must have either a very good hiding place, some form of leverage on the king himself, or both. I was puzzling over what form this could take when Lucy told me the bath was ready.

I quickly stripped off my clothes and slid into the hot water, leaning with my head back and eyes closed, trying to think. Lucy surprised me, lifting my head and pushing my shoulders forward so she could slip in behind me. She wrapped her arms around my chest and put her chin on my shoulder.

"What are you thinking?" she asked.

I explained what I turned over in my mind, then added, "My suspicion is that Farquahr has information regarding either the queen or Albert that would be damaging if it were made public."

"What could he possibly have that would be embarrassing to Lily?" Lucy asked.

"The only thing I can think of is exposing her supernatural abilities," I answered. "Perhaps he has someone who was present when she destroyed the grimoire and saw her manifest Ceridwen Sospita."

"That's fairly thin gruel," Lucy commented. "Half the kingdom would be pleased to have someone with Lily's ability protecting them from the Dark Arts. All we would need to do is bring Count Dunland forward. There are some who would be disturbed by her supernatural connections but not many."

"You're probably correct," I said with a sigh. "That means it's Albert, and I'll wager it goes back to the duPais incident, and the Black Wedding duPais was going to stage to discredit Albert."

"How?"

"Farquahr probably got his hooks into one or more of the guards who came rushing in with Prince Wim that night," I speculated. "They could twist it into an even uglier story than it was already."

"Uglier? It could hardly have been worse," Lucy commented.

"They could try to pin Wim's death on Albert, saying Albert killed his brother to keep the story from spreading," I said.

"But you killed Wim," Lucy stated.

"If they embalmed the body, which I believe they did, Farquahr could demand they exhume the corpse," I explained. "The wounds I gave him would be visible, and it would expose the lie that Wim died from falling off his horse."

"What does this mean?" Lucy asked.

"Farquahr will accuse Albert of killing his brother. If I step forward with the truth, then the king will have no choice except to have someone chop my head off, and Albert will still be smeared from his involvement with duPais. It also means I can't count on having two troops of the Castle Shield at my back when I confront Farquahr," I said. "Did Chauncey find Fenwick?"

"Yes. I think he will arrive in the morning," Lucy said. "He left Julienne to bring Mr. Balboa and Madame Hernandez back."

"If my guess is correct, the king probably has people looking for Fenwick right now. His horse will need a rest but if Tom or his uncle can find him a suitable mount and Fenwick is not too exhausted, have him follow me. He should catch me tomorrow evening because I plan to spend the night," I said. "We need to have our wits about us when we reach the city."

"What do you hope to do?" Lucy asked.

"I don't know yet," I said. "Someone once told me that dealing with men like Farquahr was like trying to juggle a ball of tar. It sticks to you, so you can't get rid of it, and it dirties everything it touches. If Farquahr has one or more of those guards under his control, he will continue to threaten the crown. He must know he is playing an extremely dangerous game. There is a piece missing."

"You will figure it out, Caz," Lucy said.

"Well, I'm going to get the money from the bank, just in case I don't," I said. "The water is cooling off. Let's get out and go to bed."

Lucy held me close. Her presence, the smell of her hair, and her warmth calmed me, and I was able to surrender to my exhaustion. I dreamed that night of the scene in the shrine below the castle and of dueling with Bergeron duPais until I killed him.

I woke with the rising sun. Lucy held me in her arms and felt I was awake. She sat up, combing her fingers through her long, curly blonde hair. It made me hate to leave.

"May I borrow Bella?" I asked. "I'm sure Andy is too fatigued."

"You may not borrow Bella," Lucy said, "because I am going with you. I can restore Andy, Fenwick, and Davy—at least enough to make it through the end of the day without injury. A full night of sleep tonight should see all of you back to rights. We will wait for Fenwick, though. I will make sure Laurie makes enough breakfast for him. He will be starving."

"Are you sure you want to come with us?" I asked.

"I *am* coming with you," she stated firmly.

I knew better than to try to oppose her. She rose and called for Hazel to fetch her saddlebags. While she was waiting for Hazel, she began pulling clothing from her armoire and a chest of drawers. While she was doing this, I dressed.

When Hazel appeared, Lucy quickly packed her things, saying, "You and Fenwick will need all the help you can get. I won't fight, but I'm sure I can assist in other ways. How, I haven't figured out yet, but something will come to mind."

She retrieved the toiletries she wanted and finished packing. After she buckled the bags shut, she indicated I should take them to the stable. I put mine on one shoulder and hers on the other. Reaching the stable, I whistled, and both Tom and his uncle George both appeared.

"We'll need Andy and Bella saddled," I instructed.

"Are you sure, milord?" George asked. "Andy looks like he could use a couple of days of rest."

"Unfortunately, I have no choice," I replied, "but I think Andy may feel better soon."

"If you say so, milord," the elder Collinwood responded, clearly not pleased with me.

I was halfway to the manor when Fenwick arrived. He and Davy both looked exhausted. He slid from the saddle and handed the reins to Tom.

"Wipe him down, brush him out, give him a new blanket and saddle him," I ordered.

George Collinwood looked as though he wanted to protest but swallowed his comment when he saw the determined set of my jaw. Fenwick looked angry but held his tongue as well. I started for the rear of the manor and beckoned Fenwick to follow me. Before Fenwick had the opportunity to unleash his temper on me, we encountered Lucy.

"Good. You're here," she said.

Lucy approached Fenwick and put her right hand on his chest. With her left, she touched her ring finger to the diamond in the center of her earring on that side. While I watched, Fenwick's look of ill-temper was quickly replaced by one of wonderment.

"What did you just do, milady?" he asked.

"Healed you of your fatigue," Lucy replied. "As I will do for Davy and Andy. I will return shortly. Please don't wait for me to begin eating."

As Lucy sailed out the rear entrance, Fenwick shook his head in slight disbelief and followed me into the dining room. He started to ask a question, but I preempted him by handing over the letter. He scanned it quickly, then looked up when he finished.

"That's the third astounding thing in the last five minutes, Caz," he said. "I'm figuring you want to leave immediately. Is Lucy treating the horses the way she just did me?"

"That would be my guess," I replied. "We are not riding straight through to the city. We will stop in the evenings. Lucy says you and I, and the horses, will be near normal with a good night's sleep tonight."

"What do you make of this?" Fenwick asked, pointing at the letter.

I shared my thoughts with him. Fenwick followed my reasoning, nodding appropriately, and gave a grunt of agreement when I mentioned I felt there was something missing. Lucy came in, and we both stood. Laurie followed on her heels with plates full of eggs, sausage, and biscuits.

"There's more when you finish that, Mr. Fenwick," Laurie said as she returned to the kitchen.

"Davy and Andy will be capable of completing today's journey without fear of injury," Lucy said, "and Mr. Collinwood is no longer upset."

"I thought you could not use the earrings in the same way as your ring and the necklace," I said.

"Something else I learned when Lily and I went to the Temple of Njörun," she said.

28

We left as soon as Fenwick finished eating. As he had skipped meals for a whole day before arriving, that took a while. Once we were underway, he told us about Chauncey's summons.

"While I was riding with Julienne, Mr. Balboa, and Madame Hernandez, Chauncey swooped down and nearly took my head off," Fenwick said. "I recognized him. He did it again, then started gliding in front of us. I asked him if I was supposed to follow him, and he hooted. As I said farewell to the others, I asked Julienne to make sure they made it back to Easton. When I rode ahead of the others, I asked if I should hurry. He hooted. Then he disappeared."

We discussed Farquahr's boldness and what it might mean. We agreed that he possessed some leverage to prevent the crown from pursuing him openly. What we did not know was whether he might have something that would protect him from Fenwick.

Certainly, Farquahr must be aware that Fenwick was now in the employ of His Majesty. He would have to know that the king would respond to any threat by sending Fenwick. Therefore, we surmised there must be something else that Farquahr possessed that would prevent the king from doing that.

That evening we stopped at an inn. All of us had stayed there several times before. Fenwick excused himself immediately after we finished eating dinner. By the time Lucy and I went upstairs a few minutes later, we could hear soft snoring from his room.

In the morning, Fenwick was awake before we were. We encountered him in the dining room, and he informed us that while he felt as though he had spent a full day in the saddle the day before, none of the exhaustion from his ride back to Easton remained. When we went to collect the horses, Andy and Davy seemed no worse than Bella.

The rest of our journey to the city was uneventful. Fenwick headed to the castle while Lucy and I went to our house. After dropping the bags, I took our horses to the Foaming Boar. It's difficult to say who was happier—Bella and Andy to see Jerry or Jerry to see them. Both animals had their heads alongside his as he embraced them both.

I found Carl inside the inn, and let him know we were boarding the horses, then asked, "Are there any men left in the city who might be available to help with some dangerous work, or did all of them join my employ last year?"

"I might know of a couple," he said. "What sort of dangerous work?"

"I don't know yet," I admitted. "When and if I need them, I will let you know. How much advance warning will they need?"

"A full day," Carl responded. "What is in the wind?"

"I can't really say yet," I replied. "It's sensitive."

When I returned to the house, Lucy was alone. She informed me Roberta dashed to the market before it closed for the day to buy something to cook for dinner that would feed Fenwick and us. He returned more than an hour later, as Roberta was just serving dinner. She quickly retrieved a plate for him.

"The first part is as you thought, Caz," he said quietly after Roberta left the room. "Farquahr has suborned two of the men who were present with Prince Wim that night. The king is furious, and Albert is despondent. In addition to the current situation with your father, if we do not resolve this, Farquahr will be a law unto himself."

"Any idea what else Farquahr possesses to protect himself?" Lucy asked.

"His Majesty and Albert have not been able to think beyond the immediate threat," Fenwick said. "The queen was able to see my point, but Farquahr has provided no hint as to what it might be."

"That would have been too easy," I commented.

"After we finish eating," Fenwick said, "I plan to find some people I know. The two of you should call on Sir Oliver at home."

Lucy had never joined me for a meeting with Sir Oliver, but I did not want to leave her at home by herself. Farquahr undoubtedly knew where we lived. Allowing him to take Lucy captive would be unacceptable.

Seven hells! He is probably watching the house already, I thought.

I reached within and tugged forth a small tendril of Bellona's essence. Using it to expand my senses, I searched the vicinity for anything that felt like a potential source of danger. It did not take long for me to feel something. A man was watching the front of our house from across the street and two houses down.

"Before we do that, Fenwick, there is someone watching the house. Would you like to ask him some questions?"

Fenwick thought for a moment before responding, "He won't know anything useful, and accosting him now would only alert Farquahr that he needs to be more careful. Let's see who he follows when we depart. That will tell us perhaps more than we would get from questioning him."

When Roberta came to clear our plates, we instructed her to lock the doors and not allow anyone in unless she was sure it was one of us. I went and closed all the first-floor windows and made sure they were latched securely. When I finished, I met Lucy and Fenwick by the front door. We left together, and Roberta bolted the door behind us.

Fenwick went to the right, Lucy and I to the left. Our watcher waited, then followed Fenwick. I informed Lucy of this.

We walked two blocks over and three blocks down to reach the street on which Sir Oliver West and his wife lived. I knew his house number but never called upon him at home. The problem was the house numbers were not in order—a quirk relating to when the homes were built hundreds of years before. Lucy and I strained to read the numbers in the dark before I realized I had an easier way. My senses were still expanded, so I just used them to feel for Sir Oliver.

He was across the street, one house away. I took Lucy across, and we knocked on the door. A servant answered after a moment.

"Lord and Lady Oritur to see Sir Oliver," I said.

The servant turned her head and hollered, "A Lord and Lady Oritur, sir."

"Seven hells!" came the return shout. "Bring them in!"

"This way, if you please," the young lady said.

She took us to a parlor. Sir Oliver and his wife stood to greet us. He introduced us to his wife, Katherine. Once introductions were complete, he offered us some brandy, and we accepted.

"You may speak freely," Sir Oliver said as he served us. "Katherine knows everything I do."

"Farquahr has my father," I said.

"I'm aware," Sir Oliver replied. "And there is nothing I can do to help you."

"I know," I stated. "That is not why we are here. We know why you cannot assist us. What concerns us is there must be something more. What does Farquahr have that he is reckless enough to make this play? Also, where is he?"

"The second question is the easier one to answer," Sir Oliver said. "He is in his usual place. A large house on the opposite side of the Kettle from Pedersen's."

The Kettle was a part of the city in a large bowl between two hills that fronted the river. While I thought the area got its name from the bowl shape of the land, another reason one could call it the Kettle is it was the hottest area of the city during the summer months. The surrounding hills prevented any sort of refreshing breeze from reaching it. The Kettle was the poorest section of the city of Aquileia.

"So bold," Lucy remarked.

"Indeed," Sir Oliver said. "He has made no attempt to hide. Your father is certainly being held there. I agree with you that Farquahr must have something else to protect him from the likes of Fenwick. My men have been beating the bushes, trying to obtain some idea of what it is. So far, all we have is some hint of a connection with the southern continent. Nagah has been mentioned, also Combrial."

"Combrial? Where is that?" I asked.

"The interior of the southern continent," Katherine replied. "Bordering Nagah."

"That is not much help," I commented.

"I know. It's all we have, though. This whole thing had been a surprise," Sir Oliver said. "Usually, I have some idea when Farquahr or Pedersen is planning something big. Not this time."

"You realize if Fenwick and I go to resolve this, Farquahr will probably not survive," I said. "The unrest in the city will be worse than when Pedersen was imprisoned."

Sir Oliver nodded.

Lucy and I thanked them for their hospitality and rose to leave. Sir Oliver escorted us to the door. I could see a look of genuine regret on his face.

"I wish the City Watch could offer more assistance, Caz," he said. "But if you decide an extra blade might be of use, I hope you'll call on me as a friend."

"Thank you," I said. "We may."

The next morning, Fenwick joined us for breakfast. His meetings after he left us produced less information than ours. At least Sir Oliver told us of some tie to the southern continent.

"The only fun I had was dealing with the man following me," he said.

"Did you kill him?" Lucy asked.

"That would have been too easy and not enough fun," Fenwick said. "I took his clothes and sent him on his way."

"Don't you worry—" Lucy started to say.

"I'm not worried about Farquahr and his people," Fenwick stated. "I'm irritated. There is a part of me that is strongly inclined to simply march over there and have it out with them."

"What? Right now?" Lucy protested.

"Majors and Minors, no," Fenwick replied. "That would be foolish. Your husband and I would be riddled with crossbow bolts before we reached the door. In the middle of the night. The more I think on it, the more I like the idea."

I shared much of Fenwick's frustration. With my father's assistance, we were pursuing the restoration project that would benefit so many people. For the debts rung up by my late half-brothers to be the cause of the current trouble added an element of disgust to my unhappiness.

"Before we march in blindly," I suggested, "perhaps we can get a better look at the building."

"I've ridden past it many times," Fenwick said. "I've been inside once. Everything I need to know, I've already seen."

"Tell me where it is, Fenwick," Lucy requested. "I understand your impatience, but there might be something you cannot see waiting for you inside."

"What do you mean?" he protested.

"There might be something supernatural waiting for us," I guessed.

"Precisely," Lucy confirmed. "The only reason I can think that Farquahr has such confidence involves magical protection, something he might have to counter the threat you represent, Fenwick."

"Fine," he snorted. "Do you have a map of the city?"

"No, but Lyle surely does," I said.

"Then take me to the bookseller's, Fenwick," Lucy said.

The two of them departed. Before they left, I checked for someone watching the house but did not sense anyone. I sat in the parlor and considered what Lucy said. We had not been able to figure out any other angle that would provide Farquahr protection. Lucy's suggestion made more sense than most of the ideas we considered.

The two of them returned within an hour. Fenwick was frowning. Lucy wasn't quite smiling, but I sensed she had proved her point somehow.

"There are two people inside who have auras with Bellona dominant," she explained. "Chauncey flew over and sensed them."

"Which is good to know but not a reason to delay," Fenwick said. "In fact, our knowledge allows us to be prepared for what we will face."

"Have you both restored the energy in your diamonds?" Lucy asked.

We both nodded.

"There is one other thing that might help," Lucy said. "If these two are powerful and skilled, as a last resort, you could try to manifest Bellona."

"Like the queen did when she destroyed the grimoire?" I asked.

"Yes. You've actually come closer to doing it than you know," Lucy stated. "Before you knew how to access Bellona, you had some duels where her power released itself."

"Yes, and left me completely drained," I said.

"You did not have a reservoir like the diamonds you both have now or tanzyan gems to channel the power, so there was not enough strength for her to manifest. She took every bit of asomatous energy you had, though," Lucy explained.

"So what do we do?" Fenwick asked.

"If you feel the battle is not going your way and you have no options left," Lucy said, "touch your ring to the diamond and access what you have stored in it and throw your connection to Bellona completely open. She will possess you for as long as there is sufficient energy."

"What will happen then?" I asked.

"If you survive the fight, you will feel as drained as you remember from those earlier incidents," Lucy said. "Weak as a pair of kittens."

"If there are others present, would we be able to defend ourselves?" Fenwick asked.

"No," I replied, shaking my head. "We will both collapse. But if Lucy is nearby, she could read the auras and send help when we need it. I think we need to go see Ollie."

"Who?" Fenwick asked.

"Sir Oliver West," I said. "If he were waiting in the wings with Lucy, she could tell them when to come to our aid."

The three of us left. Lucy and I retrieved our horses from Jerry at the Foaming Boar, then we all rode to the Palace of Justice. We tied our mounts near the administrative entrance and walked to the end of the long corridor. The same grumpy clerk was stationed there, and we asked to see Sir Oliver. he merely jerked his thumb at the door.

I led the way since I had been here many times before. When I reached his office, I knocked loudly once. Not waiting for a reply, I opened the door just as Sir Oliver was asking who was there. Fenwick and Lucy followed me in, with Fenwick shutting the door after she entered.

"Hello, Ollie," I said as I plopped down in a chair without being invited to sit. "We figured out how you can help us."

"Believe it or not, Caz, but I've missed your cheek," Sir Oliver said.

"Oh, I believe it, Ollie," I replied. "The only person I can be cheeky with these days is Fenwick, and sadly, he's better at it than I am—though it pains me to admit it."

We explained our plan to Sir Oliver. He agreed to support us. Fenwick and I would deliver Lucy here at the Palace of Justice at three o'clock in the morning. He would have a select group of men whom he trusted without reservation, and they would all ride to the corner near the building where Farquahr was. Fenwick and I would travel separately to the building. Once we knew Sir Oliver and Lucy were in place, we would begin our incursion.

29

Fenwick took off in a different direction when we finished with Sir Oliver. Lucy and I returned to the house. I unsaddled and groomed our horses but did not take them back to the stable. It was a pleasant day, and they could stay behind the house.

Lucy and I met upstairs in the bedroom. Chauncey was resting on his perch. I thanked him for his assistance. He merely blinked at me.

Lucy had a definite idea of how she wished to pass the time. She pulled me down on the bed with her. After a bit of frenetic activity, we both rested. We woke hours later, feeling relaxed and rejuvenated.

Lucy's mood the rest of the day and evening was in no way somber or apprehensive. This gave me confidence. Though she tried mightily never to betray her glimpses of the future, her pleasant demeanor led me to believe that we would have a successful outcome later. Otherwise, I did not believe she could mask her unhappiness.

Fenwick reappeared later in the afternoon with Julienne. She explained she left Mr. Balboa and Madame Hernandez at the manor. Roberta served us dinner while we explained our plans to Julienne. She insisted on joining Lucy with Sir Oliver and the City Watch. Julienne did request a bath, though. I assisted Roberta by carrying the buckets of water.

About midnight, Fenwick excused himself and went out the front door. A few moments later, we heard a yelp. Fenwick came strolling in with someone's clothes over his shoulder.

"What are those?" Julienne asked.

"Oh, some trash in the neighborhood," Fenwick answered. "Just doing a bit of tidying up."

At half past two, we woke Roberta, told her we were leaving, and asked her to bolt the doors. I saddled Bella, then Andy, while Fenwick saddled Davy and Julienne's horse, who I learned was named Millicent, or Millie. Fenwick and I escorted the ladies to the Palace of Justice and left them with Sir Oliver.

Both of us were dressed in black from chin to toe, including our gloves. We rode to the corner opposite where Sir Oliver would wait and dismounted, tying the horses to a post. Both of us accessed our abilities and cast our senses out. There was a guard outside the front door of the house Farquahr used as his headquarters. Inside the entrance were two more. Fenwick and I agreed to eliminate the one outside before Sir Oliver arrived, figuring he would surely hear Sir Oliver's men.

There were clouds scudding across the sky and only a thin sliver of moon. Fenwick and I waited for the clouds, then moved in the darkness, stopping when the cloud passed by. When the third cloud was obscuring the small amount of moonlight, we reached the watchman. Fenwick clobbered him with the guard of his sword, and he collapsed.

Even though they were quiet and well-disciplined, we nonetheless heard Sir Oliver and his men arrive. Once the little bit of noise abated, Fenwick and I waited for the next passing cloud before opening the front door. Two men were seated in chairs facing the door. Both were holding loaded and cocked crossbows, but both were sound asleep. Fenwick took the one on the left and I the right, and we dispatched them like their comrade outside.

There were four men upstairs in four different rooms. Below us, in the cellar, were four men in the same room. Fenwick and I agreed that the cellar was the goal, but we did not want anyone surprising us from behind, so we crept upstairs. We sent those four men into a much deeper sleep than what they were previously enjoying.

Fenwick and I crept down to the cellar. There was a door to the right of the stairs, opening into a room that must have been underneath the rear of the building. Light was streaming out from underneath it. I withdrew more of my power, preparing myself.

Fenwick grasped the latch and turned it slowly. He then thrust the door inward violently, but only about three inches before he caught it. Crossbow bolts thudded into the back of the door.

We stepped through quickly, swords drawn. Two of the biggest men I had ever seen were standing there, unsheathing their blades. My father was standing chained to the wall behind them, showing signs of abuse. Seated off to the side was a plump, bald-headed man.

"Did you bring my money, bastard?" he asked insultingly.

"I thought I would pay you with steel instead," I quipped, waving my blade slightly.

"You'll come up short, then," Farquahr said.

With that comment, the two huge men attacked. They were faster than even Fenwick at his best. Before I could think to cast an envelope over them to diminish their power, they were on us. I blocked the one's slash, but he continued his advance, lowered his shoulder, and launched me into the wall behind me.

Before I recovered, he was on me again. I could barely keep up with his speed. Every strike I parried nearly wrenched my sword away. When I tried to spin away, he caught me with a sweep of his left arm and sent me flying again.

He caught me against the wall, my legs wobbly. It took every bit of my concentration to parry, block, and try to move. I could not spare a split second to try to dampen his power. If I did, he would kill me.

I caught his blade on my guard. He was forcing it to my throat. I was trying to resist, but he was winning the struggle. Dimly, I heard Farquahr giggle. I went limp, trying to duck underneath and escape. The right side of my head exploded in pain as he hit me just above the ear with the guard of his sword.

The blow sent me rolling sideways, and the wall stopped my progress—mostly upside down. I had nearly lost my sword again. It was dangling in my hand, with my ring finger touching the diamond in the pommel. Lucy's advice came to me while I watched his feet crash onto the floor as he came to finish me off.

I allowed the energy stored in the diamond to flow into me unbridled while, at the same time, I opened my connection to Bellona completely. My body seemed instantly larger—of similar size to my attacker. Strength like I had never experienced filled my entire body. Without standing, I spun, twisted, and swept my legs against his and knocked him down. That enabled me to reach my own feet at the same time he recovered.

We were evenly matched now, I realized. I no longer felt overpowered, but he was still deadly fast and immensely strong. Fortunately, I was too.

What followed was no duel. It was a deadly brawl, with both of us using every tactic we knew. The two of us shuffled back and forth, striking, parrying, twisting, punching. I suddenly noticed a pattern in his movements. He would use a croisè to try to force my blade up, then attempt a thrust. The next time he did it, I let him force my blade up, but I forced his sword down with my gloved left hand.

I felt the sear of his blade as it sliced through the leather of my glove and into the meat of the palm of my hand at the knuckles. At nearly the same moment, there was a sunburst of pain in my thigh where the tip of his sword entered and sank deep. None of this mattered, though, as my backhand stroke nearly severed his head from his neck.

My attacker shrunk to a normal size as he collapsed to the ground, taking my blade with him. Farquahr was rising from his seat with his mouth agape. His expression froze like that as I withdrew my opponent's sword from my thigh and flung it backhanded at Farquahr. The tip of the blade flew into his open mouth and did not stop until the hilt slid to his teeth.

Farquahr's death brought a small feeling of satisfaction. Then I remembered I was not alone in this fight. I turned to see how Fenwick was faring but never quite made it. Before I saw him, I collapsed to the ground.

When I woke, I was in the bedroom of our city house. It was daylight and, from the angle of the sun, afternoon. Lucy was lying next to me. I could smell her hair—one of my favorite scents in the world. She must have felt my stirring and rolled to face me, laying her hand on my cheek. She leaned forward and kissed me briefly and gently.

"How are you feeling?" she asked.

"Um," I responded, stalling while I determined that for myself. "My thigh and my left hand hurt. I have a headache, and I feel like I could sleep for a week. I'm not dead, though, so it could be worse."

"Well, you've already been sleeping for two-and-a-half days," she commented. "We've treated your hand and your thigh, and you'll just need to wait for the knot on the side of your head to go away. You lost a great deal of blood, too. He nicked the primary vein when you let him poke you in the thigh."

"Hello, Your Loveliness," Fenwick greeted Lucy as he appeared at the door. "Your Somnolence," he said to me.

Fenwick was sporting two black eyes and a swollen nose. It looked as though he had broken it again. His left arm was covered in plaster from above his elbow to his fingers, and he was resting it in a sling.

"Is that the latest fashion here in the capital?" I asked him, nodding at his arm.

He ignored my quip, saying, "You used your thigh—I caught my opponent's blade with my forearm. Same end result. I will give you credit for an elegant toss at Farquahr, though."

"Oh, you saw that?"

Fenwick nodded.

"Looks like you blocked a fist with your nose again," I cracked.

"I did. Fortunately, your lady wife assures me she can help heal it in a way that enhances my peculiar style of beauty," he said.

"I didn't know she was capable of performing such miracles," I said.

"Your wit appears to be much sharper than normal this afternoon," Fenwick said. "Perhaps you should undergo near-death experiences more often."

"I think I would prefer to avoid those, even if it means always playing the dullard," I replied. "How is my father?"

"In better condition than either of us," Fenwick answered. "He is meeting with the king and representatives of the three major trading houses right now."

"And what is the mood at the castle?"

"One of profound relief," Fenwick replied. "Further cementing you in the good graces of both His Majesty and His Highness. It has also benefitted me, for which I am grateful."

"Is there anything else I should know?" I asked.

"Yes. As you may have guessed, our opponents possessed rings with tan-zyan gemstones. Neither was of as good quality as ours, but we have passed them along to the queen for safe keeping," Fenwick said. "We are allowed to keep their swords. Both are superb, though your blade remains unmatched in its excellence. Either of the two would be an improvement over what I now carry."

"Take your pick then," I offered. "I'll be happy with the one you don't choose."

"Trusting your generosity, I already did," Fenwick replied.

My stomach gave a loud gurgle just then. I realized I was ravenously hungry. Lucy laughed at the sound.

"Dinner will be ready in a couple of hours," she said, "but I can fetch you something for now."

When she left, I asked Fenwick, "Tell me how you fared in the scrap?"

"Similar to you, I expect. I had no attention to spare for anything other than my opponent," he said. "When he hit me in the nose, he drove me far enough away that I had the split-second to release my full strength. We were evenly matched then, but Caz, I must tell you, my opponent was every bit as cunning as you."

"Likewise," I agreed.

"It seemed like a good idea at the moment to allow him to skewer my forearm to trap his blade," Fenwick said, shaking his head. "He quickly twisted it and broke both the bones, but the tip of my sword was already under his chin and heading upward. I turned in time to see you nearly cut the head off your man and then hurl his sword through Farquahr's mouth. You collapsed. I will admit my legs gave way, but I remained conscious until Lucy arrived. The next day I woke at about this same time. You slept for two more days. Lucy and the queen have both been tending to you and have also helped your father and me with our wounds."

"What did they do to my father?"

"They beat him a bit. Nothing too serious," Fenwick said. "Probably more for amusement than anything."

"And Albert's problem?"

"Has been resolved permanently," Fenwick stated.

Lucy returned with a plate heaped with cold chicken already cooked. Not bothering with social niceties, I tore into it. Fenwick gave a wave and departed. When I finished, Lucy took the plate, and I must have fallen asleep instantly.

When she woke me, the shadows were longer. She brought a tray loaded with three thick slabs of roast beef and a heap of cooked spinach. Lucy watched with a bemused smile as I inhaled my food.

"Lily and I have been working on your body," she said. "Your wounds are healing nicely, but your blood supply is still quite low. Plan on spending at least the next two days in bed and doing a great deal of sleeping."

"I haven't felt this weak since—"

"Since the last time you almost died," Lucy interrupted. "At least Fenwick was on your side this time instead of trying to kill you."

Three days later, in the morning, my father came into the room. He gave me a weak smile as he crossed the room. So we could talk easily, he sat on the edge of the bed.

"Thank you for coming to my rescue," he said. "I'm sorry that your half-brothers were able to cause trouble from beyond the grave."

"That was just an excuse, father," I said. "Did Farquahr ever show you any evidence they owed him money?"

"No."

"Farquahr used you to pull me in," I said. "Along with Fenwick. He wanted to kill both of us. If he succeeded, he would have been a law unto himself."

"Surely the king—"

"For reasons I cannot share, the king would not have been able to stop him," I said.

"Huh," my father grunted. "That explains Mark's odd mood."

"Odd in what way?"

"Tired. Relieved. Grateful. He is almost apologetic, though he has nothing for which he needs to apologize to me. I thought it was strange. It was not unpleasant at all, simply not what I expected," my father said.

"Did you reach agreement with the trading houses?" I asked.

"Yes," my father said, a hint of pride coming to his face. "As good as any in the kingdom, according to His Majesty."

"Congratulations," I said. "What did you think of the property near Port Charles?"

"It's not so much what I thought of it," he said, "but rather what Mr. Balboa felt. He is excited. We wandered all over, and he examined the soil in dozens of places. He feels we will easily exceed his production estimates. His only remaining concern is the length of the growing season. He was also excited by the two stone tanks we found. They are perfect for treating the harvested plants. We will begin rebuilding the structures once Port Charles is reopened, and we can ship the materials in."

"Do you plan on rebuilding the main house?" I asked.

"I have not made up my mind yet," he said. "Fortunately, we will have the funds to do so if we wish. His Majesty indicated to me that the contract he issued to us for the roadwork should provide the March enough income to pay for restoring the entire operation. Do you have any objections to that idea?"

"None, sir," I replied.

Once he departed, I thought about asking for a bath so I could get out of bed for the day. I sat up and stretched my legs over the side. Before I stood, I suddenly saw our outpost at Bannock Hill from a lofty vantage point. Reaching within, I found the node for Shasha.

Where have you been?

"I was injured. The past few days, I have been sleeping most of the time while my wounds heal."

This is not the time for sleep, Caz, Shasha said. *People have come.*

ABOUT THE AUTHOR

John Spearman (Jake to his friends and colleagues) is a Latin teacher and coach at a prestigious New England boarding school. This book is the sixth of the *FitzDuncan* series.